Poetic Animals and Animal Souls

Poetic Animals and Animal Souls

Randy Malamud

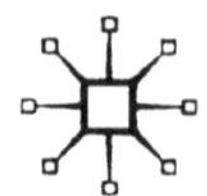

First published 2003 by
PALGRAVE MACMILLAN™
175 Fifth Avenue, New York, N.Y. 10010 and
Houndmills, Basingstoke, Hampshire, England RG21 6XS.
Companies and representatives throughout the world.

PALGRAVE MACMILLAN is the global academic imprint of the Palgrave Macmillan division of St. Martin's Press, LLC and of Palgrave Macmillan Ltd. Macmillan® is a registered trademark in the United States, United Kingdom and other countries. Palgrave is a registered trademark in the European Union and other countries.

ISBN 0–40396–178–6 hardback

Library of Congress Cataloging-in-Publication Data
Malamud, Randy, 1962–
Poetic animals and animal souls/by Randy Malamud.
p. cm.
Includes bibliographical references (p.).
ISBN 1–40396–178–6
1. American poetry—20th century—History and criticism. 2. Animals in literature. 3. English poetry—20th century—History and criticism. 4. Moore, Marianne, 1887–1972—Views on animals. 5. Pacheco, José Emilio—Views on animals. 6. Human–animal relationships in literature. I. Title.

PS310.A49 M35 2003
811'.509362dc—21 2002030830

A catalogue record for this book is available from the British Library.

Design by Newgen Imaging Systems (P) Ltd., Chennai, India.

First edition: March, 2003
10 9 8 7 6 5 4 3 2 1

Printed in the United States of America.

For Benjamin Simonds-Malamud

(whose animal soul may be a bunny)

Contents

Acknowledgments

I want to acknowledge the advice and support of a group of colleagues, fellow travelers in ecocriticism and anthrozoology whose work inspires my own and whose insights I have always valued monumentally: Ralph Acampora, Steve Baker, Charles Bergman, Erica Fudge, Cheryll Glotfelty, Gary Gossen, Dale Jamieson, Rod Preece, Harriet Ritvo, Marian Scholtmeijer, Julie Smith, Kenneth Shapiro, and Molly Westling.

Without Margaret Sayers Peden's masterful translation of Pacheco, I could not have appreciated fully the power of his poetry.

At Georgia State, a cadre of wonderful administrators, colleagues, and students have been—as always—immensely supportive of my work. I am grateful to be able to work in such a rich intellectual climate. I thank especially Ahmed Abdelal, Lauren Adamson, David Blumenfeld, Bob Sattelmeyer, Matthew Roudané, Marta Hess, Tammy Cole, Heather Russel, Greg George, and the English Department WIP (works-in-progress) group 2001–02, among many others. And I have appreciated immensely Lisa Anderson's outstanding editorial contributions that have improved every page of this book.

I have always written, ultimately, for my family, whose influences permeate all my work: thanks to Daniel and Judith Malamud, and Lisa, Paul, Owen, and Emma Apostol, for helping me to get to . . . wherever I have gotten to. Dorothy and Sol Disner and Jack and Jennie Malamud, to whom I dedicated my first book, are always with me; Jacob Simonds-Malamud, to whom I dedicated my last book (in part so that I would have to write another one for his brother) never ceases to amaze me. Wendy Simonds's contribution to my work, and my life, is infinite and virtually inexpressible . . . but: thanks.

A version of chapter 2 appeared in *Society & Animals* 6.3 (October 1998), and a version of chapter 3 appeared in *Comparative Literature and Culture: A WWWeb Journal* 2.2 (June 2000).

Excerpts from "The Jerboa," "No Swan So Fine," and "The Buffalo" from *The Collected Poems of Marianne Moore*, copyright © 1935 by Marianne Moore, copyright renewed © 1963 by Marianne Moore and T. S. Eliot, are used by permission of Scribner, an imprint of Simon & Schuster Adult Publishing Group, and Faber & Faber Ltd. Excerpts from "The Rigorists," "He 'Digesteth Harde Yron,' " and "The Pangolin" from *The Collected Poems of Marianne Moore*, copyright © 1941 by Marianne Moore, copyright renewed © 1969 by Marianne Moore, are used by permission of Scribner, an imprint of Simon & Schuster Adult Publishing Group, and Faber & Faber Ltd. Excerpts from "The Wood-Weasel" and "Elephants" from *The Collected Poems of Marianne Moore*, copyright © 1944 by Marianne Moore, copyright renewed © 1972 by Marianne Moore, are used by permission of Scribner, an imprint of Simon & Schuster Adult Publishing Group, and Faber & Faber Ltd. Excerpts from "His Shield" from *The Collected Poems of Marianne Moore*, copyright © 1951 by Marianne Moore, copyright renewed © 1979 by Marianne Moore, are used by permission of Scribner, an imprint of Simon & Schuster Adult Publishing Group, and Faber & Faber Ltd. Extracts from "Tom Fool at Jamaica," "The Arctic Ox," "Blue Bug," and "Tippoo's Tiger" are used by permission of Penguin Putnam Inc.

Excerpts from "Parrot," "The Zoo," "This is Disgraceful and Abominable," "Death Bereaves our Common Mother / Nature Grieves for my Dead Brother," "Nature and Free Animals," "Sunt Leones," "Friends of the River Trent," "My Cats," and "My Cat Major," from *Collected Poems of Stevie Smith*, copyright © 1972 by Stevie Smith, are used by permission of New Directions Publishing Corp. and the Estate of James MacGibbon.

Excerpts from "What Happened Here Before," "Coyote Valley Spring," "Prayer for the Great Family," "The Dead by the Side of the Road," "Mother Earth: Her Whales," "The Call of the Wild," "The Hudsonian Curlew," and "Introductory Note," from *Turtle Island*, copyright © 1974 by Gary Snyder, are used by permission of New Directions Publishing Corp.

Excerpts from "Rapture of the Deep: The Pattern of Poseidon's Love Song," "Mousefeet: From a Lecture on Muridae Cosmology," "Abundance and Satisfaction," "Fractal: Repetition of Form over a Variety of Scales," and "Animals and People: The Human Heart in Conflict with Itself," from *Song of the World Becoming: New and Collected Poems, 1981–2001*, copyright © 2001 by Pattiann Rogers, are used with permission from Milkweed Editions.

Excerpts from "Address to the Beasts," from *W. H. Auden: The Collected Poems,* copyright © 1976 by Edward Mendelson, William Meredith and Monroe K. Spears, Executors of the Estate of W. H. Auden, are used with permission from Random House, Inc. and Faber & Faber Ltd.

Excerpts from "The Man with the Blue Guitar," from *The Palm at the End of the Mind* by Wallace Stevens, are used with permission from Random House, Inc. and Faber & Faber Ltd.

Excerpts from "The Fish," "Egrets," and "The Snakes," from *American Primitive* by Mary Oliver, copyright © 1978, 1979, 1980, 1981, 1982, 1983, are used by permission of Little Brown and Company, Inc.

Excerpts from Philip Larkin's *Collected Poems,* copyright © 1988, 1989 by the Estate of Philip Larkin, are used by permission of Faber and Faber Ltd. and Farrar, Straus and Giroux, LLC.

Excerpts from Seamus Heaney's *Selected Poems, 1966–87,* copyright © 1990, *Opened Ground: Selected Poems 1966–96,* copyright © 1999, and *Seeing Things,* copyright © 1991, are used by permission of Faber & Faber Ltd. and Farrar, Straus and Giroux, LLC.

Excerpts from José Emilio Pacheco's *An Ark for the Next Millennium* (trans. Margaret Sayers Peden), copyright © 1993 by the University of Texas Press, are used by permission of Margaret Sayers Peden.

Part One
An Ecocritical Ethics of Reading

Chapter 1
On Knowing (and Not Knowing) Animals

Thinking Outside the Box

The relationship between people and nonhuman animals is codified in social culture as hierarchical and fundamentally impermeable: we are in here, they are out there. People are alienated from animals, with only token points of connection that are so heavily conscribed and artificial as to hinder any significant experiential association across the divide. The classical construct of a Great Chain of Being, or its near-variant, the ladder of evolutionary progress, endures essentially unchallenged: all creatures are linked together in some cosmic schema, in which some pigs (us!) are considerably more equal than other pigs. The predominant Western moral code positions humanity with regard to animals as unilaterally supremacist: "And God said, Let us make man in our image, after our likeness: and let them have dominion over the fish of the sea, and over the fowl of the air, and over the cattle, and over all the earth, and over every creeping thing that creepeth upon the earth. . . . And God blessed them, and God said unto them, Be fruitful, and multiply, and replenish the earth, and subdue it: and have dominion over the fish of the sea, and over the fowl of the air, and over every living thing that moveth upon the earth" (Genesis 1: 26–8).

From the beginning God authorizes an ecologically perverse hubris. Epistemologies of the world fortify the rift between people and animals. Nature is the vehicle "through which humanity thinks its difference and specificity," according to philosopher Kate Soper (155). This idea of nature—in which animals are, of course, a constituent element—presupposes a barrier that differentiates and separates us from it. In everyday terms, Soper argues, people conceive of nature as oppositional to accultured and civilized surroundings: "the urban or industrial environment" contrasts with "'landscape,' 'wilderness,' 'countryside,' 'rurality'" (156).

Civilization is the privileged term here, with nature and animals relegated to the status of subaltern. (By "animals" I mean to denote, following the chauvinistic prejudice that alienates people from other living creatures in the popular idiom, "nonhuman animals.") Jean Baudrillard relates the rise of humanist civilization to inhumane treatment of animals: "animals were only demoted to the status of inhumanity as reason and humanism progressed" (133). In modern culture, animals have become commodities, resources to advance human enrichment. "The destruction of habitat, the enslavement into medical research and creation of industrial husbandry regimes," writes Adrian Franklin in *Animals and Modern Cultures*, "were always justified through their contribution to the greater (human) good" (3). Alan Bleakley suggests that "the more civilized the society the worse are its attitudes towards animals," citing Freud's description in *Civilization and Its Discontents* of a civilized state as one in which "wild and dangerous animals have been exterminated" (30).

Structural anthropologists believe that one of the main functions that animals serve in human culture is precisely to stake out the perimeter of that culture: "humans use animals in order to specify clearly who they are and where the differences lie between themselves and the natural world, particularly between themselves and animals" (Franklin 12). Animals are vehicles, burdened with the anthropocentrically symbolic projections of our own minds. We engage animals in a fashion that keeps them distinct from us, as we define ourselves against them. One could hardly imagine an orientation less amenable to harmonious and ethical coexistence with animals. Claude Lévi-Strauss's dictum in *Totemism* that animals are good to think with (89) describes a paradigm of imaginative exploitation. We conceive of animals as means to an end, as guinea pigs—by which I mean figurative "guinea pigs," not the literally designated creatures. *Q.E.D.*: the guinea pig's symbolic identity trumps its biological identity. The primary connotation of this animal's name invokes the rampant and unbridled performance of human operations upon animals. The guinea pig—as a species and as a figure of speech—illustrates our manifold use of animals in the enterprises of advancing our cultural and intellectual ambitions. The appellation is a self-fulfilling prophecy of exploitation: a mere guinea pig per se is a cog, a device. (Compounding our conceptual distortions of the animal, it "is not a pig and . . . does not come from Guinea" [Palmatier, 178].)

Animals, as we envision them from our side of the border, are largely constructs—mad dogs, dumb bunnies, busy bees, raging bulls—that service an array of cultural and imaginative needs. Such figurative appropriation is not the smoking gun in our imperious exploitation of animals; it is merely one indicator of our subliminal convictions that animals are marginal and malleable. Idiom demarcates cultural difference at the border between human and nonhuman.

When people do attempt to cross this borderline between "culture" and "nature" in order to broach animals, we tend to do so at our own pleasure and without interrogating the implications of these borders. If we are interested in animals, we are inclined to bring them into our world rather than meeting them on their own terms and in their own territory. Indeed, we assert that they have no "terms"—no a priori claim to an ethos or a logos, no rights, no property, no soul—and we have colonized and polluted beyond recognition, and beyond ecological viability, the lion's share of their territories. By "the lion's share," I mean, of course, *the people's share*; do lions ever actually get the lion's share? Assume that every animal metaphor I use is ironized: our language, like most human cultural systems, relegates lions and guinea pigs, along with all their other furry cousins, to the slough of irony.

As an example of how people relate to animals across this frontier, in which solely human considerations mediate the encounter, consider the logic underlying the exhibition of captive animals in zoos. Keepers remind spectators that many of the animals on display cannot survive in their native environments, which have been desecrated; thus, zoos are supposed to testify to our society's benevolent concern for these animals taken into protective custody in a small, artificial compound far from their natural habitat and profoundly restrictive of their normal instinctual behavior. *How* exactly did the animals' habitats get destroyed? What cultural dynamics connect the destruction of animal habitats and the enjoyment that we reap as we bring these animals—these "monkeys in the middle"—into our ken, surrounded by souvenirs, popcorn, parking lots, and all the other trappings of *our* habitual comforts? Doesn't the whole enterprise actually encourage benign neglect toward the environmental pillaging (out in the imperial provinces) that supports our consumptive appetites, and reward such large-scale ecological insouciance by justifying the small-scale extrication from the plundered biota of a few, token exotic animals—charismatic megafauna, in zoo parlance—who are relocated to a setting where *it is very convenient for us to see them*?

Our cognitive attempts to imagine and experience animals are, in the main, inaccurate: riven with the prejudices consequent upon our fierce determination to live inside the box we have constructed for ourselves and to reify the boundaries that separate us from the animal-other.

The physical and conceptual borders that separate people from animals facilitate the indignities we wreak upon them. "The plight of animals worldwide has never been more serious than it is today," write Jennifer Wolch and Jody Emel in *Animal Geographies*. "Each year, by the billions, animals are killed in factory farms; poisoned by toxic pollutants and waste; driven from their homes by logging, mining, agriculture, and urbanization; dissected, re-engineered, and used as spare body parts; and kept in captivity and servitude to be discarded as soon as their utility to people has waned" (xi). Yet, the reality of animals' suffering "is mostly obscured by the progressive elimination of animals from everyday human experience, and by the creation of a thin veneer of civility surrounding human–animal relations" that serves "to minimize human awareness of animal lives and fates" (xi). We situate animals beyond the pale, out of sight and out of mind, making it easier for us to sublimate their various plights.

Paul Shepard, too, perceives a geographical/spatial distancing from animals when he despairs that "the planet is becoming a city," and we have convinced ourselves that we live in "a world too small for animals" (*Thinking Animals* 1). Inside our box, we miss so much of animals' lives—the beautiful and amazing aspects of their existence as well as the more tragic circumstances that Wolch and Emel detail—across the divide. Human cultural designs fantasize a vast emptiness outside our box: we imagine a realm ripe for the projection of our own conceits (e.g., the inscription into the frontier landscape at Mt. Rushmore of American "manifest destiny"), and we are untroubled by the fact that our fantasies displace and destroy whatever might actually inhabit that uncharted territory. "To read most geographical texts," write Wolch and Emel (who are geographers), "one might never know that nature was populated by sentient creatures" (xv); and the same holds true, I would argue from my perspective as an English professor, for most literary texts.

It seems unlikely that in the present undertaking I am significantly less encumbered by the blinders of personhood than most of my fellow human beings whose anthropocentrisms I critique; still, in good faith and with some trepidation, I will attempt to suggest ways to reform our epistemological habits and assumptions: to think outside the box. I seek a connection between people and animals that runs counter to a culturally pervasive segregationist mind-set and challenges the dynamics that pervade most of our engagements with animals. This connection will be not so much a discovery as a rediscovery—Barbara Noske reminds us that "the human–animal relationship is first of all one of ancestry, of biological kinship, since it is from animals that the human species is descended" (1), and notes ironically our inclination "to define ourselves as distinctly non-animal" despite the fact that "Western science is revealing an increasing number of aspects of commonality between humans and animals" (40).

A Bat out of Hell . . .

"What is it like to be a bat?" This was the title, and the subject for deliberation, of a philosophical investigation that Thomas Nagel presented in 1974. "I assume we all believe that bats have experience. After all, they are mammals, and there is no more doubt that they have experience than that mice or pigeons or whales have experience," he writes, and "the essence of the belief that bats have experience is that there is something that it is like to be a bat." But Nagel does not finally resolve the question his essay poses. "Our own experience provides the basic material for our imagination, whose range is therefore limited. It will not help to try to imagine that one has webbing on one's arms, which enables one to fly around at dusk and dawn catching insects in one's mouth. . . . In so far as I can imagine this (which is not very far), it tells me only what it would be like for *me* to behave as a bat behaves. But that is not the question" (437–8).

Nagel states that "It would be fine if someone were to develop concepts and a theory that enabled us to think about" what it is like to be a bat, "but such an understanding may be permanently denied to us by the limits of our nature" (440). Possibly the human imagination might allow us to "transcend inter-species barriers" (442), but since this could be done only from our own (and not the bat's) point of view, it would be only a partial understanding. We would be committing anthropomorphic fallacies, Nagel implies. Ultimately, he concludes, we would need "to form new concepts and devise a new method—an objective phenomenology not dependent on empathy or the imagination" (449).

Personally, I would love to know what it is like to be a bat. I am more receptive than Nagel to the empathizing imagination that, in my opinion, is epitomized by art: I believe that art has the potential to present a valuable (if not complete and flawless) account of what it is like to be a different animal from ourselves. Indeed, I think that simply the expression of *wanting* to know what it is like to be a bat is the beginning of actually achieving that knowledge, and this expression of cognitive desire may quite possibly represent the incipient motive for creating (and for experiencing) an artistic representation of an animal. I have a strong faith in the powers of our intellectual aspirations when they are honestly and diligently exercised and especially when they are crystallized in our most sublime modes of expression.

José Emilio Pacheco, the contemporary Mexican poet who is the subject of chapter 3, has written what I think is a very good poem about a bat, "Investigation on the Subject of the Bat": rampantly subjective and imaginative, certainly full of anthropomorphic fallacies. Yet it tells us a great deal about bats—not in the (Baconian, positivistic) way that we generally expect to receive and process such information, with encyclopaedic detail or biological terminology. Instead, the poem encourages us to watch the play, the associations, the imagery that a poet generates from his ruminations on an animal. The poem inspires—and I would argue, *empowers*—Pacheco's readers to perform our own imaginative interactions with bats, which is a step toward experiencing what it is like to be a bat.

> It is obviously mammiferous, but I prefer to think of the bat as a
> bewitched neolithic reptile interrupted in transition between
> scales and feathers, in its now-thwarted desire to become a bird.
> It is, of course, a fallen angel, and has lent its wings and costume to the
> legion of devils.
> Blind (as we know what), it loathes the sun. And melancholy is the
> primary note in its disposition.
> Clumped in clusters, it inhabits caverns (silky sound of flight in the
> darkness) and eons ago learned the delights and hell of being an
> anonymous face in the crowd.
> It is probable that it suffers from that illness theologians call accidie—
> such indolence may engender nihilism—and it is not illogical to think it
> spends its mornings musing on the profound inanity of the
> world,
> foaming its anger, its rabid rage, at what we have done to its
> species. (51)

As the poem describes and imagines the condition of bats in our world, we may perceive that bats do not especially *belong* in our world. Seeing them in "our-worldly" terms is not the best way to meet them: they are, for example, ensconced in clichés—"Blind (as we know what)"—a shoddy mode of language from which we recoil as readers of poetry. A bat doesn't really experience the spiritual anxieties formulated by human theologians; it is not well-served by the anthropomorphic traits that we clumsily grasp for (melancholy, nihilism) in our attempt to understand this odd animal; and, worst of all, bats are furious at us! Pacheco's bat, it should be fairly noted, may not especially closely resemble a real bat. Indeed, the poem depicts primarily Pacheco's own idiosyncratic cultural and psychological associations with bats.

Certainly Pacheco's orientation has hermeneutic inadequacies, but also advantages. Pacheco's bat enjoys a figurative polyvalence: while obviously mammalian, it also evinces reptilian and avian elements, not to mention a trace of the existential philosopher. Pacheco's poem pushes us away from itself: we are trying to look at a bat, but we are simultaneously inundated with a sense of its elusive, uncertain, unknowable presence in this poem. If, as he implies, *our world* is not ideally suited for the sublime experience of bats, then we might escape beyond the text (as limited by human language and cultural habits), to another place, another consciousness. The animal's vivid presence amid the forces of Pacheco's poetry is a step in the process of shucking conventional and delimiting conceptions of bats: clearing the decks and brainstorming up a fresh set of cognitive and perceptual tools for "Investigation on the Subject of the Bat" so that we can begin anew in the endeavor of attempting to know bats and know what it may be like (if not what it *is* like) to be a bat.

Our mainstream experience of animals consists of "banal stereotypes," writes Paul Shepard in *The Others*, and "radical ways of revisioning, at once unromantic and free of the old logic of hierarchy, are necessary" to get beyond this (12). To paraphrase T. S. Eliot, the end of all our exploring will be to arrive where we started and know the bat for the first time. As a bird-reptile-nihilist bat, the subject of Pacheco's poem is poised to transgress the boundaries that an imaginatively impoverished discourse—for example, the pinpointing scientific vocabulary of Linnaean taxonomical classification with its absolute hierarchies encoded in a dead language—might impose upon it. The bat meets us halfway in our attempt to know it, and Pacheco situates both the human being and the bat in this meeting place, outside the box.

Pacheco's bat is empowered, exuberant, hyper-animated, in this poem and beyond this poem. Nagel's bat, the bat of the well-meaning but ultimately irremediable anthropocentrist, remains inaccessible, mute, hypothetical—relegated to the eternal holding pen of philosophical theory. I agree with Nagel that we should "form new concepts and devise a new method" in order to expand our experiential and epistemological sense of animals, but I discount what he deems the limitations of human empathy and the human imagination in this endeavor. The empathizing imagination can be enlisted to enhance the awareness of sentient, cognitive, ethical, and emotional *affinities between people and animals*, and it is the potential for enhanced appreciation of these affinities that makes me want to know what it is like to be a bat.

In the very moment that Nagel asks his titular question, it is a foregone conclusion that we will not learn what it is like to be a bat if we follow him in the processes of his treatise. I do not mean to single out Nagel as a whipping boy: he simply reiterates the course of enlightenment/rationalistic epistemology when it comes to consciousness of the other. When powerful white Christian Victorian men posed The Negro Question or The Woman Question or The Jewish Question, it was similarly inevitable that The Negro, The Woman, and The Jew would not receive satisfactory Answers. I prefer not to get bogged down in The Bat Question, but instead, to use the occasion of its emergence as an impetus to fly away from it and to outfox its rationalist discourse. We can do better than Nagel in terms of our attempts to know animals; someone like Pacheco, whose animals are vast and contain multitudes, points us in the right direction.

Instead of a single overbearing Animal Question, I will scatter generously throughout my investigation a range of questions—sometimes vague and general, sometimes loaded, sometimes unanswerable—intended to foster a perspective and a discourse that will help to broach most effectively the inter-disciplines of anthrozoology (human–animal studies). Here are some of the most basic questions that we may begin with: Who are *they*? Who are *we*? How do we relate to each other? How can we connect with each other? What are the terms that can facilitate this dialogue (if dialogue is even an appropriate term, in light of the language barrier between people and animals), this process of discovery? Nagel, an eminent philosopher, is probably right—within the terms of his discourse—when he demurs from answering the question he asks: what is it like to be a bat? But why *does* he ask it? It seems as if he wants to affirm a wider trope of knowledge and connection across species-barriers but feels limited in this aspiration by his obligations to established human rational (philosophical) methodology. Perhaps he raises a question that he declines to answer himself so that someone like Pacheco, or someone like me, can take up his challenge with a leap of faith across the species-divide. Indeed, faith, as contrasted with the conventional tropes of science, is an important mode for my investigations here. The praxes of spiritual conviction offer an alternative discourse to scientific rationalism in mediating the relations between people and animals. I will try to show in part 2 how we may find, in poetry, a secular analog to the power more conventionally perceived in the realm of spirituality: a power that I invoke in my attempt to assert a currently ineffable sense of affinity between people and animals. Poetry "must take the place / Of empty heaven and its hymns" (Wallace Stevens, "The Man with the Blue Guitar" 135).

The rationalistic constraints that afflict Nagel leave Gilles Deleuze and Félix Guattari uncowed (and again: remember—these are *ironized* cows! but watch out for them nevertheless... they may leave messy ironic cowpies all over the place). In *A Thousand Plateaus*, Deleuze and Guattari propound a conceptual model that challenges the segregation of human vs. animal sentience—and also challenges Judeo-Christian dominionism—via a consciousness they call "becoming-animal." It is abstractly elusive, as theoretical philosophy can often be, and as human-voiced accounts of human–animal connection must be if they are to escape the entrenched conventions that reinforce our diminution of and separation from animals. The notion of people becoming animals is inherently paradoxical—we are already animals... in a sense, but also not, in a sense; when we say "animals," we signify *them*, as opposed to us.

Akira Mizuta Lippit explains the subversive implications of *A Thousand Plateaus*: "In Deleuze and Guattari's reinvention of the world as becoming-animal, the subject of a human system is also exposed to the forces that other systems... impose upon it. Humanity's being is opened to animal being. . . . The work of Deleuze and Guattari seeks to map, against every convention of mapping, a terrain open to animal being" (128).

"Becoming-animal" invokes a fluidity between and among species, a permeability—eschewing the boundaries—that consecrates the affinities and interactivity between human and nonhuman animals. Deleuze and Guattari begin by noting, in the safely contrived genre of myth, the prevalence of inter-species transformations, transmigrations, metamorphoses: "in his study of myths, Lévi-Strauss is always encountering these rapid acts by which a human becomes an animal at the same time as the animal becomes... (Becomes what? Human, or something else?)" (237, ellipses in text). Myth initiates a challenge to rigid species distinctions. But "becoming-animal" is not merely mythic symbolism or metaphor: "not a correspondence between relations... neither is it a resemblance, an imitation, or, at the limit, an identification. . . . Becomings-animal are neither dreams nor phantasies. They are perfectly real. . . . becoming is not an evolution, at least not an evolution by descent and filiation. Becoming produces nothing by filiation; all filiation is imaginary. Becoming is always of a different order than filiation. It concerns alliance" (237–8). The idea of *alliance* between people and other animals is at the core of the consciousness that I am trying to elucidate; thus, intrigued by Deleuze and Guattari's formulation here, I am encouraged to proceed further.

In their conception of animals, Deleuze and Guattari privilege action—intensity, dynamism, becoming—over mere form. "Part of Deleuze and Guattari's particular concern about form is their suspicion that in handling animal form, artists are merely *imitating* the animal from a safe distance," writes Steve Baker. "Mere imitation has nothing to do with the intense and thorough-going experience of becoming animal. Artists cannot remain detached, but... are caught up in the lines of flight their work initiates" (*Postmodern* 139). Deleuze and Guattari's animal metaphor, "lines of flight," affirms the synthesis and potential transcendence that effective art enacts: the art initiates these lines of flight, and the artists become caught up in this—as if they are flying themselves; as if these lines (lines of paint perhaps, or poetry, or music) are their ticket to a higher plane of consciousness, beyond the merely human.

Deleuze and Guattari's formulation here resembles what I earlier defined as art in the valence of empathetic imagination, art that connects us with other species in a meaningful way that is inaccessible in the default cultural modes. An animal in a certain artistic incarnation represents, and enables, a departure above and beyond the canvas... or outside the text. The achievement of this art is not imitation, not fidelity to form, but something dynamic and supra-dimensional: beyond merely the length and width of the canvas; beyond the frame; beyond the colors and composition of the static text, and into—*becoming*—something more intense; metaphysicality... resonance... inspiration... epiphany. Such art takes the viewer into a higher cognitive/experiential/epistemological realm. It points us toward a place where we might learn, for example, what it is like to be a bat.

Deleuze and Guattari illustrate the distinction between mere imitation and more profound and experientially affective representation of animals in art by reference to Alfred Hitchcock's film, *The Birds*: "Becoming is never imitating. When Hitchcock does birds, he does not reproduce bird calls, he produces an electronic sound like a field of intensities or a wave of vibrations, a continuous variation, like a terrible threat welling up inside us" (305). Hitchcock's birds are alien, threatening, and in many ways not at all like real birds (as Pacheco's bat diverged in many ways from a real bat)—but I think the appeal of Hitchcock's terrible birds to Deleuze and Guattari lies in their power, their otherworldliness, and thus their capability to shatter our *idées reçues* about birds. Hitchcock compels us to consider that there may be much more between the beak and the tail than meets the eye. Deleuze and Guattari celebrate the threatening terror with which Hitchcock infuses his birds, because this force inspires us to revisit the dull old images, static and two-dimensional, that have surrounded most earlier representations of birds.

In their account of a dance, Deleuze and Guattari offer another example of the activity and interactivity—involving motion and action;

transcendence of the passivity that characterizes our habitual cultural experiences—that is necessary if we are to approach the animal, become-animal:

> The tarantella is a strange dance that magically cures or exorcises the supposed victims of a tarantula bite. But when the victim does this dance, can he or she be said to be imitating the spider, to be identifying with it...? No, because the victim, the patient, the person who is sick, becomes a dancing spider only to the extent that the spider itself is supposed to become a pure silhouette, pure color, and pure sound to which the person dances. One does not imitate; one constitutes a block of becoming. Imitation enters in only as an adjustment of the block, like a finishing touch, a wink, a signature. But everything of importance happens elsewhere: in the becoming-spider of the dance, which occurs on the condition that the spider itself becomes sound and color, orchestra and painting. (305)

The vital engagement of vibrant animals (as opposed to our cultural default, the domesticated subjection of animals rendered virtually inanimate) demands transgressing static boundaries, conceptual and cognitive restrictions on border-crossings between people and animals. To achieve this, Deleuze and Guattari describe an epistemological fusion: interdisciplinary, multimedia, inter-species. Bird as electricity; spider as orchestra. To approach these animals, to become these animals, we become something outside ourselves: more than just time- and place-bound spectators, consumers, of images, art, animals. It is not even sufficient to dance with the animals, but more radically, we must *dance the animals*. Animals must shock us, viscerally and literally, with the sort of electric force that Hitchcock's birds convey. The crux of becoming-animal is the becoming, the process; Deleuze and Guattari will not designate the outcome of this process as either human or animal: it is instead some fantastic synthesis of hitherto segregated identities, and this process so powerfully challenges the delimiting *boxes* of our consciousness—the borders, the boundaries, the manifold geographies that separate people from animals—because it is, pointedly, "an *absolute deterritorialization* of the man" (*Kafka* 35); there is "no longer man or animal, since each deterritorializes the other" (Baker 124). This apotheosis uncompromisingly nullifies the historical territorial constraints of animals and the corollary territorial monomanias of people.

Becoming-animal enables us to see the human–animal relationship as versatile rather than dogmatic and hierarchical. It is not "about the linear and progressive narrative of human evolution," write Lynda Birke and Luciana Parisi, but about "processes of interchange with environments and of 'making them over.' It is about the creation of change" (65).

> We can think of the example of ecosystems—although not as assemblages of individuals or populations of different species as they are sometimes described. Instead, we might emphasize the transformations of energy central to ecosystems . . . Through these transformations, entities are continuously in states of becoming: even apparent equilibrium is dynamic. . . . Deleuze and Guattari's notion of becoming . . . allows us to begin to think differently about ourselves and about animals. These ideas move beyond simple dualisms by insisting on connections and flows rather than individual entities, and by insisting on transformation and change rather than essence. Becoming animal, in Deleuze and Guattari's work, is to experience interchange. (65–7)

A passage from Gary Snyder's "Straight Creek—Great Burn" strikes me as a superb illustration of Deleuze and Guattari's concept of becoming-animal—an aesthetic approximation of their theoretical construct. The poem sets out lines of flight that propel the reader from the art into the experience of the animal:

> A whoosh of birds
> swoops up and round
> tilts back
> almost always flying all apart
> and yet hangs on!
> together;
>
> never a leader,
> all of one swift
>
> empty
> dancing   mind.
>
> They arc and loop & then
> their flight is done.
> they settle down.
> end of poem. (53)

The poem ends when the birds stop flying. The birds—their flight, their movement, their energies, their lives—are captured in the poem, one might conventionally say: and yet, here, one wants a more felicitous description than "capture" to describe the poetic presence of these birds. We might say, the moment of the poem corresponds with the birds' action, as it reflects their lives: the poem flies with the birds, and it settles down and ends with them, too. As we watch the birds, with Snyder's evocative guidance, *we* fly with the birds; we fly the birds. Snyder describes both the literal details of their movement and, as well—with the exclamation point—the human experience of this: our perception, our response to them, our interaction with them, our flight with them. As they swoop, we exclaim! In one short, imagistic stanza—"empty / dancing mind"—Snyder conjoins human choreography, our art, with bird-flight choreography, their art, and our sentience (our mind) with theirs. When the dance is over, when the flight is over, the poem is done—and Snyder hits us on the head as he announces the end of the poem, "end of poem," as if to bring us back from our trance, from our experience of flight, from our becoming-animal. The art (the poem) is the flight; the end of flight is the end of poem.

One final point of interest from Deleuze and Guattari is their contention that the animal is always multiple: "A becoming-animal always involves a pack, a band, a population, a peopling, in short, a multiplicity. . . . We do not become animal without a fascination for the pack" (239–40). Perhaps this is because we conventionally abrogate unto ourselves a monopoly on singularity, unique individuality, and leave for the animals only the *dehumanizing* pack-status—as, for example, a "wolfpack" of people metaphorically denotes an assembly that is vicious, subhuman, threatening because of its size, but also because the participants have "devolved" into "subhuman" behavior. But for artists who enact a becoming-animal, this multiplicity becomes an empowering attribute rather than a pejorative limitation. To return to Hitchcock, again, and the power of his filmic animals: one bird is just . . . a bird; it is *the birds*, in the plural, that transcend their banal innocence, their innocuous subjectivity, and become able to challenge and modify human social behavior. In Hitchcock's hands, given the nature of his discourse in the thriller genre, this multiplicity manifests itself in fear and threat; but in the hands of the poets I will discuss later—especially José Emilio Pacheco (in chapter 3) and Marianne Moore (in chapter 4)—it is the multiplicity, the power consequent upon experiencing animals in a pack, that facilitates the most dazzling assemblies of poetic animals.

On the other hand, overemphasizing the collective force of animals may neglect their individual significance, which may be a disservice especially because it is already so difficult, generally, for people to perceive this sense of particularity in other animals. My earlier deliberation about the portrayal of bats in the cultural imagination, for example, was pervaded on all sides with a sort of generic distancing: as we mull over pluses and minuses about the theoretical representation of bats, what does all this have to do specifically with that skinny bat hanging up there on the rafter, the third one from the left? A given poem may approach the representation of animals by celebrating their multiple energies, or by highlighting and illuminating a single representative example. In the first two stanzas of her poem "Abundance and Satisfaction," Pattiann Rogers thoughtfully explores the case for both the multiple and the individual consideration of animals:

> One butterfly is not enough. We need
> many thousands of them, if only
> for the effusion of the wayward-
> swaying words they occasion—blue
> and copper hairstreaks, sulphur
> and cabbage whites, brimstones,
> peacock fritillaries, tortoiseshell
> emperors, skippers, meadow browns.
> We need a multitude of butterflies
> right on the tongue simply to be able
> to speak with a varied six-pinned
> poise and particularity.
>
> But thousands of butterflies
> are surfeit. We need just one
> flitter to apprehend correctly
> the will of aspen leaves, the lassitude
> of lupine petals, the sleep
> of a sleeping eyelid. To examine
> adequately one set of finely leaded,
> stained wings of violet translucence,
> one single sucking proboscis (sap-
> and-sugar-licking thread), to study
> thoroughly just one powder scale, one
> gold speck from one dusted butterfly
> forewing would require at least
> a millennium of attention to all melody,
> phrase, gravity and horizon. (*Bread* 63)

Wallace Stevens famously considers the multiplicity versus the individuality of animals in "Thirteen Ways of Looking at a Blackbird," where the title animal is simultaneously singular and plural, unique and polyvalent. His Cubist sensibility puts the onus on the viewer, the one who is looking, to determine whether s/he is looking at one bird or a series of birds. As Hereclitus might have said, one can never look at the same blackbird twice. Does this mean that the concept of the blackbird (and of any animal in art, in our imagination) is inherently multiple? Are all these writers—Stevens, Rogers, Deleuze and Guattari—even talking about the animal per se or only the medium of perception (poetry, vision, consciousness), as they try to balance and reconcile animals' singularity/plurality?

Literary Formulations of Animals

At the beginning of the twentieth century, President Theodore Roosevelt's "naturalist" adventures helped inspire an American back-to-nature movement. Different cultural arbiters offered competing representations of nature. The type of first hand, physically intense experience epitomized by Roosevelt's grandiose African hunting expeditions vied with other models of experiencing animals and nature: "The emergence of environmental preservation organizations such as the Audubon Society and the Sierra Club, the federal government's preoccupation with conserving the nation's natural resources, the push for nature study in the public schools, and the growth of landscape architecture initiated by Frederick Law Olmstead's work... all reflected an interest among the nation's urban middle class for greater contact with nature" (11), writes Gregg Mitman.

This interest in nature also produced "a large market... for the realistic wild animal story made famous by writers such as Jack London, Ernest Thompson Seton, Charles D. Roberts, and William J. Long," Mitman explains. "The popularity of animal stories such as Seton's *Wild Animals I Have Known*, which went through sixteen printings in four years, and London's best-selling novel *The Call of the Wild*," testified to the national attraction to nature (10). But some questioned whether literary representations were at all relevant to real animals:

> In March of 1903, the acclaimed Catskill nature writer, John Burroughs, used the pages of the *Atlantic Monthly* to lambaste the growing literary genre that he dubbed "mock natural history." In Burroughs's evaluation, literary naturalists such as London, Long, and Seton had simply seized on the public's fascination with nature and turned it "into pecuniary profit." Burroughs disdained the sentimentalism and anthropomorphism found in books such as Seton's *Wild Animals I Have Known* and Long's *School of the Woods* that claimed to be faithful and accurate representations of nature. . . . Any nature writer faces the danger, Burroughs wrote, "of making too much of what we see and describe, of putting in too much sentiment, too much literature, in short, of valuing these things more for the literary effects we can get out of them than for themselves." (Mitman 11)

Impressed by Burroughs's critique, Roosevelt "questioned the veracity" of some of these popular depictions of animals, and "feared that Long's books, which were particularly popular in the public schools, would ultimately hinder public appreciation, study, and preservation of nature. 'If the child mind is fed with stories that are false to nature,' Roosevelt argued, 'the children will go to the haunts of the animal only to meet with disappointment, . . . disbelief, and the death of interest.' . . . Roosevelt championed the knowledge of the hunter over those whom he regarded as armchair naturalists. Roosevelt found 'real' nature through the touch of a steel trigger and the sight down a gun barrel, rather than through the poet's pen" (12).

I have rather more confidence than Roosevelt did in the poet's pen, as opposed to the steel trigger, as a medium to facilitate our cultural engagement with animals. But the issues that Roosevelt and Burroughs raised a century ago remain potent today: what is "real" nature, and—assuming that we can determine this—how do literary representations relate to nature? What do we expect of the animals that we may encounter in literature? Our culture has conditioned us to expect that our animals will be copiously present to treat as we please: whether we want to eat them, or wear them, or dissect them, or just look at them. And in our aesthetic enterprises, we demand of animals a similar accessibility and ubiquity of service, as metaphors, symbols, vehicles, toys, fodder for contemplation, backdrops, flatterers of our omnivorous cultural grasp. Certainly most literary representations sustain this conceit of the subject animal's availability, boundless pliability, and unproblematic implication in whatever text at hand happens to require a quack-quack here or an oink-oink there. Consider, as comparable cultural constructs, such types as the contented slave, the stage Irishman, and Harriet (Mrs. Ozzie) Nelson. But there are rare and interesting exceptions, in which the animals overcome their subordinate subjectivity, in a trope where they do not figure as the happily second-class foils that we have come to expect, and refuse to proceed submissively into an abattoir of cultural mauling.

Literature is emotional, prettified, fallacious, delusory, delusional, passive, distanced, disengaged, cheap, weak, and tepid. These prejudices presumably underlie the accusations that Burroughs and Roosevelt launched against the "armchair naturalists" who enjoy nature through the mediation of a text. On the other hand, a more felicitous attitude toward the conjunction of literature and nature comes from Jonathan Bate, who implores his readers in *The Song of the Earth* to live with "an attunement to both words and the world, and so to acknowledge that, although we make sense of things by way of words, we do not live apart from the world. For culture and environment are held together in a complex and delicate web" (23). In this vein, I will propose a defense of literary value, and not just on cerebral or intellectual merits, but as a springboard for ethical replenishment: a platform for real-world improvements of our modes of engaging with nature.

Aesthetic interactions with animals leave them untouched by people—untrammelled, unexploited—or, so I hypothesize. It may be true, as some aboriginal cultures believe, that to take a likeness is indeed, literally, to "take" it—to colonize, to steal the spirit that the likeness represents. But the utility in aesthetic representations of animals may serve as an antidote to more invasive, distorting ways of interacting with animals that run rampant in our culture. In the hopes of discovering a *maximally insightful and harmless* aesthetic ethos, I will survey different modes of perception and cultural experience that surround our encounters with animals.

What licenses are we taking when we implicate nature as a subject in human culture? Surely, the "literary effects" that Burroughs warns against are rampant in the works I study—indeed, as a literary critic, I may be drawn to such works primarily by those effects. What drawbacks accompany literary effects? Is there, as Burroughs worries, "too much literature" here? Do we experience and canonize aesthetic animals at the expense of real ones? And even if we *do* do that, is it necessarily a bad thing? Perhaps it works, ultimately, to the protection of the animal—the literary animal may serve as a "beard," or decoy, while the real one can prosper unconstrained by human cultural systems.

My topic is, specifically, animal poetry. "Animal poetry," I explain to people who ask about my interests and are momentarily confused by my response, refers to poetry *about* animals, not *by* animals. But the other is an intriguing concept as well. I suppose I'm insufficiently attuned to animals to appreciate the poetry that they generate, though I have no doubt that it's there; I wonder how we might access it. . . . if anyone has discovered anything like this, please e-mail me, rmalamud@gsu.edu.

Where does an 8000-lb. Elephant Sit?

But if I may indulge my digression and consider further the concept of art by animals: I am intrigued by the activity of elephant painting that has become popular in zoos lately. In attempts to extract art from animals, zookeepers have placed paintbrushes in elephants' trunks and set up canvases in front of the animals, to generate "paintings" that sell for considerable amounts of money. This money is often used to support the zoo: the animal thus works to advance the institutional instrument of its own imprisonment. Once again, we see how the animal in human culture is invariably ironized.

According to Vicki Croke, the most famous painting elephant is Ruby, "an eight-thousand-pound elephant at the Phoenix Zoo whose paintings provide money for the institution and apparently contentment to the elephant herself. She chooses her colors with authority, and her vivid compositions sell for $1,000 each" (66–7):

> Keepers give Ruby a canvas on an easel and several choices of brushes and jars of nontoxic acrylic paints in red, blue, yellow, green, orange, turquoise, magenta, and purple. With her trunk, which contains fifty thousand separate muscles and can weigh as much as a man, Ruby delicately points to her selection of brush and color. . . . The brush is dipped in her color choice and handed over to her. She decides when to freshen the brush or switch color. She decides when the work is complete. When Ruby is finished, she either refuses to select another color or backs away from the work. . . . According to a paper written by one of her trainers . . . Ruby's early paintings were "composed of smears, but as the activity progressed, the paintings seemed to develop in composition with linear, triangular, and circular motions being noted." Ruby uses as much or as little of the canvas as she pleases and will not be swayed to change her area of concentration. She will also superimpose one mark on another using different colors. All of this may reveal compositional control and visual organization. (68)

Croke is an apologist for zoos, so when she notes that the elephant's trunk contains 50,000 muscles, for example, she's suggesting, implicitly, that painting is thereby a valid, appropriate activity for Ruby to be performing with some of those otherwise-dormant muscles. And when Croke describes how "Ruby *delicately* points to her selection of brush and color," we're meant to savor the elephant's exquisite delicacy: she's so sensitive, just like a *real* artist! (By which we would mean, of course, a human artist.)

As a counterforce to Croke's tacit endorsement of Ruby's lot, a poem by Stevie Smith comes to mind, called "This is Disgraceful and Abominable." The title alone—certainly one of the most blatantly polemical in the history of poetry—conveys Smith's unabashed fury at how people engage with animals.

> Of all the disgraceful and abominable things
> Making animals perform for the amusement of human beings is
> Utterly disgraceful and abominable.

> Animals are animals and have their nature
> And that's enough, it is enough, leave it alone. (79)

But people are usually unable to "leave it alone," leave animals to their own nature. Performing animals draw enthralled audiences, and Ruby's accomplishment generated an epidemic of imitators: "Word of Ruby's success spread like wildfire among elephant trainers, and soon zoos across North America began plying their elephants with paint-soaked brushes, pushing them in front of blank canvases, and waiting for the spark of genius," write Vitaly Komar and Alexander Melamid in *When Elephants Paint.* "The ranks of elephant artists were growing rapidly: there was Scarlett O'Hara in Atlanta, Siri in Syracuse, Kamala in Calgary, Annabelle in Alaska, Mary in Little Rock, Winky in Sacramento, Sri in Seattle—about twenty in all, each churning out abstract canvases that bore an uncanny resemblance to the messy, all-over, expansively gestural work of American artists of the 1950s, such as Jackson Pollock, Willem de Kooning, and Franz Kline" (10).

Painting is *our* art form; why do we make an elephant do it? Because it's cute: look at the animal, pretending to be like us. . . . as delicate as us (though we know she never could *really* be—but we've dressed her up, as if. . . .). The elephant's paintings are, by our standards, pathetic, primitive, meaningless. We look at them to confirm our own presumption that we have a monopoly on the imaginative vitality necessary to produce "real" art. These scrawls amuse for a few moments and then confirm by negation—by their distance from "real" art—the boundary that separates, on the one side, animals' ignorance, and on the other side, our own sublimities. If people speculate that the elephants' canvases somewhat resemble those of Pollock *et al.*, finally we regard the resemblance as merely coincidental (or, perhaps, we wonder to ourselves whether those artists are just overglorified animals). Elephant "art" does not really, essentially, convince people that elephants share human talents. Rather, it reiterates the proverbial monkey-in-front-of-a-typewriter phenomenon: eventually, we know, the monkey would type *King Lear*, but this is a statistical rather than an intellectual incident; it doesn't mean that there's a bard of monkeydom comparable to William Shakespeare.

An organization called the Asian Elephant Art & Conservation Project sponsors several elephant painters, residents of various preserves and safari parks. Its website features biographical critiques of each animal's art, and I cannot quite tell whether they are straight or parodic—probably some of both, depending on the reader's perspective.

Judge for yourself:

> As a second generation domesticated elephant, with a background in the entertainment industry, there was never any doubt that Ramona would succeed as an artist. . . . Within two days, she was making confident strokes, deep in concentration before the canvas. Her brush strokes are delicate and measured, and she has a preference for darker colors. She has a true artistic temperament.
>
> [Seng Wong] began learning to paint by making slow measured marks on the paper, which was laid on the ground. After moving to the easel, his style developed and the brush strokes became more free, although he maintains his early cautious manner and appears to be deep in concentration when at the canvas.
>
> Aided by her handsome young mahout, Juthanam favors a palette of clear, bright colors which she applies with thick, meandering, wormlike brushstrokes. Critics have commented on the elemental, organic quality of Juthanam's wandering lines, noting their uncanny resemblance to the interlocking strands of DNA molecules. (Asian Elephant Art & Conservation Project)

Nor are elephants' cultural endeavors limited to the painting arts: apparently, they also possess musical talents. Under the direction of David Soldier and Richard Lair (human beings), the "Thai Elephant Orchestra" enjoyed extensive international publicity when it released a CD from Mulatta Records in 2000. The six orchestra elephants live with several dozen others in the Thai Elephant Conservation Center, in Lampang. They once worked in government logging camps hauling teak, but when that was banned they began "earning their keep," as NPR reporter Renee Montagne put it, by painting and giving rides to tourists. Soldier, an avant-garde composer, trained some of these animals to use cymbals, harmonicas, gongs, thundersheets, and drums. "The idea wasn't exactly, you know, let's see if elephants can play like John Coltrane," Soldier says. "The idea was to see, if you give them the instruments, and it's comfortable for them and they learn how to control them, what are they going to come up with?" (Montagne). "Two things make it hard to deny that they're real musicians," says Montagne, and Soldier explains why he believes the animals exhibit "artistic intent": "One is that, as soon as they learn how to play the instruments, they're not hitting randomly. They'll learn where the instrument sounds good and they'll always repeat it at that spot." And second, "I've never seen an elephant walk over to one of the instruments and start playing spontaneously. However, once they do start playing with them . . . many of them, you tell them to stop and they won't." Lair describes the music as "difficult to listen to but compelling, full of subtleties and variations"; Soldier calls it "both challenging and bizarre" (Strickland). Lair addresses the ethical issues: "Many people will say that these noble elephants should not be forced to mimic human activities. I agree. Elephants should not be in captivity but sadly, virtually all elephants in Thailand must work for a living. Being allowed to bang on musical instruments and make gorgeous noises of their own volition and invention is at worst very soft duty and for most of them is quite clearly a great pleasure. So these elephants are unjustly incarcerated—but what better job than to be in the prison band?" (Strickland).

How do we evaluate this output? Is it art? Is it animal abuse? Is the resulting artifact "beautiful" (and what standards of beauty do we use in this adjudication)? What are the implications of the *production*, the "artistic" performance, that generates this "art?" What does it mean for us to make animals make art? And if, as I presume, this art is fundamentally human art (even though it happens to be produced by an animal, or more accurately, *via* an animal), is there any such thing as truly animal art? Do these performing elephants bring us in any way closer to such art?

The human organizers of the elephant orchestra seem at least somewhat more humanely attuned to animals' welfare and integrity than zoo promoters such as Ruby's masters, who seem more like circus ringleaders. The orchestra leaders have thought about the ethics of what they are doing, while there is no indication that Ruby's keepers have done so. Soldier and Lair are working to discover, or perhaps just to rationalize and profit from, the elephants' unique potential for creative performance. I am not convinced by the criteria that they use to assess the animals' artistic intent, but at least they are aware that this is something they need to consider if they are to avoid being "merely human" about all this, and simply harvesting one more clever artifact from dumb-animal subjects. In the final analysis, it is hard for me to get beyond a conviction that elephants are not "supposed" to be cutting CDs, and it is difficult to see how this enterprise can generate anything other than anthropocentric culture featuring the latest incarnation of the dancing bear.

In response to NPR's story about the musical elephants, an incisive exchange arose on the discussion listserve of the Association for the Study of Literature and the Environment (archived at its website, www.asle.umn.edu). I would like to quote, as a sort of forum, several of these contributors, who illustrate the range of responses to the complex issues involved here.

> Anyone hear the NPR segment on today's "Morning Edition" about the Thai Elephant Orchestra—six pachyderms that have just released their

first CD? . . . The story caught my attention because of the unselfconscious regard that the musicians working with the elephants seemed to have for the elephants' music. True, the musicians set the elephants up with human instruments, but the interspecies interaction via a shared medium was still fascinating. (H. Lewis Ulman)

I mean this as a legitimate instigation of social/personal reflection, not merely as a snotty comment: did anyone ask the elephants if they wanted to perform? to "release" a CD (which implies agency)? to play "their" music on "human instruments?" Sorry (not really), but this news story really bothered me, especially the way that so many people I know thought that it was cute without thinking it through. To me, animal music is composed of the sounds they make when not lined up, moderated, and with objects attached to their bodies. (Sandra Leigh Matthew)

Good question, to be sure. Just the sort question we should be posing (and I should have posed in my original message) about such treatment of animals. But the answer seems to me more complicated that my original posting or Sandra's response suggest.

If I remember the story correctly, the elephants were "laid off" from the logging industry by environmental controls. For better or worse, they were already domesticated animals, and I can't easily quarrel with the event that led to this experiment. Also, I don't think the musicians working with the elephants tried to teach the elephants to play the instruments in a particular way or to play "human" music to entertain humans; rather, they built oversized versions of drums, cymbals, and harmonicas, presented them to the elephants, and watched to see what would happen. They seemed sensitive to individual variation among the animals (some of the elephants seemed to like playing more than others).

. . . I want to thank Sandra for raising questions that I pondered but didn't have the time or patience to include in my original message. I wonder if anyone has read more about the story. The real work to be done lies not in our immediate response to the gist of the story (which I should have acknowledged) but in detailed analysis of the circumstances and discourses surrounding it. Assuming, of course, that we don't have an a priori objection to animals and humans working together but rather to the conditions of that work. (H. Lewis Ulman)

I would suppose that they really DO have agency, in that no one can really *make* an elephant stand still if they don't want to, and if they don't want to cooperate with the instruments, they won't. (Just ask a parent of any small child how a mammal responds when it doesn't want to do something . . .) Humans seek out and enjoy the interspecies interactions with so many creatures, must we assume that the pleasure isn't returned in some instances? Cooperation looks a lot different than indifference or anger—and would I think be apparent. The choices would be no response, flight, or bites. (Maggie Dwyer)

I heard this report as well. If my memory is correct, these were elephants who were used in the Thai logging industry. That industry is apparently

> drying up. So the elephants were already used/exploited/trained by humans prior to their current activities. This doesn't make the situation better or worse necessarily, but it adds another wrinkle to the situation. (Tom Dean)

> In the story, they made it very clear that the elephants were being cared for in a sanctuary because they had been laid off from logging. The people involved seemed genuinely interested in the animals (for example, they used instruments tuned to the Thai scale because it was what the elephants were familiar with). They decided to give them instruments because, apparently, elephants respond readily to music. They wanted to see if they would make music. One of the musicians involved said that after playing around with the instruments a little, the elephants would repeat passages that were "musical." E. O. Wilson has suggested that it is our capacity for appreciating art that separates humans from animals ("The Poetic Species"). Perhaps we are even closer than we thought. (Kaye Adkins)

> According to what I gleaned from the NPR piece, the elephants apparently enjoyed making music (on human instruments) and sought out the opportunity to do so once the instruments were available. The musicologist got the idea to make instruments for them because he noticed that they seemed to enjoy human music. If I'm remembering correctly, when he left harmonicas for them, they picked them up of their own accord. When the musicologist returned the next day, he could hear the elephants walking around their patch of jungle, playing harmonicas. That image delights me. Perhaps I'm being hopelessly naive, but the whole thing seemed not so much the tacky manipulation of a circus act, but something more in the spirit of an invitation to the elephants to join in the music-making.
>
> And it could have been worse. The elephants could have been given accordions. (Ian Marshall)

> If only elephants could persuade us to learn to play their music, if such a concept applies in the lives of elephants. What instruments do elephants use to play "music," I wonder. Jeffrey Moussaieff Masson discusses animal music in *When Elephants Weep*, by the way.
>
> And what's wrong with accordions? (Robert Mellin)

These postings reflect bemusement at the possibilities that the enterprise offers and a desire to find some redemptive sense of value in the music, but this is tempered by a wariness about what can happen to animals—what *usually* happens—when they get sucked into human culture. Our track record testifies to a panoply of indignities and inanities that we commit when we compel animals to do things that they don't normally do—things that people find cute or funny; unnatural activities that we think, somehow, can nevertheless illuminate how people and animals relate to each other; things that may entertain us precisely because they are so counterintuitive. These activities threaten animals' integrity: they exemplify what Alan Bleakley calls "another way to exterminate the animals: by denying their animality, their bestiality. . . . in Baudrillard's term, we extract a 'confession' from them that demonstrates that they are no longer bestial (and then incomprehensible and mute), but both comprehensible and able to communicate with us (on our terms, through our invented languages). Once the confession is obtained, then we can rest easily in our beds, for the animals are no longer dangerous Other, but incorporated into the ever-expanding human domain" (23).

Erica Fudge analyzes what happens when we bring animals, gratuitously, close to human cultural processes in her discussion of sixteenth-century monkey-baiting at the Bear Garden in London. A monkey rides in the saddle of a horse, which is attacked by a half dozen dogs. An Italian observer recorded: "it is wonderful to see the horse galloping along, kicking up the ground and champing at the bit, with the monkey holding very tightly to the saddle, and crying out frequently when he is bitten by the dogs" (11). Fudge explains: the spectator's image of the monkey

> is obviously and disturbingly anthropomorphic. There is a sense of recognition: the monkey is a creature similar to the human. . . . [The monkey] may well have been dressed up to underline its likeness to the human. By staging the anthropoid nature of the animal in such an obvious way the spectator was invited to perform two forms of recognition: to recognize the anthropoid nature of the animal, but also to recognize that anthropoid only ever means human-like, it can never mean human. At the moment of sameness difference is revealed and the disturbing spectacle of the screaming monkey on horseback becomes a reminder of the superiority of humanity. The monkey can only ever achieve a comic imitation of the human. There are parallels between Homi Bhabha's work on colonial literature and this reading of monkey-baiting. Bhabha discusses the notion of "Anglicizing," noting that the Indian native is only ever Anglicised, never made English, and that "to be Anglicised is *emphatically* not to be English." Similarly, in the Bear Garden, to be anthropoid is *emphatically* not to be human. (12)

Can performing animals attain the status of cultural players? Can they ever be more than comic mockeries of themselves? Whatever affinities link people and animals via art, we are not likely to approach them with painting elephants or monkeys on horseback. Consider the fable of the blind people trying to figure out what an elephant is by feeling its different parts, but unable to comprehend the animals' entire being: so they proclaim the trunk a snake, the ear a flag, the leg a tree, and so on. I think we reiterate this erroneous appraisal of an animal if we try to know an elephant by this brushstroke, that harmonica chord. . . . like the people in the fable, we are blind to the totality of the animals that we haphazardly grope. We cannot know an animal, a whole animal, within the limitations of our own perceptual consciousness, and CDs, zoos, circuses, and monkey-baiting typify the profoundly limiting cultural situations—the *blinders*—that render us incapable of seeing, and knowing, elephants.

Animal Poetry

Before I ran into the elephants—and everybody knows that an 8000-lb. elephant sits wherever it wants—I was about to discuss animal poetry. To return to my main track: there is a great deal of animal poetry, a profusion of possible texts. Most poetry about animals induces a brief, simple, and predominantly anthropocentric moment of contemplation of our fellow creatures. It is usually harmless enough, except to the extent that it displaces the more rigorous consideration of animals that we should be undertaking. Mainstream animal poetry may mildly scent, but does not very keenly acknowledge or celebrate, the subjects' authenticity, complexity, and nobility. An ur-poem, for me—a representative failure in the canon of animal poetry—is W. B. Yeats's short and mean poem, "To a Squirrel at Kyle-na-no":

> Come play with me;
> Why should you run
> Through the shaking tree
> As though I'd a gun
> To strike you dead?
> When all I would do
> Is to scratch your head
> And let you go. (155)

The most pronounced trope that undercuts the value of most animal poetry is a sense of imperial mastery over animals: they exist for us to use as we please, in our life and in our poetry. Yeats epitomizes this attitude by playfully positioning himself alternately as tormentor and friend—only hypothetically as tormentor, but of course the suggestion, even in its negative case (as the speaker's demurrals assert: what makes you think I would kill you?), implies the possible advance to actuality

(I *could* kill you—and, in fact, here's how I'd do it: get my gun, . . .). The poem presumes that the encounter between the poet and animal is inherently on the poet's own terms—the squirrel is his subject to treat badly or kindly. The speaker's privilege, obviously, massively inflects the poem's political situation, the relationship between man and animal. The writer of a poem like this may *believe* he is recounting an enlightening and equitable interaction with an animal, but this conceit is self-evidently insupportable.

It may seem fairly obvious that Yeats as an animal poet is a wolf in sheep's clothing, but he is no straw man: his poetic pervades the great majority of animal poems. Animal poetry, in the main, uncritically accepts the idea of human power over animals. It exhibits a sense of (often facile) benevolence that always inherently includes its antithesis—here manifest, though usually more quietly implicit: the option of harming the animal if the mood hits the human poet/reader/actor. The animal subject exists for our pleasure and at our pleasure. We use the animal in poetry, as we use it in industry, agriculture, science, to accomplish a specific purpose and satiate a specific desire.

Wanting to assist my research, people frequently pass on to me their favorite animal poems. A colleague says I should look at Ogden Nash's animal poems. My kids suggest: "Fuzzy Wuzzy was a bear. . . ." I didn't spend six years in graduate school to write books about Ogden Nash and Fuzzy Wuzzy, I demur. But still, I start thinking . . . Fuzzy does, interestingly, problematize the issues of naming and definition, and of our perceptions of animals and relations to animals as mediated by the poetics of our culture. Who is this bear? How do we see him or her? Bears are supposed to be fuzzy—that's why we encourage our kids to cuddle with them, and again Theodore Roosevelt (Teddy Bear's namesake) returns as an influence here. How did Fuzzy "lose" its hair? (I don't mean to be biologically pedantic, but bears are covered with fur, not hair—I suppose the rhyme-word is more important than zoological accuracy.) Hairless, it's certainly true that Fuzzy Wuzzy, by definition, wasn't fuzzy, was he? But the ditty also suggests, via textual identity-pun, the possibility that Fuzzy Wuzzy wasn't Fuzzy Wuzzy. Who was he, then? Wuz his identity wholly dependent upon his cultural attraction of fuzziness? Who wants an unfuzzy bear? What/who is a bear, or any animal, when it runs afoul of the cultural pattern, the type, the niche, to which we have relegated it?

The rhyme conveys an interesting existential uncertainty about animals that is not wholly irrelevant here. Who is any animal that fails to satisfy our expectation of it? What happens to a cute zoo-exhibit, a lion cub or a baby elephant, when it outgrows its cuteness? Can you spell "surplussing?" That's the euphemism zoos use to denote what they do with the animals who have outlived their usefulness as exhibits. . . . and it doesn't mean going to live with a nice family in the country. How does an animal go from "is" to "was"?—Fuzzy Wuzzy *was* a bear. What is he now? An ex-bear? Remember the Monty Python skit that features John Cleese banging a defective bird-corpse on the pet shop counter and screaming, "What we have here is an ex-parrot!" What is any animal after we are done with it—after it has served our cultural purposes, had the culture sucked out of it?

And Nash: he wrote dozens of animal poems, "light verse"—yet no less revelatory than "heavy (?) verse" about how conventional human expectations of animals overwrite the animals and about our tendency to exploit them for a cheap snicker. He touts the comic grotesqueness of animals—by human standards of aesthetics, of course—as in "The Rhinoceros":

> The rhino is a homely beast,
> For human eyes he's not a feast.
> Farewell, farewell, you old rhinoceros,
> I'll stare at something less prepoceros. (27)

The context of this poem, presumably, is a zoo: that is where people stare at animals, and Nash's dismissal of the animal here takes the form of the speaker's determination to stare at something else. The withdrawal of the imperious human stare, for Nash, equates with rejection of the animal: we vote with our eyes—so as we look away and move onto the next cage, the poem ends, and the animal (for all intents and purposes) disappears: farewell, farewell. Could there be any more blatant expression of solipsism? This solipsism is directed here at a single example of an animal that (for some vague reason) fails to satisfy us; writ large, however, it typifies the solipsism that humanity in general fosters, inside our box, with respect to the "prepoceros" creatures outside. For Nash, the function of animals is often elusive, irrelevant, to the point of meaninglessness, as in "The Fly":

> God in His wisdom made the fly
> And then forgot to tell us why. (214)

Nash mocks animals, especially the features that differentiate animals most strikingly from people. In "The Firefly," he writes, "I can think of nothing eerier / Than flying around with an unidentified glow on a person's posteerior" (193). Remember Thomas Nagel's query, "What is it like to be a bat?" Here Nash illustrates how to fail, monumentally, at the question of "what is it like to be a firefly?" And in "The Centipede," Nash offers his version of the latent death-wish that surfaced in Yeats's "To a Squirrel," reiterating the human proclivity to adjudicate any creature's right to exist:

> I objurgate the centipede,
> A bug we do not really need.
> At sleepy-time he beats a path
> Straight to the bedroom or the bath.
> You always wallop where he's not,
> Or, if he is, he makes a spot. (145)

As Yeats's poem suggests, we kill the animal subject, or we don't—but either way, it is in our sights, always dead meat potentially if not actually.

Any cultural incarnation of animals, however apparently innocuous, nevertheless fascinates me: what are these animals doing here? And what are we doing with them? Nash's amiable nonsense may seem culturally insignificant, but it taps into a widespread and unchallenged sensibility that has, in the aggregate, concretely dangerous manifestations. Nash's poetry contains all the ingredients, in frivolous trappings, which we see in cultural expressions that are obviously more dangerous, such as racism, prejudice, and propagandistic manipulation of the masses. Nash's is just one of many voices that cajoles us to approach animals with a demeanor predisposed to mockery, trivialization, subordination, violence, contempt. It's hard to resist deconstructing Nash's animal poetry: like shooting goldfish in a bowl. But I have bigger fish to fry—with apologies for the pescatorial carnage, meant to emphasize, just once more, the pervasive aggression toward animals in the exploitative, consumption-oriented idiom that permeates our language hook, line, and sinker—so I will move on to some more serious animal poetry.

There is a vast menagerie of animals in poetry, most of which fails to serve my purposes. In order to possess what you do not possess, as T. S. Eliot writes, you must go by the way of dispossession. Such works as John Hollander compiles for his Everyman's Library Pocket Poets edition of *Animal Poems*, an anthology typical of the dozens in this genre, exemplify what I dispossess. Hollander surveys some lightweight representative animal poetry by writers who have cordoned off a niche for a few animal poems in canons that mainly concern *other*—more important, worldlier—things.

Examples of inadequate animal poetry pervade the opening section, "Householders," featuring poems about the most familiar domesticated animals, cats and dogs. Works by otherwise noteworthy poets testify to their own mediocrity—such as Robert Penn Warren's "English Cocker: Old and Blind":

> With what painful deliberation he comes down the stair,
> At the edge of each step one paw suspended in air,
> And distrust. Does he thus stand on a final edge
> Of the world? Sometimes he stands thus, and will not budge... (19)

or Charles Baudelaire's sonnet "Cats": "Dozing, all cats assume the svelte design / of desert sphinxes sprawled in solitude" (24); or Hardy's "Last Words to a Dumb Friend":

> Pet was never as mourned as you,
> Purrer of the spotless hue,
> Plumy tail, and wistful gaze
> While you humoured our queer ways... (35)

This poetry is tame, predictable, contrived. It rings false with regard to animals, because the poems are about people—about our sensations when we happen to be around (our) animals. The poetry assumes a possessiveness that diminishes the integrity of the animal subjects and any insights into their sensibilities; its demeanor casts animals as foils, springboards for our own deep and sensitive cleverness. They are bad animal poems for the same reasons they are simply bad poems: they pander to us, rather than challenging us, or surprising us, or shaking their fists at us. They may *describe* animals, as in Robert Frost's "The Cow in Apple Time,"

> She runs from tree to tree where lie and sweeten
> The windfalls spiked with stubble and worm-eaten.
> She leaves them bitten when she has to fly.
> She bellows on a knoll against the sky.
> Her udder shrivels and the milk goes dry. (43)

but they do not substantially approach or interact with animals. Animals in these poems are curiously Emersonian, for example, in Ralph Waldo Emerson's "The Humble Bee":

> Insect lover of the sun,
> Joy of thy dominion!
> Sailor of the atmosphere;

Swimmer through the waves of air;
Voyager of light and noon;
Epicurean of June;
Wait, I prithee, till I come
Within earshot of thy hum,—
All without is martyrdom. (59)

or Lawrentian, as in D. H. Lawrence's "Tortoise Gallantry":

Making his advances
He does not even look at her, nor sniff at her,
No, not even sniff at her, his nose is blank.
Only he senses the vulnerable folds of skin
That work beneath her while she sprawls along... (159)

or Dickinsonian, in Emily Dickinson's poem about a caterpillar:

Its soundless travels just arrest
My slow—terrestrial eye
Intent upon its own career
What use has it for me— (154)

Many animal poets who look nice and ecofriendly still fall short under scrutiny. Mary Oliver serves as an example here. She has written dozens of animal poems, and "Egrets" typifies her poetic. Oliver arrives, by the end of that poem, at an illuminating image of the birds, but begins—and this beginning clearly establishes the poem's trajectory and focus—

Where the path closed
  down and over,
    through the scumbled leaves,
      fallen branches,
through the knotted catbrier,
  I kept going. (19)

The poem depicts her voyage, her quest, her arduous confrontation with nature, her... finally, just *her*. The egrets are a quest-object; they are exhilarating (for her!) when she finally arrives at their pond-nest. It is as if they exist to formulate the climax of her poem; they are dignified by her fascination in them—but if she happened not to have found them, not to have persevered bravely through scumbled leaves and catbrier, what then would have been their significance? The poem fails to address this contingency. In the same vein, Yeats's best-known animal poem, "The Wild Swans at Coole," features animals as merely a device to prompt the poet's own introspective flights of self-assessment. At the end, the birds' migration to another place—away from Coole and far out of Yeats's line of vision—relegates them to an imaginative void, and the poem concludes on the assumption that the audience will be content to remain with the poet and yet another of his elusive questions about himself or other men, but not, in any substantial sense, the swans.

Oliver's relationship to the egrets in her poem, and her use of them, typifies what John Tallmadge characterizes as "the excursion format" (also called a "ramble" in Thomas Lyon's taxonomy of nature writing)—the trope "begins in Gilbert White's *Natural History of Selbourne* as a simple neighborhood walk during which the curious naturalist merely records observations. A religious and psychological dimension enters with Wordsworth, for whom nature provided lessons in the conduct of life and the motions of the mind. Henry Thoreau combined these two approaches to create a deliberate practice in which walks followed by reflective journalizing provided scientific awareness, moral and psychological understanding, and prophetic social critique" (197).

But the problem with the excursion format is that it represents a corrupt fantasy of detachment from the rewards and pitfalls of natural encounters. The excursion implies a departure from and return to a fixed place that is logically discrete from—outside, above, beyond—the place in which we excurse. Things wonderful and terrible may befall the walker in the woods, but they are, ultimately, somehow separable from what happens in the rest of our lives. John Elder calls Oliver "a poet who prospects for wildness in the foreground of her life" (217), and, though he does not intend an exploitative resonance in the idea of "prospecting," he accidentally highlights the aspect of Oliver's poetic that I find troubling: her *use* of nature—like the mining and harvesting that typifies the prospector—seems too fundamentally selfish.

The excursion mode pervades a great deal of animal poetry: animals are creatures that poets meet on adventures of one sort or another. They serve the purpose, mainly, of occasioning the poem—the conclusion of which coincides with the termination of the excursion. For the reader, too, animal poetry brings us into contact with the animal only for the duration (which tends to be short) of the time that we are reading the animal lyric at hand. The experience is contained, constrained. A higher aspiration for animal poetry would be to situate poet/reader and animal as coterminous; cohabitants; simultaneous, and thus ecologically and experientially equal. The conclusion of the poem should not signify the

closure of the relationship between person and animal, but rather, ideally, should initiate and inspire the *beginning* of an imaginative consideration and reformulation of who these animals are and how we share the world.

Like many ecologically conscious people who brake for squirrels and eat low on the food chain, I find Oliver's poetry pleasant enough, and I'm sure I'd enjoy an excursion in the woods with her. I don't mean to imply that she's a bad person or sadistic toward animals (which, I suppose, is what I *do* feel about Yeats after reading "To a Squirrel"), but still, her work does not break through the presumptions of anthropocentrism. The reader is not made to feel that the animals of which she writes exist, or that their existence is important, when she has stopped looking at them, when she is done *using* them, when the poem is over.

A conspicuous giveaway is simply the too-prominent presence of the poet herself: an egocentrism that invokes the corollary anthropocentrism. This glorification of the human consciousness is not the sole reason I disqualify Oliver's poetry from "breakthrough" status, but it certainly poses a significant obstacle to a poetic that aspires to extend beyond speciesist self-obsession. A poet who writes about animals and uses a first-person (human) voice must explicitly confront and resolve what that voice means with respect to the rest of the world, if the poetry is to transcend the tradition of regarding animals as unpoetic (except as subjects, backdrop), unvoiced, culturally disenfranchised. The danger of the human "I" with respect to animals—real, or cultural representations thereof—is what we might call, after Yeats, the everpresent threat to "strike you dead." Unless the poet consciously orients herself otherwise, the poetic "I" is inherently exploitative of nonhuman animals; superior to them; uniquely expressive, sentient, privileged in the world that the poetry delineates. It is an I that speaks for people to people, and essentially about people, albeit with a cast of thousands of minor characters from other species. The logical endpoint of this "strike you dead" human stance in animal poetry is narcissism and speciesist isolationism. As sensitive and delicate as Oliver may be, she hasn't crossed the Rubicon, say, from sympathy to empathy: a distinction that oversimplifies the ideal potential of animal poetry, but which will serve, to begin with, as a rough standard.

Oliver's "The Snakes" begins, "I once saw two snakes," and I continue reading with a diminished expectation that the two snakes she once saw will transcend the frame, the subjugation, of the poet's gaze, even though the remainder of the poem offers an intricate and compelling account of these snakes. Her poem "The Fish" begins, "The first fish / I ever caught..." (and includes an expression I find especially irritating, gratuitously pantheistic: "Now the sea / is in me: I am the fish, the fish / glitters in me..." [56]). Again the human presence, the human sense of control, is paramount. If a tree fell in the forest and nobody heard it, would it make a noise? (Yes.) If an animal lives in the forest or river, and a poet like Oliver does not see it, does it make a noise? (Yes, but we wouldn't know it from her poetry.)

Not Knowing Animals

I don't feel that I, personally, know a great deal about animals. I'm keenly cognizant of the limits that affect my relationships with animals as a consequence of the habits of life that I've chosen—urban living, bookish career, and the like; and on some level I'd like to transcend these, but I haven't. I *could* go out into the woods and sustain habitats for endangered creatures, or chain myself to trees in clearcut plots, but I don't. I read books, try not to do too much harm to the ecosystem, and hope to change, for at least a few people, some cultural attitudes that seem to me demonstrably undesirable.

I suspect that lots of creators and consumers of cultural representations of animals, like me, don't know a great deal about animals—or, to put it another way, the blinders or cultural biases that color the things they know about animals and the ways they experience animals result in a sum experience that's more artificial than natural, more misinformational than informational. I think it would be useful for more people to confront, as I've done just now, how much we don't know about animals, and to accept the limitations of our epistemologies—instead of the alternative: faking it; masking our ignorance in self-centered fantasies; perverting natural and ecological paradigms to flatter the centrality and omniscience of our own existence.

Reading literature about animals, I've become very interested in them, and *wish* I knew them better, knew more about them; but at the same time, I become more convinced of the difficulties, the distances, between us and them. While I lament the pervasive borders that our culture has constructed between people and animals, nevertheless, I cannot deny that these borders are potent constructions and as difficult for me to transcend as they are for anyone else.

An anecdote about one of the ways I've come to know-but-perhaps-not-know animals: I signed up my 5-year-old son for something called "bug camp" at our local science museum one summer, which offered a wonderful example of bad cultural engagement with animals. After three days, the campers hadn't actually seen a bug (except when one camper had the idea of bringing in a cricket in a box . . . at which the teacher recoiled). They made bug-shaped candy and spider webs out of yarn, and listed random thoughts about bugs on the blackboard—but no bugs. It's just silly not to know bugs, not to look directly at bugs, in bug camp; I don't mean to suggest that campers should be led on aggressive bug-hunting in the mode of Nabakovian butterfly collecting expeditions (which is often the model for human interactions with bugs—if we are going to expend our attention on any creatures so small and trivial and ubiquitous, we feel compelled to inscribe the enterprise in the adventuring tropes of safaris or other quests for the *rara avis*, and to collect insects the way we collect coins and stamps . . .). I believe that people shouldn't be looking at giraffes and lions if they live, as I do, in a North American city, because this distorts our perceptual ecological balance; but *not* looking at bugs, which of course live all around us, is as perverse as *looking* at the animals that don't live around us. The disinterest in looking at bugs is probably related to the interest in looking at lions: people flock to zoos to see what we shouldn't see—what we're not meant to see in our own native habitats and environs. The corollary of the craving to know animals that don't belong in our ken of perception is the resistance to knowing the animals that do belong around us. Bugs, squirrels, pigeons: dull, low-rent attractions.

So anyway, I pulled Jake out of the program and home-schooled (home-camped?) him. We found, as I suspected we would, many interesting bugs in our backyard and had lots of fun observing them, leaving food for them, keeping track of what bugs we saw in which areas at various times of the day, and so forth—a range of observational experience about the insects that cohabit with us in our immediate ecosystem. For me, one of the most memorable rewards of our ad hoc bug project was coming to appreciate, especially richly, a piece of poetry I'd had in my mind: Marianne Moore's "Critics and Connoisseurs," which celebrates the life processes of an ant as contrasted against the backdrop of human "high culture." Her poem concludes:

> I have seen ambition without
> understanding in a variety of forms. Happening to stand
> by an ant-hill, I have
> seen a fastidious ant carrying a stick north, south,
> east, west, till it turned on
> itself, struck out from the flower-bed into the lawn,
> and returned to the point

> from which it had started. Then abandoning the stick as
>   useless and overtaxing its
>   jaws with a particle of whitewash—pill-like but
> heavy, it again went through the same course of procedure.
>   What is
>   there in being able
>   to say that one has dominated the stream in an attitude of
> self-defense;
> in proving that one has had the experience
>   of carrying a stick? (38–9)

I don't think I can easily explain what this dense poem finally means—how, exactly, it adjudicates the relationship between animals and human culture, though I feel certain that it does address this relationship, importantly. (I don't mean to evade my critical responsibilities here—let me simply defer, at this time, my approach to the somewhat daunting Miss Moore with a promise to undertake exegesis more diligently when I get to her in chapter 4.) I found myself overwhelmed by the poem, impressed by the depth of what I think it might mean, and—most notably—significantly more engaged with the poem after hours spent looking at ants.

So my attempt to know animals began with what I conceived as a conventional naturalistic program of observation, but metamorphosed into another discourse (or, became usurped by a different mode of cognition): that of humanism, aesthetics, poetry. This aesthetic mode of interaction—just a fancy way of describing what happens when we read literature about animals—is not the only way, certainly, and quite possibly not even one of the better ways, to know animals, but it is one way... my way. I resist facts, taxonomies, culturally-constructed ways of knowing animals, in favor of a more picaresque epistemology. Understanding Moore's poem better after two days of watching ants is, for me, a great accomplishment, although I realize that it remains an open question with regard to the issue of knowing animals if this is an adequate result—or if it represents a cultural evasion, a retreat to my safe ground, the world of textuality. Did I learn about ants, or did I learn about poetry (about ants)?

Most of what I know about animals, like most of what I know about everything, I've learned by reading literature. This means that what I know may or may not be right—*may* be factual and accurate, or may be essentially correct in spirit if not in actuality, or may, in fact, be completely fictitious, swamped in poetic license. I don't intend to argue against the possibility of people's actually knowing animals—certainly some do, very well—but I think that many people, however well-meaning they may be, are uncritically inclined to presume a level of knowledge that they may not possess or to mistake their own *interests* in animals for bona fide knowledge.

My thoughts on knowing and not knowing animals are indebted to John Berger's seminal discussion, "Why Look at Animals?" Animals have been "co-opted into other categories so that the category *animal* has lost its central importance" (13), he writes. The ways in which we look at animals have resulted in their becoming culturally marginalized, "transformed into spectacle," which is akin to their having disappeared.

> The camera fixes [animals] in a domain which, although entirely visible to the camera, will never be entered by the spectator. All animals appear like fish seen through the plate glass of an aquarium. . . . Technically, the devices used to obtain ever more arresting images—hidden cameras, telescopic lenses, flashlights, remote controls . . . —combine to produce pictures which carry with them numerous indications of their normal *invisibility*. The images exist thanks only to the existence of a technical clairvoyance. . . . animals are always the observed. . . . They are the objects of our ever-extending knowledge. What we know about them is an index of our power, and thus an index of what separates us from them. The more we know, the further away they are. (14)

Berger's last sentence is the seed of what I'm developing here: *The more we know, the further away they are.* Perhaps, then, our assumptive knowledge—as facilitated via lenses, webcams, "technical clairvoyance," and all the other media that mediate our animal sightings—isn't really knowledge: merely a hyperintense form of *seeing*, but without understanding. (As T. S. Eliot puts it: we've had the experience but missed the meaning.) In some ideal sense, I believe that an increased knowledge of animals can only bring us closer to them, and so if Berger's ironic final assessment is correct, then the *quality* of the knowledge per se must be defective. On the other hand, perhaps such distancing consequent upon knowledge simply reflects the distance people have constructed between our world and theirs: this is the sort of response that I had to Pacheco's poem about a bat. The more we contemplate animals, the more we come to understand the impossibility of any meaningful, interactive experience with them amid the ineluctable solitude of our own cultural location: inside the box. I think both these extrapolations of Berger's statement, though they may seem contradictory, are valid at least in part.

At the risk of positing a head-in-the-sand, "ignorance is bliss" epistemology, I suggest that we might at least consider the desirability of knowing animals, in the future, *less* than we have done in the past and present—to spare them the fate that is consequent upon our knowing them increasingly intently...knowing them to death. We should, for instance, stop knowing them in zoos. It is better not to see an elephant at all than to see one in a zoo. The kind of knowledge we get in zoos is negative, flawed knowledge: misinformation. Zoos teach us precisely the wrong things about elephants—that they live in cages in London and Atlanta. I think that we want to know animals, at least partly, because we believe that knowledge equals control; but we have demonstrated our control over animals, when we exert it, to be capricious and destructive. We should consider whether our compulsion to know-and-master nature is what motivates our environmental sensitivities, and, if so, what implications this has. John Fowles writes that the human fixation with knowing all there is to know about nature often amounts to "treating nature as some sort of intellectual puzzle, or game"—and the consequences of such a condescending construction of nature are self-evident.

Seamus Heaney's "Death of a Naturalist" is a propos here: his poem about a boy, entranced by the spring frogspawn, who wanted to *know* the tadpoles, the frogs, the lives of the animals that inhabited the world just around him, and wanted to know them in the ways his culture had provided for him (inquisitive, intrusive, domineering Baconian biology). Using the vocabulary of the schoolboy scientist, Heaney writes of bringing "jampotfuls of the jellied specks to range on window-sills at home, on shelves at school," describing what the teacher taught them about the frogs' lifecycle and how you could tell the weather by the frogs—all ways of asserting a kind of epistemological mastery and control. But then, the poem offers a striking peripateia, where the boy realizes that he can't control, can't know, the frogs on his *own* terms; he can't frame them within his domesticating tropes:

> one hot day when fields were rank
> With cowdung in the grass the angry frogs
> Invaded the flax-dam; I ducked through hedges
> To a coarse croaking that I had not heard
> Before. The air was thick with a bass chorus.
> Right down the dam gross-bellied frogs were cocked
> On sods; their loose necks pulsed like sails. Some hopped:
> The slap and plop were obscene threats. Some sat
> Poised like mud grenades, their blunt heads farting.
> I sickened, turned, and ran. The great slime kings
> Were gathered there for vengeance and I knew
> That if I dipped my hand the spawn would clutch it. (5–6)

The poem viscerally expresses the *fear* we may have of animals when they don't behave the way we want them to; when they get messy; when they defy us or scare us; when they stink; when they taunt us with their unknowability. Perhaps this latent fear is a factor in our cultural hostilities toward the nonhuman "other." The ubiquitous surface-level affection that we claim toward our furry friends may mask a deeper ambivalence about them, and one that stems from a subconscious awareness of their resistance to our tropes of knowledge.

The more determination we exert trying to get to know animals in the way that we know the things in our world, heedless of their own independent existence and integrity and processes, the more we are disappointed by the failure to achieve this. They will defy being known in that way—and so we can either "mis-know" them: capture them, punish them, tame them, put them in cages, humiliate them, marginalize them. . . . or, as Heaney does here, we can confront the limits of our epistemologies: we can stop our heroic march toward omniscience and unbounded experiential conquest, and pause to reflect on what it means for us to know (or try to know) animals. Writing—or reading—a poem like "Death of a Naturalist" is an act of reflection. I find it a disturbing but honest, and thus admirable, poem about knowing animals. Like Oliver, Heaney embarks upon the enterprise of knowing the animal from a position of privileged entitlement and an assumption of inherent mastery. But in Oliver's poems, despite any compelling experiences involving animals, the speaker concludes pretty much just as she started. While she is affected and moved by the experiences, she is not fundamentally changed: she has only accumulated a bit *more* of what she already had a lot of: nature-smarts, animal-points. Her excursions—like those of most people who take field trips (whether real or imaginative) outside our box for an occasional encounter with the animal-other—are carefully mapped, assured of completion, without surprises or challenges or obstacles. But Heaney describes a real transformation, and reform. What began for him as an excursion to play with animals ended up as a lesson about the inadequacy of the path.

What can we gain from interaction with animals? I think a sense of compromise is essential as we consider this question: beyond a certain point experience and knowledge become exploitation and constraint. This is as true for animals we encounter in literature as it is for animals we encounter in reality. Poetry can set out "lines of flight," in Deleuze and Guattari's words, that point us toward vital insights about animals, but it must also stop, at a certain point, in acknowledgment of our limitations, our hubris, our humanness. Of course, we want it all: omniscience by the bucketful, a consummately dazzling epiphany in every couplet . . . but *we can't have it all.* I advance this simple proposition—which I hope doesn't seem too facile or obvious—as the crux of a new ecological vision that we might do well to develop in the third millennium.

Art (not all art, but selected pieces here and there) can help us understand and believe in this imperative for compromise, for accepting less than we have become accustomed to having. The prospect of bounded insight, diminished aesthetic stimuli, reduced imaginative bedazzlement, flies in the face of current cultural trends, which promise more, more, more: more channels on broadband, more kilobytes per second of streaming media, higher definition TV, better digital resolution. But coming to terms with a necessary retrenchment of our high-powered cultural expectations will help acclimate us to the need for compromises that are looming on other fronts: learning to settle for less energy, less land, less extraction, less meat, less air conditioning, and so forth.

I offer a hypothetical conjecture about composite American culture-consumers—a stereotype obviously, but one that I think accurately reflects significantly prevalent attitudes and convictions of the contemporary cultural audience. What these readers crave from aesthetic encounters with animals is, ideally, to know what it is like to be a bat, and an elephant, and a firefly, and a squirrel, and more. They want to have all these experiences, all these vicarious thrills, quickly and easily (not more than a couple of pages of blank verse, with only a few not-too-difficult metaphors . . .): one at a time or heaped together on a smorgasbord, as the mood suits, while still enjoying the power that comes with being consciously human—that is, the cultural consumers don't wish to give up or trade in any of the privileges of humanness in order to access the animal, but rather, want to supplement the human with a side-order of animal. Animals in art allow these audiences to indulge a fantasy of picking and choosing from among dozens, hundreds, of different animal experiences, vistas, moments, as if flipping channels on a remote control: stepping in and out of various animal-consciousnesses as befits various whims. These people would like to take on the power of animals, especially with regard to the things that animals can do and people cannot. They know what it is like to be a person, to locomote and emote as a person does, to feel the fears and thrills that people do. They are sometimes a little bored with this; they want more—want to know and to experience, via art, also what it is like to slither in the leaves, and to learn to fly from a nest, and to see through the darkness; to hunt, and also to be hunted; to be king of the jungle and also to be brought low, denuded, ironically, of what had seemed to be a limitless natural power. They want to shuck their skins (briefly). And they want to do all this in the excursion mode, and come home to sleep in warm, comfortable beds when it's done.

But this presumption of aesthetic/imaginative entitlement is, I think, excessive. Instead, from a perch of compromise, we should ascertain what we can more reasonably expect from our art—and by *reasonably*, I mean, as informed by a reasonable conception of our symbiotic relationship with all the elements of our ecosystem. Just as excessive physical consumption of resources is unsustainable and depletes the ecosystem, so, I believe, excessive imaginative appetites carry comparable costs. Mary Oliver wants it all; Seamus Heaney's poetic reflects his acceptance of a sense of compromise. He takes what he can get: a good poem, a sincere and vital formative experience, but not, ultimately, an omnipotent aesthetic-cognitive mastery of the frogs—their lives, their cosmos—as his initial greedy possession of the jampotsful of frogspawn had led him to fantasize.

An overweening confidence in literary experiences of animals can be dangerous: "I am leery of my own enthusiasm for writing," Paul Shepard confesses. "Our bookstores and libraries are fat with accounts of the natural world, yet nature writing is flawed. The flattery of the printed word . . . makes nature a subject matter and becomes a secret enemy of the natural world. . . . Nature writing nourishes the view of nature as esthetic abstraction . . . and captivates its readers with a spurious substitute for experience in the natural world" (*Others* 10–11). Shepard brings us back full circle to President Roosevelt's wariness of literary authority and motive. But balanced against all these caveats, Shepard broaches a potentiality: "art can never replace, certainly not explain, that adventure among the Others [i.e., nonhuman animals] which remains central to our lives, though it is the principal means of evoking it" (11).

The poems that I have chosen to discuss in part 2 help illuminate what Shepard characterizes as "that adventure among the Others"; they can help show us this "certain point" that I fuzzily referenced above: the point that marks as far as we can go in our effort to know animals . . . or, alternatively, as close as we can get to them. (Are we "going far," or "getting close?" I will leave these two spatial contradictions standing clumsily together, as a reminder of the indeterminacy about the direction, or the path, that will take us to animals.) I believe there is a point of equilibrium between people and animals—although I am not sure exactly what it is—that represents the most enlightened possible relationship: the point of greatest knowledge, and least "static." While the poems discussed in part 2 will certainly not answer all the questions that are brimming up here in part 1, about how and where we should situate ourselves with respect to animals, I think they will help us at least begin to answer them.

An Ecocritical Aesthetic Ethic

To resist the cultural marginalization of animals, I propose an ethic that centers animals and advances an advocacy methodology. I start from the premises, in the mode of Marxist or feminist criticism, that,

1. the subject at hand (the proletariat, women . . . here, animals) is profoundly and systematically oppressed;
2. any cultural expression that features these subjects as a major or minor presence can be maximally understood only if the history of their cultural exploitation is foregrounded; and
3. the only humane response to such an understanding, to a cultural encounter of any kind involving animal subjects, is the development of the consciousness that we, as a species, have behaved badly, inexcusably, toward our fellow creatures, and must behave better.

We must understand and appreciate animals more extensively, more intelligently; cultural expressions can help—*or hinder*—in this enterprise. I believe that the natural consequence of a more intelligent understanding of animals will be, to reiterate, the realization that we must behave better. We must accord nonhuman animals more respect and develop a deeper sense of their integrity, their wisdom and importance on their own terms—not as judged by the criteria of human utility or aesthetics. Ultimately, this is the preeminent lesson that we can learn from encountering animals in literature. We may inculcate a biocentrism as opposed to the anthropocentrism that now conscribes our vision; we may learn to value an art that promotes the ethos of conserving rather than exploiting our habitat and all its constituent elements.

It is not the case that all people always exploit all animals, but our history as a species, and especially recently, and especially as affluent Americans, is a shameful one, and I believe that it behooves us, in every encounter we have with animals in the flesh or in the imagination, to atone for our past record and to seek a better path for the future. In my own small field of proficiency, I have tried to resist and reverse the hegemonic subordination of animals: to identify the destructive representations of animals—derogatory and demeaning, encouraging disrespect and trivialization—that pervade our culture and that certainly impact our real world conception and treatment of animals. The countervailing aesthetic that I propose should inspire people to work to rescue animals from the degradations, the manipulations and decontexualizations that they suffer in so many of our cultural processes and products.

Why do animals matter in art? What relation do cultural representations of animals have to real animals? What ethical relationship and responsibility does the artist have to the animal subject? How can art about animals serve as a metaphor, or a testing ground, or a microcosm, for our real-world interactions with animals? Animal poetry teaches me that we should interrogate our received ideas with respect to animals and seek perspectives that push us outside our default perspective. Once we have attuned ourselves to a vantage point that does not obscure the animal's integrity, its self-sufficient force, we should attempt with determination to sustain this point of view as persistently as possible: beyond just the small, quick space of a poem, and on into the world we share with animals.

I present some explicit goals of an ecocritical aesthetic. My ideal is to achieve and experience, via art, enlightened interaction with animals: easy enough to say, but what does this mean? The ethics of such an aesthetic entail:

1. Encouraging people to see animals without hurting them (without hurting them literally, *or* spiritually, metaphysically); without capturing them; without constraining them. Appreciating, then, the richness of seeing them artistically, culturally (instead of physically).
2. Understanding how animals exist in their own contexts, not in our contexts, and without impinging upon or damaging their contexts in the process. This may seem to contradict my first point: isn't seeing animals through art seeing them in *our* contexts rather than theirs? But I think that, in the case of the sensitive and determined artist or poet, we *can* see animals in their contexts in our contexts. . . . yes, there are "framing" issues to be considered here. My equivocation may seem quibblesome, but I can attest, from my personal experience of reading certain poetry, that this *can* happen; I will offer examples in part 2.
3. Teaching about animals' habits, their lives, their emotions, their natures, as much as can be done from our limited and biased perspective. Aesthetic representations can do at least a good job of this, even if they cannot provide complete insight. In Heaney's poem, for instance, the primary "lesson" has to do with the fearful experience of retreat from the farting frogs, a failure that is exaggerated into the titular death of the naturalist. But in fact, some naturalism does survive: Heaney *did* learn something (which he teaches to his readers) about frogs and their lifecycles and habitats.

4. Advocating respect for animals, on their own terms—not because of what they can do for us or what they mean to us. Steve Baker writes in *Picturing the Beast* that we can hope a careful and enlightened study of cultural representations of animals may stimulate our concern for "the circumstances of actual living animals in that same culture," and may enable animal rights advocates "to develop and promote a less contemptuous and condescending attitude to animals throughout the culture" (x). At times, this will involve using the aesthetic artifact at hand to advance a polemical exposé, a condemnation of the suffering that animals and their habitats have experienced at human hands.
5. Knowing animals, somewhat: learning who they are and how their lives relate to ours; developing a culturally and ecologically complex, problematized vision of what an animal means. Using our aesthetics, our cognitive and perceptual vocabulary, to establish and embellish, to the fullest extent possible, a contact zone with the nonhuman animals who share our world with us, but accepting also that there exist considerable venues on either side of this contact zone that are, on the one hand, only human, and on the other hand, only nonhuman. Differentiating between what we can know and what we cannot, and then forsaking modes of knowledge that are ecologically and ethically shady.

In condensed form, the basic elements of my ecocritical aesthetic are: seeing animals without hurting them; seeing them in *their* contexts; teaching about animals; advocating respect for them; and finally *knowing* them, richly but also incompletely.

This aesthetic should not engage in gratuitous human-bashing: still, at least as an initial corrective, there must be a prominent expression and condemnation of animals' historical victimization. It is necessary to proclaim animals' moral innocence and humanity's moral shame by comparison, along the lines of W. H. Auden's encomium/apology to animals in "Address to the Beasts":

very few of you
find us worth looking at,
unless we come too close.

To you all scents are sacred
except our smell and those
we manufacture.

How promptly and ably
you execute Nature's policies,
and are never

lured into misconduct
except by some unlucky
chance imprinting.

Endowed from birth with good manners,
you wag no snobbish elbows,
don't leer,

don't look down your nostrils,
nor poke them into another
creature's business.

Your own habitations
are cosy and private, not
pretentious temples.

Of course you have to take lives
to keep your own, but never
kill for applause. (in Muldoon 2)

One doesn't need to read much poetry in this vein—it makes people feel too guilty and soon becomes tedious—but it's a starting point. We begin to see ourselves, to know ourselves, and to realize how distorted are our perceptions of ourselves with relation to animals: our self-flattering but vacuous sense of superiority, privilege, isolation. From that point, we may proceed to the issue of how we are going to know animals and how we are not going to know them. We should renounce the temptation to know animals in most of the ways that our culture sets out for us: for example, in zoos and other animal-themed entertainment compounds... circuses... cockfights... bestial pornography... vivisection... smuggling and commercial fetishization of exotic and endangered species... hunting sports... fur "fashions"... tusk harvesting... taxidermy... live animal trade for the pet industry... and on and on. Dead or alive—or, most often, somewhere in between life and death—the animals that serve as the subjects of these activities testify to the vast spectrum of harm that we visit upon animals in the cause of our own vanities.

For another instance, as an exemplary illustration of badly knowing animals in art, consider the work of the English artist Damien Hirst. Hirst is famous for displaying in art museums the mutilated carcasses of animals preserved in formaldehyde, or simply rotting, with overly clever titles, which are ironically understated, innocent, culturally cliché-ridden—almost as if he's playing on the titles, challenging us to wonder whether our culture at large, not Hirst himself, is the real desecrator of animals. A 1996 diptych of two halves of a pig, cut through the middle, displayed in separate tanks, is titled "This Little Piggy Went to Market" and "This Little Piggy Stayed at Home." "Away From the Flock" is the title of a 1994 work featuring a lamb in formaldehyde. In "Mother and Child, Divided," 1995, two tanks of formaldehyde hold, suspended, the two halves of a whole cow, with a fetus still in its womb, bisected perfectly so that the viewer can walk through the middle of the dead animals. Others of his installations feature dead butterflies stuck to painted canvas and a severed bull's head rotting with maggots and hatching into flies. The enterprise is not unremunerative: Hirst's "artworks" sell for amounts in the range of £25,000.

Hirst's displays epitomize the use of animals for our clever aesthetic games, heedless of the animals' integrity and their own presence. Hirst's art illuminates how witty we think we're being, at the animals' expense; how little it matters what ends up happening to them—how they suffer, physically or imagistically, for our amusement, or our intellectual exercise. The phenomenon of Hirst's prominence in the art world demonstrates how absolutely our culture is primed to detach ourselves from animals—from connection to them—from any sort of natural, empathetic bond; how tremendously we have "othered" them; what barbarities we are capable of committing and what epistemological rifts—ecologically and ethically absurdist rifts—we are capable of constructing; how confused our notion of art has become with regard to animals.

Hirst is the endpoint of a continuum that reflects our cultural projections of animals—or, I hope, at least he's near the endpoint: I can't conceive of anything much worse we could do to animals in our art; but he is not, I think, *sui generis*. He embodies our fantasies about animals and how we can manipulate them in the enterprise of art. Capturing... gawking... transforming... disfiguring... exulting over their pathetic mortality. Hirst embodies all of our uses of animals, dignified with the aura of art: to tell us, whatever we've done to animals, it's okay—it's clever; it's somehow advancing the cause of civilization. It can be made to seem harmless, no matter how brutal it essentially is. A webpage, for example, describes Hirst's work as "an exploration of mortality, a traditional theme which Hirst has updated and extended with wit, verve, originality, and force." We can aestheticize and intellectualize animals, and thus, we can do what we want with them. "Animals," as Harriet Ritvo puts it, "never talk back" (5). *They* can't aestheticize *us*, so the systemic cultural relationship we have with them—*at* them—is destined to endure, at least until such time as we forcefully reject artists who reify the exploitation of animals. Just as male artists have done for centuries with women in their art (nudes reclining, supple and compliant—the eternal sex object, plaything; gazing in a way that situates women as subaltern and disempowered. . . .), so Hirst figures at the vanguard of a rich and deep tradition of Western culture that excludes animals from parity in an impermeably anthropocentric cultural nexus; a Great Chain of Being whose greatness inheres absolutely at the apex where we have enthroned ourselves. The task for us is to resist and reform this cultural conspiracy.

Part Two
Poetic Animals

Chapter 2

Mesoamerican Spirituality and Animal Co-Essences

> We need another and a wiser and perhaps a more mystical concept of animals. Remote from universal nature, and living by complicated artifice, man in civilization surveys the creature through the glass of his knowledge and sees thereby a feather magnified and the whole image in distortion. We patronize them for their incompleteness, for their tragic fate of having taken form so far below ourselves. And therein we err, and greatly err. For the animal shall not be measured by man. In a world older and more complete than ours they move finished and complete, gifted with extensions of the senses we have lost or never attained, living by voices we shall never hear. They are not brethren, they are not underlings; they are other nations, caught with ourselves in the net of life and time, fellow prisoners of the splendor and travail of the earth.
>
> (Henry Beston)

> Animals are among the first inhabitants of the mind's eye. They are basic to the development of speech and thought. Because of their part in the growth of consciousness, they are inseparable from a series of events in each human life, indispensable to our becoming human in the fullest sense.
>
> (Paul Shepard)

> There are few things uglier than a lack of reverence for animals.
>
> (Jane Harrison)

Building upon cultural anthropological studies of Mesoamerican beliefs about nonhuman animals, I want to present a model for appraising animal poetry. The Mesoamerican conception of "animal souls"—the idea that a person's soul is explicitly connected with an external animal counterpart, or co-essence—suggests an expansive paradigm for human–animal relationships in my own culture. The richness of the Mesoamerican system of animal beliefs inspires me to juxtapose them against a discourse with which I am more familiar: poetry, which, in different ways, offers comparably rich insights into how people and nonhuman animals may coexist. I want to show how animal poetry might inculcate its readers with some of the sensibilities held by those who believe in animal souls. This poetry might thereby provide a medium through which Western industrial-world readers, at present uninitiated, can tap into some portion of the worldview evinced by those societies that possess a more sophisticated sense of how people and animals relate to each other. Examining animal poetry in the light of Mesoamerican animal beliefs promises to provide insights that industrial-world readers have sublimated or simply missed, but that I believe are, nevertheless, recoverable. If we investigate foreign sensibilities and then return to study our own poetry from this perspective, we may transcend our received ideas, and discover starting points that lead toward other ways of regarding animals.

Mesoamerican philosophies about animals differ strikingly from those prevalent in Western industrial culture, which disdains animals' integrity, disregards their importance in the ecosystem, and refuses to grant them any semblance of parity. Our anthropocentric view of the world barely registers its nonhuman inhabitants. Looking at animal poetry through the lens of animal souls may reinforce our appreciation of its potential power and inspire us to believe in the possibility of reforming our speciesist chauvinism: setting out a righter path and resisting—even if only in homeopathic measure—the damage done on so many other fronts.

I have chosen to focus on the Mesoamerican conception of animals from among a wide array of attitudes that are fascinatingly, refreshingly distinct from our own. Numerous other cultures, past and present, offer enlightened perspectives on animals and ways of including animals in their ontological consciousness that pay greater heed than contemporary Western culture does to the equity and the sanctity of the animal in this encounter. Their interactions with animals, at least at first glance, often seem (to me) better than our own habits, though perhaps finally they are just different. Medieval French societies believed that certain animals had legal status and involved them in court proceedings. In ancient Egyptian culture animals appear ubiquitously, closely associated with every aspect of people's lives; they represented the recurring cycle of renewal in nature and were believed to have superhuman powers. Animals existed in the divine sphere, and many deities took animal forms. Mummified animals were buried along with people—in death as in life, the Egyptians were close to their animals.

Animals have an intense spiritual potency in numerous Native American cosmologies. Howard Harrod's *The Animals Came*

Dancing: Native American Sacred Ecology and Animal Kinship describes the rituals of Northern Plains tribes that consecrated people's spiritual relationship with animals. Many Native Americans believed (and believe) that people share with animals a close and mutual divinity, established through "guardian spirits" that cross species boundaries. A Seneca elder, Grandmother Twylah Nitsch, describes in *Creature Teachers* how animals lead people who embark upon vision quests to wisdom.

Much African art features motifs that testify to people's sense of connection with animals and to the insight and power that people can access via animals. "The animal form in art has been an ancient leitmotif in Africa," writes Charles Davis. "It has served as a clan symbol to a people closely tied with the powers of nature. Animals were and are a medium for man's understanding of natural processes. The inexplicable was often perceived as the workings of an animal spirit. Equally important, however, was man's self-interpretation, his view of his own animal nature. Almost every human action could be illustrated by an animal action" (4).

Buddhists believe that all lives, human and nonhuman, are equal. "There is in Buddhism more sense of kinship with the animal world, a more intimate feeling of community with all that lives, than is found in Western religious thought," writes Anagarika P. Sugatananda. "This is not a matter of sentiment, but is rooted in the total Buddhist concept of life. It is an essential part of a grand and all-embracing philosophy which neglects no aspect of experience.... So in the Buddhist texts animals are always treated with great sympathy and understanding. Some animals... are used as personifications of great qualities."

Many cultures could serve as counterpoints in terms of how their consciousness of animals compares and contrasts with that of the contemporary Western industrial world. I have chosen the Mesoamerican system because, for the purposes of the enterprise I undertake here, it expresses most simply, clearly, and absolutely the potential parity between people and animals. I wanted to posit a model of human–animal interaction predicated upon equality, and I felt that I had found this when I discovered Gary Gossen's account of animal souls in the anthropological scholarship that has been his life's work.

I am sensitive to charges of cultural imperialism and aware of the possible distortions and errors inherent in imperfectly transposing a set of beliefs and expressions from one culture to another. I acknowledge the sort of possible objection raised eloquently by Rod Preece in *Animals and Nature: Cultural Myths, Cultural Realities*: that "the customary depiction of... Aboriginal concerns for the nature realm... has been greatly overdrawn" (xi). His book is a valuable corrective to some current unexamined presumptions. The tendency to idealize non-Western societies and fantasize that they evince an ecological sensitivity that is superior to our own may well be simply inaccurate; certainly it is an overgeneralization. "It is rarely clear what is meant by those who claim that certain societies are at one with, or in harmony with, nature," Preece writes; "at least sometimes those who make the claims for harmony are conceptual Humpty Dumpties who make words mean whatever they want them to mean and change the meanings to suit their ideological bent" (xi). I hope that in my work here the ends justify the means: that the opportunity afforded by the juxtaposition of Mesoamerican spirituality and Western poetry will provide an insight into our own cultural expressions, practices, and potentialities, as well as those of the Mesoamericans, in a way that is vital enough to justify this intercultural exercise.

Animal Souls

"Mesoamerican souls are fragile essences that link individuals to the forces of the earth, the cosmos, and the divine," writes Gossen. "They provide this link because they originate outside the body of their human counterpart, often in the bodies of animals" ("Mesoamerica" 81–2). Mesoamericans believe in "a private spiritual world of the self that is expressed through the concept of animal souls or other extrasomatic causal forces that influence their destiny" ("Olmecs" 555). The specific culture that Gossen studies, the Chamula Tzotzil community of Southern Mexico (descendants of the ancient Maya), shares with the vast majority of over 15 million Amerindians in Mexico and Central America "a pan-Mesoamerican indigenous belief in what is generally known as *nagualismo* or *tonalismo* in the anthropological literature of the area" (Gossen, "Animal Souls" 448). The two terms are kindred; *nagualismo* signifies the transformation of a person into an animal, and *tonalismo* refers to a person's companion animal or destiny, which everyone is believed to possess (Adams and Rubel 336).

"An animal-soul companion, of a particular species and of the same gender as the human counterpart, is assigned to each individual at conception," Gossen explains. "The destiny of each animal soul—health, injury and sickness, wealth and poverty, life and death—is shared with its human counterpart and is the object of supernatural intervention on the part of the shamans" (*Telling* 183). The Mesoamerican belief in human–animal co-essences is of ancient provenance, and these beliefs are historically linked with power and destiny. A statuette dating from the second century C.E., "probably a representation of a shaman who is calling up an animal-soul companion," is inscribed with glyphs that have been deciphered as "The animal soul companion is powerful" (*Telling* 231–3). And the Mayan Popol Vuh—the epic history apparently transcribed from a hieroglyphic text in the sixteenth century that subsequently disappeared—"contains literally hundreds of passages that can easily be interpreted within the matrix of the Maya variant of Mesoamerican *tonalismo* and *nagualismo*" (*Telling* 234).

A Tzotzil creation account, in a narrative text conveyed by a storyteller and part-time shaman named Xun Méndez Tzotzek (transcribed and edited by Gossen during his ethnographic fieldwork with the Chamula in 1969), offers a firsthand rendition of the system of animal souls:

> At the time when people first began to multiply,
> Jaguars started to be born,
> Coyotes started to be born.
>
> Animals started to be born.
> All the animals there are on the earth started to be born.
>
> The jaguar was the first. Next came the coyote,
> Then came the lion and the bear.
>
> The jaguar was the first to come out.
> You see, that is how he came to be the animal-soul companion of half of the people.
> The other half had the coyotes as their animal-soul companions.
> This was because the large animals came first.
>
> You see, the people were occupied in increasing their numbers.
> So it was when the first people emerged.
>
> Later it came to be that jaguars accompanied some of them;
> Coyotes accompanied some;
> Weasels accompanied others.
>
> But those whom the jaguars accompany,
> These are richest.
>
> Those whom the coyotes accompany,
> These are not so rich.
>
> Those whom the weasels accompany,
> These people are poorer.
>
> Those whom the foxes accompany,
> These are the poorest,
> Rather like those of the weasel.

As for the human counterparts of both the fox and the weasel,
These unlucky ones do not live very long.

There was once a person whose baby chicks had been eaten by some animal.
The owner of the chicks saw this.
He shot the culprit, a weasel, with a shotgun.

After the weasel died,
It was only a matter of three days until the owner of the chicks died also.
He had shot his own animal soul, and so died quickly himself.
So also with the fox.
He who has the fox as a soul companion does not live very long.

This one, the fox, likes to eat chickens.
When the owner of the chickens sees that the fox is catching his baby chickens,
The fox quickly meets his end at the point of a shotgun.

Then, when the fox dies of shotgun wounds,
He who has this fox as a soul companion lives for only three days.

The person who has the fox as soul companion may be a man or a woman.
So it is, whoever we are, we die just as our soul companions do.

You see, long ago it was Our Father who thought about all of this.
Our Father long ago gave us dreams about our animal-soul companions.

That is why it remains the same even today,
That not all of us have jaguars as animal souls.

There are several kinds of animals that Our Father has given to us as soul companions.

For this reason it is often unclear which soul companion Our Father has given to us.
Whether it is a jaguar,
Whether it is a coyote,
Whether it is a fox,
Whether it is a weasel.

These, then, are the kinds of soul companions that Our Father provides.
That is our heritage, even into our time.
You see, long ago it was this that occurred to Our Father,
At the time when he started to make the earth ready for us. (*Telling* 73–4)[1]

Rigoberta Menchú's Guatemalan Quiché culture affirms animals' interdependence with people via a spiritual system closely resembling that of the Chamula. She explains: "Every child is born with a *nahual.* The *nahual* is like a shadow, his protective spirit who will go through life with him. The *nahual* is the representative of the earth, the animal world, the sun and water, and in this way the child communicates with nature. The *nahual* is our double, something very important to us... The child is taught that if he kills an animal, that animal's human double will be very angry with him because he is killing his *nahual.* Every animal has its human counterpart and if you hurt him, you hurt the animal too" (18).[2]

"The thread that unifies these various expressions" of the Mesoamerican human–animal spiritual affiliation "focuses on the predestination and life history of the self that lies outside the self and is thus not subject to individual control," Gossen writes ("Animal Souls" 83). Events beyond the jurisdiction of our immediate influence have always compelled people to identify some domain or entity that mediates these issues—God, Zeus, the Fates, the planets. For Mesoamericans, it is animals who embody this domain.

Mesoamerican animal beliefs evoke some of the enticements I find in poetry. Poetry taps into a realm of consciousness beyond our immediate, quotidian perceptions and senses. Mesoamerican metaphysical representations of human ties to the earth, nature, and fate, as mediated by animals, may illuminate a power underlying some Western poetic inscriptions of animals.

Animals and Poetry

"When animals are transformed into art they often become reflections on the human condition, adjuncts of human thought," writes Howard Morphy. This challenges my claim for the importance of animal poetry: it would be, then, just one more narcissistic avenue by which our culture celebrates ourselves. But beyond aesthetic animal representation as merely adjunct to human thought, Morphy continues, "there are two-way processes involved in the relationships between [people] and animals, art and reality, for in using animals for certain purposes and encoding them in particular ways people inevitably affect the concept of a animal that they have" (14). In the processes of both creation and reception, art may help shape the world from which it emanates. Art may educate its audience about how the society treats the artistic subject, culturally and intellectually; it may profitably elucidate the implications of the relationship between *we* who watch and create, and *they* who are looked at and comprise the content of our creations. Art may foreground the ethical and behavioral conditions affecting how we might improve upon our relationship with the subject animals. My critique presupposes that animal poetry is not a one-way street, not entirely about people; I would like to explore how it can be about animals, too.

While animal poetry may facilitate an enlightened outlook toward animals, the poet who writes about animals risks succumbing to the temptation of hubris. As David Weiss writes, "Adam's naming of the creatures is connected with his birthright of dominion over them. . . . The danger is this: to name is to cage; to preserve is to kill" (238). The singular poets are those who, in Weiss's construction, "refuse to name" (234)—who manage to evoke and poeticize animals without colonizing them and without constraining them in the methods and limits of our own knowledge system. Not all animal poetry succeeds in, or even should aspire to, advancing an ecocultural epiphany; but I believe that the best of it may provide at least a hint as to how art may facilitate our *better* understanding and appreciation of animals (and thus, of nature and the world around us at large)—better than our performance record in most of our political, economic, and cultural practices.

Some critics have suggested, or intuited, that poetry is somehow a privileged genre when it comes to nature writing and literary representations of animals. A few have advanced explicit hypotheses for why this might be so, and others (myself included) proceed more inductively: as it happens, I have found in poetry a great deal of material useful to my investigations about animals, so I assume that poetry must represent an especially amenable genre for the engagement of animals. Perhaps poetry is the farthest from "normal" human modes—certainly the novel and drama are more directly implicated in our social processes. Poetry is odd: books of poetry sell significantly fewer copies than those in other genres; people are often afraid of poetry. Poetry is relatively less trammeled culturally—it exists, fairly inconspicuously, far from the madding crowd. Poetry is conventionally regarded as a direct path to the solitary contemplative consciousness, which seems important in the process of thinking about animals: it is desirable to step away from our accreted social experiences in order to encounter animals more open-mindedly, more equitably. Plays and novels are, of course, full of people—human intrigues, social complications, civic and political allegories, all of which are well-served by those more public social genres. What remains for poetry? By default, perhaps, poets are left with nature.

Poetry, John Elder writes, has the potential to be "in ecological terms the *edge* between mankind and nonhuman nature, providing an access for culture into a world beyond its preconceptions" (210), a "mediation" between the realm of the human and that of the nonhuman. As an example of what such poetry may achieve, Elder cites Robinson Jeffers's "attempt at a vision of 'inhumanism.' Jeffers's hope was to locate his poems beyond the narrow circle of human understanding, to speak past his own humanity" (210). Poetry may facilitate ecological insight and reform if its creators, "rather than domesticating nature, . . . are themselves assimilated into its ever-emerging and overwhelming particularity." In such an instance, "Poetry's landscape is an ecotone"—an ecological community of mixed vegetation formed by the overlapping of adjoining communities—"where human and natural orders meet" (210).

Poetry is in some ways closer to music than to speech, Paul Shepard suggests, and thus, like music, "establishes connectedness and flow" (22) akin to the rhythms of the ecosystem. He notes the profusion of animal images in our speech and observes that such images are particularly abundant in the mode of metaphor. Poetry is the aesthetic trope that uses metaphor most comfortably and in which metaphor is the most fundamentally integral, which suggests another reason for its special value as a literary portal into the world of animals, the world beyond human boundaries. The hundreds of animal metaphors that enrich our language—"to be a horse's ass," "to play possum," "horse about," "wolf your food," "quiet as a mouse," "bull in a china shop" are just a few examples Shepard offers (27)—testify to the same energies that, I believe, poetry possesses in its ability to describe animals, and to reach animals, with a power that few other human cultural endeavors can match.

In "Seeing in Nature What is Ours: Poetry and the Human–Animal Bond," Elizabeth Lawrence argues for the special insights of animal poetry. She laments "the inexorable intellectual heritage and social conditioning of the Western world" (47) that has distanced human from nonhuman life. If we aspire to "restore, preserve, and enhance the human bond with animals" (47), we must recognize that this bond

> emanates partly from the deep levels of our consciousness, originating from the same kind of experience as myth, folklore, and poetry, whose languages are symbolic. Tapping into a special aspect of the psyche, these forms of expression articulate truths that are more profound than observable "fact." . . . Of all the forms which celebrate and illuminate the bond between animals and people, poetry possesses the most immediacy. Its expressions are composed of spontaneous outflows of affirmation for life, untempered by dependent variables. The symbolizing of animals that is

> peculiar to poetry contributes an essential key to the age-old search for "man's place in nature." (47–8)

In support of her argument, Lawrence cites Edward O. Wilson, who believes people

> exhibit "biophilia," an inherent tendency to focus on and affiliate with other forms of life. If he is right—and there is good evidence in support of his hypothesis—human relationships with animals take place at a most fundamental level of our existence. Perhaps because it operates at that level, the innate bond we share with animals is more amenable to poetry than to any other medium. Wilson explains: ... "Mankind ... is the poetic species. The symbols of art, music, and language freight power well beyond their outward and literal meanings. So each one also condenses large quantities of information. Just as mathematical equations allow us to move swiftly across large amounts of knowledge and spring into the unknown, the symbols of art gather human experience into novel forms in order to evoke a more intense perception in others." (51)

Animal poetry edifies readers, Lawrence believes, as no other medium can; people

> may understand their own or even their species's feelings about animals, but it is far more difficult for them to comprehend equally well the animal's half of the relationship. To fully understand human–animal interaction, the most important requirement is empathy. It might be said that this quality is the poet's stock in trade. A gifted poet communicates intimate feelings for the other beings ... Literary critic Geoffrey Moore wrote of the poet John Keats: "When he saw a sparrow pecking about on the gravel, he did not merely identify with the bird, he became it." (48)

I resist the suggestion that the consummate function of animal poetry is for the poet to "become" the animal (Figuratively? Empathetically? How can this happen? Would it be the ideal outcome? Doesn't it disregard the profound artifice of human culture, and dismiss fundamental biological realities?). Deleuze and Guattari's trope of "becoming-animal," discussed in part 1, is a process considerably more complex than just watching an animal and writing a poem about it—even a very good poem. Still, Lawrence presents a useful model of how animal poetry might allow readers to transcend the limitations inherent in an epistemology that uniquely privileges human consciousness and sensibilities.

When I read animal poetry, I ask what it reveals about people's relationship with animals and about how human culture frames this relationship. I seek some formulation that answers Henry Beston's call in *The Outermost House* (a naturalistic account from the 1920s of the cycles of life and nature as observed during a year on Cape Cod) quoted at the head of this chapter: "We need another and a wiser and perhaps a more mystical concept of animals" (25). Mesoamerican communities have confronted the issue of human–animal relationships, and arrived at a simple, compelling awareness: they believe that human existence is directly related to and dependent upon the fortunes of other creatures. The conception of animal souls that underlies their spirituality exemplifies Beston's "more mystical concept of animals" and inspires me to integrate Mesoamerican sensibilities, in some adaptation that fits literary culture, into the consideration of animal poetry. In Western industrial culture, we and our poets fumble around more tentatively, lacking a widespread, vital system of belief and knowledge about the relationship between human and nonhuman animals.

Yet, I hypothesize that animal poetry may embody a displaced realm of contemporary Western spirituality—one that, like Mesoamerican spirituality, emanates from the natural world that exceeds the merely human realm. Animal poetry, highly varied in scope and quality, is a trope so common and perhaps even exhausted, that we may be inclined to discount its potential force. But I believe that we may be able to rediscover and recenter a repressed "biophilia" (as Wilson terms it) by situating animal poetry alongside animal souls and, more generally, reading it through the program of ecocriticism.

Michael Branch describes the platform for ecocriticism as "explor[ing] new ways of belonging to the world, new ways of developing an ethic of caution and reciprocity in our interactions with nonhuman nature" (xiv). Ecologically enlightened poetry, "sustainable poetry" as Leonard Scigaj terms it, "addresses our connection to the natural world" and treats nature not "as a convenient background for human concerns but acknowledge[s] that it sustains human, as well as nonhuman, life in ecosystems that have been deeply bruised by human exploitation and pollution" (7). Branch's sense of *reciprocity* and Scigaj's invocation of *connection*, both of which are central to any sane conception of ecological harmony and equilibrium, inhere firmly in the tradition of animal souls.

The concept of *animal souls* takes on broader latitude as I import the term from its original context into literary criticism. In its precise denotation as a characteristic of Mesoamerican culture, the animal soul describes the animal component, or complement, of a human soul: what is on some level a shared existence, a symbiotic human–animal consciousness. Cultural anthropologists understand "animal souls" to refer implicitly to *people's* animal souls—that is, the part of the human spirit situated in an external animal. It would be disingenuous to deny, in this formulation, the privileging of the human being in this human–animal relationship: as if, in some sense, a degree of *human* sentience is franchised out, transposed into an animal host, but nevertheless a constituent of our own domain of consciousness. The dynamics of the human–animal bond encompassed by animal souls can be interpreted in two different ways: either granting animals a potent parity with humanity by acknowledging their spiritual force and their equitable, intimate interaction with people; or, conversely, representing animals as colonized subjects, outposts of our own central empire of self. Certainly the same is true of poets who use animals in their art—and we must examine carefully what it means to "*use*" animals, even in the seemingly innocuous mode of artistic representation.

I believe it makes sense to examine the presence of animal souls in an assembly of poetic animals based on my presumption that certain poets evince some approximation of the fierce conviction demonstrated by Mesoamericans: that animals crucially matter and that they embody a spiritual and ecological potency on their own terms rather than simply figuring as supporting players in an anthropocentric fantasy. I am aware of the great distance (in terms of geography, culture, academic disciplinarity, genre) between poetic representations of animals and Mesoamerican spiritual ideologies. I do not mean to assert any explicit connection between poetic animals and animal souls, but merely to look at the former through the lens of the latter: to borrow from Mesoamericans (and, I hope, not to appropriate too insensitively or haphazardly) a belief system, a consciousness, that resonates with the poems I discuss.

For Mesoamericans, animal souls is a way to describe and affirm animals' spiritual value. In the animal poetry I examine, depictions of animals are sometimes imbued with forthright spiritual veneration, although—given the absence of prominent Western cultural traditions that endorse animal reverence—the expression is usually more tentative. I want to be suggestive and approximate rather than literalistic about attributing animal souls to poetic animals. Some poets, indeed, clearly convey the divinity they believe inheres in animals; others regard and, via their poetry, "worship" animals in a less theologically explicit mode. Like Mesoamericans, some poets (and readers of poetry) in our culture have tried to embrace the notion of co-essentiality with nonhuman animals: the conviction that people are not alone as sentient creatures on the earth, but rather, that we share a common nature and partake of a common life-force. *Tonalismo* and *nagualismo* embody the tenets of co-essence for Mesoamericans, and I have come to believe that poetry may embody a comparable set of expressions.

The metaphysic of animal souls offers a vocabulary and an ethos unavailable elsewhere. The poetic animals in the following chapters represent such a visionary breakthrough beyond most of the animal art our culture creates that it becomes necessary to transcend familiar intellectual and aesthetic methodologies to find a reference point, a touchstone, that adequately contextualizes it. The belief in animal souls is uniquely capable of offering such a context. The great cultural and cognitive distance between Mesoamerican spirituality and modern poetry is, finally, an advantage rather than a drawback, precisely because the orientation that one may bring to poetry from this foreign belief system is so unusual: as an outsiders' discourse, it is untainted by Western industrial-world cultural marginalizations and trivializations of animals. Looking beyond established ways of appraising animals and describing anthrozoological interaction in our culture will help generate a more equitable way of achieving enlightened coexistence. I offer here, for better or worse, the elaboration of my cross-cultural meditations on poetic animals and animal souls.

Animals and Ethics

We ought to respect animals more and appreciate more keenly their significance in the world we share with them. Paul Shepard suggests in *The Others* that animals make us human. The end of his book presents a letter written in the voice of "the others," the nonhuman, explaining the urgency of the human–animal connection. At first, the others recall, "We nurtured the humans from a time before they were in the present form. . . . In ancient savannas we slowly teased them out of their chauvinism. In our plumage we gave them esthetics. In our courtships we tutored them in dance. In the gestures of antlered heads we showed them ceremony and the power of the mask. In our running hooves we revealed the secret of grain. As meat we courted them from within" (331).

But as human civilization has advanced, Shepard's letter continues, people have valued the others less, and human debts to animals have been neglected. "They still do not realize that they need us," the others write,

> thinking that we are simply one more comfort or curiosity. We have not regained the central place in their thought or meaning at the heart of

> their ecology and philosophy. . . . Sometimes we have to be underhanded. We slip into their dreams, we hide in the language, disguised in allusion, we mask our philosophical role in "nature esthetics," we cavort to entertain. We wait in children's books, in pretty pictures, as burlesques in cartoons, as toys, designs in the very wallpaper, as rudimentary companions or pets. We are marginalized, trivialized. We have sunk to being objects, commodities, possessions. . . . Their own numbers leave little room for us, and in this is their great misunderstanding. They are wrong about our departure, thinking it to be part of their progress instead of their emptying. When we have gone they will not know who they are. (333)

It does not require a very piercingly critical analysis of our culture to see the myriad ways in which we mistreat animals, physically as well as metaphysically (aesthetically, intellectually, ethically). Our speciesist discourtesy betrays the cultural prejudices that we manifest as citizens of the Earth; it is my hope that these prejudices can be somehow reformed. If "the others" have had to be underhanded to preserve their presence in our world, as Shepard writes, this is so because of the diminutive physical and imaginative space we have allocated for them, but *tonalismo* and *nagualismo* illustrate an alternative model. Mesoamerican animals need not become devious to ensure their survival: they are welcomed into the course of life as full and equal partners, with no expectation that they demean themselves in the "dancing bear" trope. I believe it is possible and desirable to achieve, universally, the ethos of parity that Mesoamericans embrace. Poetic animals offer a valuable signpost pointing toward this ethos and a reformative response to the underhanded existence that people have imposed upon animals.

A profoundly respectful environmental sensitivity—inculcated even prenatally—accompanies a belief in animal souls. Menchú explains that a pregnant woman "talks to the child continuously from the first moment he's in her stomach. . . . She'll say, for instance: You must never abuse nature' " (8). After the birth, the community symbolically affirms that "the earth is the mother and father of the child" (9). In Quiché agricultural rituals, the harvest fiesta "really starts months before when we asked the earth's permission to cultivate her" (52). Even when animals threaten their agricultural livelihood and children are posted guard to prevent birds and rodents from eating seeds after they have been sown, Menchú writes, "We set traps but when the poor animals cry out, we go and see. Since they are animals and our parents have forbidden us to kill them, we let them go after we've given them a telling off so they won't come back" (53). Menchú recounts numerous customs testifying to the pervasive reverence for the nonhuman world that her culture promotes:

> We worship—or rather not worship but respect—a lot of things to do with the natural world, the most important things for us. For instance, to us, water is sacred. Our parents tell us when we're very small not to waste water, even when we have it. Water is pure, clean, and gives life to man. Without water we cannot survive, nor could our ancestors have survived. The idea that water is sacred is in us children, and we never stop thinking of it as something pure. The same goes for the earth. Our parents tell us: "Children, the earth is the mother of man, because she gives him food." ... So we think of the earth as the mother of man, and our parents teach us to respect the earth.... [During] prayers and ceremonies... We evoke the representatives of the animal world.... We say: "Mother Earth, you who give us food, whose children we are and on whom we depend, please make this produce you give us flourish and make our children and animals grow.... We do not abuse you, we only beg your permission, you who are part of the natural world and part of the family of our parents and our grandparents." This means we believe, for instance, that the sun is our grandfather, that he is a member of our family.... [The Quiché] must respect the life of trees, the birds, the animals around us. We say the names of birds and animals—cows, horses, dogs, cats. All these. We mention them all. We must respect the life of every single one of them. (56–8)

Of course, Menchú's people do not hold a monopoly on respect for nature—every religion, mythos, and culture contains tributes to the earth and the animals. Certainly American parents, like their Quiché counterparts, plead with their children not to waste water while brushing their teeth. Indeed, American culture resonates with expressions (albeit sublimated—lacking the unabashed veneration Menchú describes) of totemic or individual affiliation with animals in appreciation of their natural power. Consider, for example, one of our most universal and intense cultural activities:

> Sports have always used animals as logos, mascots, nicknames, and metaphors. Baseball has teams named the Cubs, Tigers, Bluejays, Orioles, and Cardinals.... There have been players nicknamed "Bull," "Mule," "Iron Horse," "Cat," "Big Cat," "Moose," "Goose," "King Kong," and even "Penguin." Basketball has teams named the Bulls, Bucks, Hornets.... In football, the animals multiply and become even more ferocious, for the most part, befitting the combative nature of the game. There have been players with the nicknames of "Bronco," "Bull," and "Bulldog," and teams named the Bears, Bengals, Broncos, Colts, Eagles, Falcons, Lions, and the Rams. (Ardolino 47)

Such team identities (which become, also, geographical, commercial, and institutional identities) represent one way of expressing a connection with animals. Sports fans acknowledge a vitality ascribed to animals, believing that we are somehow, even if only figuratively, like these animals with which we identify.

Another way in which we link human heroic prowess with animals—literally draping ourselves with the force of animals—appears in a strain of characters (real and fictional) who appear bedecked in their skins: John Seelye enumerates such figures as Davy Crockett "portrayed in a hunter's fringed-leather jacket, trimmed with fur, and wearing a hat made from a wildcat, its head and tail intact. . . . [James Fenimore] Cooper's Leatherstocking likewise wore a fur hat, to which he added buckskins borrowed from Daniel Boone." Robinson Crusoe appears "clothed in his homemade costume of goatskins," Tarzan appears with "his privates concealed by a loincloth made from the skin of a lion or leopard," and even Ben Franklin "in a famous French portrait" poses "in a fur hat," all of which semiotically signify that "the wearer [of animal skins] is a true Child of Nature, a tradition that emerges from an ancient European archetype, the 'Wild Man' " (155–7). These men demonstrate an intimate physical connection with animals via the affinity of animal-skin clothing: the wearer of dead animals' pelts wishes to take on the vitality of animals. However one appraises the implications of such a use of animals (and I am not inclined to endorse this fashion as enlightened pan-speciesism), it offers one more indication of our desire to connect with animals.

Evidence in every culture indicates at least an inkling of animals' spiritual potency and some aspiration to tap into this. But communities such as the Chamula and Quiché seem sincere in their intimate, respectful acknowledgment of animals' importance on a wide scale and with a conviction that vastly exceeds the experience of Western society. "The concept of animal souls and other co-essences goes well beyond being a mere evaluative vocabulary," Gossen explains. "These ideas matter. They constitute a key node in Indian cosmologies and beliefs about health and general well-being" ("Olmecs" 555).

In my own culture, generally, interest in animals rings hollow; it is rote or merely symbolic, possessing a diminutive cultural currency. Animals and animal imagery are ubiquitous, but the importance we accord them is shallow; aesthetically and sociologically, the animal is perpetually subaltern. For Mesoamericans, animal souls are real, immediate. They live out, at the heart of their belief system, a valorization of animal life. The "set of beliefs and language for talking about [animal souls] reside at the very core of what might be called a native metaphysics of personhood in Mesoamerica," Gossen writes; "the language of souls has fundamentally to do with Mesoamerican construction of self and social identity, destiny and power, as much now as has apparently been the case for two thousand years in Mexico and Central America" (556), and constitutes for Mesoamericans a salient element of the most central aspects of human nature: "strength... frailty... vulnerability... inequality, and even our unwitting capacity to destroy ourselves" (566).

Parallels/Connections

Animals and people lead "parallel lives," John Berger writes in "Why Look at Animals?" This observation cuts two ways: the parallelism can be an empowering association, as it is in Mesoamerican culture, or it can be more segregationist, which is how Berger describes the alignment of animals and people in Western culture. A person looks at an animal, he writes, just as the animal may look back at the human observer, "across a narrow abyss of non-comprehension" (3). The animal "is distinct, and can never be confused with man. ... a power is ascribed to the animal, comparable with human power but never coinciding with it. ... always its lack of common language [with people], its silence, guarantees its distance, its distinctness, its exclusion, from and of man. Just because of this distinctness, however, an animal's life, never to be confused with a man's, can be seen to run parallel to his" (3–4).

Berger's parallelism is mutually exclusive: either human or animal, with no common ground. This sensibility accurately describes the mainstream Western attitude toward animals: people live in houses, cities, communities, *culture*, while animals live "out there" in woods, wilds, preserves, *nature*; and in most other ways, too, we conceive ourselves as living at a binary-opposed distance from animals. Berger's account of human–animal parallelism contrasts with a Mesoamerican parallelism that is consummately permeable and mutually inclusive: immensely more affirming of the shared claims between people and animals in the ecosphere. The Mesoamerican parallelism, if visually graphed, might resemble a ladder: two straight lines, representing the life-courses of human and nonhuman animals, with copious rungs connecting these two lines; Berger's appraisal would lack the connecting rungs.

Animal poetry offers an opportunity for discovering within our culture an incipient sensibility—embracing a sound, interdependent relationship with animals—approximating attitudes more prevalent in societies outside the Western sphere. Even if we probably cannot finally achieve the faith in animal souls that other cultures have, we may nevertheless try to learn from and emulate those who have attained keen insights about inter-species relationships. We might strive to embrace some of their perceptions, and to celebrate some areas in our own culture where we may have already taken a step in the right direction. We might try to understand and value the natural world more than we do in our environmentally hostile communities, where animals are marginalized, incomprehensible, because our habitats' antinatural forces—artificial climates, toxic emissions, plastic flowers, synthetic foods, and on and on—displace animals' presence and vitality. We might celebrate in animal souls what is inexplicable in our own cultural processes. Gary Kowalski explains in *The Souls of Animals* how he conceptualizes animals' spiritual potentiality: "My contention is that spirituality is quite natural, rooted firmly in the biological order and in the ecology shared by all life. . . . To me, animals have all the traits indicative of soul. . . . No one can prove that animals have souls. But if we open our hearts to other creatures and allow them to sympathize with their joys and struggles, we find they have the power to touch and transform us. There is an inwardness in other creatures that awakens what is innermost in ourselves" (3, 5).

Independent of Mesoamerican tenets but congruent with these sensibilities, Kowalski concludes, "Animals are our spiritual colleagues and emotional companions. We know this to be true less through debate than through direct experience" (108). Asking people to open our hearts to animals and greet them as soul mates, Kowalski writes, "The things that make life most precious and blessed—courage and daring, conscience and compassion, imagination and originality, fantasy and play—do not belong to our kind alone" (111).

Animal poems represent a contact zone with animals, within which writers may attempt to discover what Mesoamericans possess as part of their ingrained epistemology. This poetry hints at poets' (and readers') attempts to find something similar to what Mesoamericans recognize as their animal souls. If we can accomplish an approximation of the Mesoamerican metaphysics, we will have ventured much closer to the rhythms and workings of the natural world than we usually do in Western industrial acculturation. Animals are very important to our lives in so many ways, and yet we largely construct our world and our lives as necessarily, "naturally," separate from theirs. We should feel compelled to think about them, understand them, both on their own merits and in terms of how their existence and their survival impacts our lives.

Like canaries that accompanied miners into the tunnels, dying of gas inhalation before the people could smell the danger, all animals possess an acute survival instinct that may serve to warn us of impending threats. But there need be no dead birds to enable our survival; we should aspire to learn from animals—as every society has done to some degree—without leaving them poorer, crippled, displaced, captured, contaminated, or dead. At the vanguard of the modern intellectual/industrial world, people's naturalistic perceptions are so crudely stinted, insensitive, that we overlook imminent natural hazards. Our prosperous cultural systems seem to be proceeding just fine, so we tune out the ecosystem's warning alarms: global warming, acid rain, eroding shorelines, dying trees, polluted oceans, overharvested fisheries, evaporated rivers, disappearing nature. It is possible to look at the world from the perspective of our immensely sophisticated technoculture and not notice what's wrong. It is less possible to do this if we are clearly attuned to animal consciousness and perspectives. Like animal souls, animal poetry fosters transcendence of anthropocentrism. "As we inhabit the twenty-first century, we will need a poetry that does not ignore nature or simply project human fears or aesthetic designs on it. Nature must have its own voice, separate and at least equal to the voice of humans, in the quest to create a balance where both humans and nature can survive into the next century" (Leonard Scigaj, *Sustainable Poetry* 5).

I find in poetic animals a corpus that allows this balance, that eschews the sort of anthropocentrism that pervades most human art. The "human fears" that Scigaj mentions connote the everpresent anxieties of the empowered class: that our hegemony will be somehow challenged, undercut; that acknowledging the subaltern threatens our own primacy; that confronting our historical legacy will reveal our tyranny—the habitats we have ruined, the animals we have destroyed in the indulgence of imperious vanities.

The concept of "sustainable poetry" asserts a compelling connection between art and nature that we might ideally achieve. Scigaj begins with a conventional definition of ecological sustainability: a condition in which human births and deaths are in balance, tree cutting does not exceed tree planting, the number of cattle on a range does not exceed its carrying capacity, carbon emissions match carbon fixation . . . Sustainable poetry, as he describes it, "offers exemplary models of biocentric perception and behavior" (78–9): it inspires a mode of existence that will allow the earth to remain safe and ecologically prosperous.

Sustainable poetry "does not subordinate nature to a superior human consciousness," Scigaj continues. What he calls "establishment poetry," on the other hand, represents the status quo: it "systematically naturalizes nature into reliably benign, National Park landscapes and regularly sanitizes the text by systematically editing out specific social and economic concerns, while restricting interest to aesthetics and language theory." Establishment poetry is unsustainable because it "attenuates our grasp of important referential realities"—that is, the threats to the real world of nature that this poetry stylizes and sanitizes. Sustainable poetry "sustains a connection between the inner and outer world," where the inner world refers to the realm of human art and the human mind, and the outer world consists of trees and animals and so forth (79).

> A sustainable poem . . . is the verbal record of an interactive encounter in the world of our sensuous experience between the human psyche and nature, where nature retains its autonomy—where nature is not dominated, reduced to immanence, or reduced to a reliably benign aesthetic backdrop for anthropocentric concerns. . . . an ecopoem becomes a tool for altering the reader's perceptions from the anthropocentric to the biocentric, and many ecopoems model biocentric behavior. Ecopoems help us to live our lives by encouraging us to understand, respect, and cooperate with the laws of nature that sustain us. Today we very much need sustainable poetry. (80–1)

Scigaj illustrates the ethos of sustainable poetry with a comment from W. S. Merwin in response to a discussion of some highly theoretical, self-reflexive academic trends surrounding the contemporary poetry industry. "Merwin smiled ruefully and said, 'I thought poetry had something to do with living' " (79).

I share with Scigaj and Merwin the conviction that poetry has an ecological ethical potential, and an ecological ethical burden. Art can help, or harm, the world we live in, and we must *choose* (which is the praxis of ethics) which of these visions we would endorse. The tenuous condition of animal life and animal habitats today is such that the middle road, a Platonic vision of art as neither helpful nor harmful but merely neutral (escapist, otherworldly, intentionally irrelevant to reality), is not viable: those who are not with the animals are against them.

Poetic Animals

Most animal poetry strikes me as either manifestly and immediately offensive, or more seductively and insidiously blindered in the mode of the examples discussed in part 1 (W. B. Yeats, Mary Oliver, Ogden Nash *et al.*). Rarely, I find poetry that breaks through the solipsistic restraints of anthropocentrism: where animals enjoy a respectful prominence on their own terms, irrelevant of what they can do for us (or what we can do to them). A few exceptional poets exemplify a more valuable strain of animal poetry, offering a literature that substantially serves both aesthetic and ecological interests. Their poetry honors animals without implicating them in human cultural models. It attempts to confront animals as they are, instead of as they appear to us or as they suit and flatter our habits. I signify (and dignify) the apotheosis by identifying this achievement not with the term "animal poetry," but rather, "poetic animals." In the analysis that follows, I will set out a working process for reading and evaluating poetry according to a certain set of criteria, which will illustrate how readers might use poetic animals to achieve a degree of insight into human–animal relations that transcends conventional modes of engagement.

The poetry of Marianne Moore (1887–1972) features animals that are unique and splendid, yet which tend to appear somewhat opaque, weirdly elusive to us. Readers may initially resist or fault Moore's verse because her animals are hard to relate to; it is difficult to penetrate her poesis and feel a keen sense of knowing control over the animals she describes. But gradually, Moore's ideal reader comes to appreciate that this effect, intentional, serves to teach people about nonhuman animals and their difference from us. We are not *supposed* to revel in the omniscient dominance that we usually expect to experience when we read animal poetry. Moore extols the eloquence of animals in their habitats; she teaches her readers to respect animals in their own places, on their own terms, and not (like so many other appropriative representations of animals) transposed into our distorting, artificial constructs for our more convenient cultural consumption. "The Fish," Moore writes, in the strikingly watery poem of that title,

> wade
> through black jade.
>   Of the crow-blue mussel-shells, one keeps
>   adjusting the ash-heaps;
>   opening and shutting itself like
>
> an
> injured fan.
>   The barnacles which encrust the side
>   of the wave, cannot hide
>   there for the submerged shafts of the
>
> sun,
> split like spun

glass, move themselves with spotlight swiftness
into the crevices—
in and out, illuminating

the
turquoise sea
of bodies. (32)

Moore's poetic animals march to their own beat; her poetry, however humanly and artificially, at least tries to suggest how animals *really* look and act. The syntactic, prosodic, and conceptual difficulties of Moore's poetry formally evoke people's difficulty in understanding animals and in situating ourselves in a cognitive perspective that is not human-centered. At the same time, her rich, indirect complexity tantalizes readers with the insights we may reap if we transcend our conventional sensibilities. Enigmatically, her poetic animals embody a promise of the fascination that exists profusely all around us and that we can share if we learn how to look at animals as Moore does.

Looked at by daylight,
the underside's white,
though the fur on the back
is buff-brown like the breast of the fawn-breasted
bower-bird. It hops like the fawn-breast, but has
chipmunk contours—perceived as

it turns its bird head—
the nap directed
neatly back and blending
with the ear which reiterates the slimness
of the body. The fine hairs on the tail,
repeating the other pale

markings, lengthen until
at the tip they fill
out in a tuft—black and
white; strange detail of the simplified creature,
fish-shaped and silvered to steel by the force
of the large desert moon. (14)

Like Pacheco's overdetermined polyvalent bat (reptilian, avian, nihilistic, and so forth) discussed in part 1, Moore's jerboa—the animal this excerpt describes—enjoys a more-than-jerboa animality: fish-shaped, bird-headed, chipmunk-contoured. This animal overflows with the enthusiasm that engages Moore as she marvels at its strange simplicity and, via poetry, transforms its literal physical details into an artistic homage. The dignity of Moore's attention to animals, and her expansive, delicate meditation on their lives and habits, suggest she is one of the rare industrial-world citizens who believes in animals' force as devoutly as Mesoamericans. Moore is the type of poet who seems at least roughly comparable to the believer in animal souls because it is obvious that her vocation is one she embraces seriously, unwaveringly, and, let us say, religiously; the *quidditas* of her poetry is a profusion of noble, soul-infused animals.

Gary Snyder (b. 1930) imbues his poetic animals with spirited, feisty integrity. Awestruck, he acknowledges animals' own lives and processes—while aware that the awe itself is part of the human construct, the artifice inherent in the way we look at animals. An unabashed reverence for animals' power is always implicit in his poetry, and is often intoned explicitly, as in "Prayer for the Great Family": "Gratitude to Wild Beings, our brothers and sisters, teaching secrets, / freedoms, and ways; who share with us their milk; / self-complete, brave, and aware" (24). Snyder powerfully counterpoises animals and people so as to depict, one the one hand, their majestic presence, and set against this, human habits of interaction with them that result in their distance and loss from our lives. The pathos is self-evident in his poem "The Dead by the Side of the Road," a catalog of animals carelessly slain by people that ends:

> The Doe was apparently shot
> lengthwise and through the side—
> shoulder and out the flank
> belly full of blood
>
> Can save the other shoulder maybe,
> if she didn't lie too long—
>
> Pray to their spirits. Ask them to bless us:
> our ancient sisters' trails
> the roads were laid across and kill them:
> night-shining eyes
>
> The dead by the side of the road. (7–8)

Again in "Mother Earth: Her Whales," Snyder juxtaposes animals' magnificence with people's dishonorable treatment of them:

> The whales turn and glisten, plunge
> and sound and rise again,
> Hanging over subtly darkening deeps
> Flowing like breathing planets
> in the sparkling whorls of
> living light—

And Japan quibbles for words on
  what kinds of whales they can kill?
A once-great Buddhist nation
  dribbles methyl mercury
  like gonorrhea
      in the sea. (47)

Like Mesoamericans, Snyder is keenly attuned to the intricate links between people and animals, the interstices of our worlds. In his effusions of gratitude toward animals—in the prayer for does' blessings, in the ecstatic experience of whales in motion—Snyder exhibits a spiritual reverence as intense as the Mesoamericans'. But when he extrapolates animals' connection with people, the shot deer and poisoned whales produce a jarring discordance. His poems provide more unsettling accounts of the human–animal relationship than believers in animal souls might affirm, testifying to the distance our culture must travel before we can achieve the metaphysic that Mesoamerican spirituality evinces.

José Emilio Pacheco (b. 1939) shows the variety and complexity of animals' lives in *An Ark for the Next Millennium*, a collection featuring dozens of individual creatures. Like Snyder and Moore, Pacheco evokes an acutely rapturous vision of animals' quotidian existence far from the range of normal human perception. He writes in "Octopus":

Dark god of the deep,
fern, mushroom, hyacinth
among rocks unseen by man, hidden in the abyss
where at dawn, against the fire of the sun,
night falls to the bottom of the sea where the octopus
absorbs its murky ink through the suckers of its tentacles
Radiant, nocturnal beauty, it pulses
through the caliginous brine of mother waters
it perceives as fresh and crystalline. (23)

As in Snyder's poetry, Pacheco's attribution of spirituality to this "Dark god of the deep" is not a gratuitous construct, but conveys an honest conviction in the divinity of animals. Pacheco offers a humbling perspective that reflects his fascination with all the other species that exist in our world; human beings slip down a few notches as the poet's attunement to all the other life on our "ark" corrects our pervasive egocentrism. Pacheco paints the conditions of his subjects with a pragmatic simplicity, and tries to inform readers of what is going on in our world with respect to animals. He writes in the prose poem "Augury":

> Until just recently I was awakened by the sound of birds. Today I realized they're no longer there. Those signs of life are gone. Without them, things seem much drearier. I wonder what may have killed them—pollution? noise? starving city dwellers? Or maybe the birds realized that Mexico City is dying, and have flown away before the final ruin. (37)

Like Mesoamerican spirituality, Pacheco's poetry alerts us, quietly yet ominously, to the importance of animals in our biosphere and the danger implicit in their absence.

The chapters that follow examine the poetic animals of Pacheco, Moore, and Snyder, along with those in the works of Stevie Smith, Philip Larkin, Seamus Heaney, and Pattiann Rogers. I will consider aesthetics and ethics at the crossroads of nature and culture, animals and animal poetry. Ultimately, I seek to delineate a poetic that transcends any of these individual writers and stands as the touchstone of an ecologically ethical apotheosis. Informed by the kind of relations that can exist between people and animals in Mesoamerican animal souls, we might try to replicate some of these relationships via aesthetic representations of animals. We may find, or at least approach, our own animal souls through these poetic animals.

Chapter 3
José Emilio Pacheco: "I saw a dying fish"

An Ark for the Next Millennium is the title of Margaret Sayers Peden's 1993 translation of José Emilio Pacheco's poems originally published as *Album de zoología* (1985). Her edition, the text I shall discuss here, presents nearly 80 poems, each featuring a specific animal, divided into sections representing the elements that the animals inhabit: water, air, earth, and fire. The lyric subjects include, for example, crabs, fish, octopus, and whales in the realm of water; sparrows, owls, buzzards, mosquitoes, flies, bats, and moths in the air; monkeys, lions, horses, scorpions, boars, ants, and mice on earth; and a lone poem about a salamander, which mythically inhabits the flame, comprises the final section. Pacheco's "ark" is certainly one of the richest poetic assemblies of animals ever created—throughout the course of my research on animals in literature, I have found no other poet who has engaged animals with as much determination and focus. Pacheco, as a Mexican poet, is geographically proximate to the Mesoamerican communities that embrace animal souls, although I see no explicit or intentional connection between his ideas about animals and theirs—it is only coincidental that Pacheco's system of beliefs about people, animals, and their shared existence rivals the philosophical and ethical intricacy of animal souls.

A keenly-honed consciousness of animals pervades Pacheco's canon. His first collection, *Los elementos de la noche* (*The Elements of the Night*), from 1963, includes "animals, later to populate many of Pacheco's most memorable indictments of man, lurk[ing] in these opening lines," writes Michael J. Doudoroff (265). *No me preguntes como pasa el tiempo* (*Don't Ask Me How the Time Goes By*), from 1969, includes a section called "The Animals Know," 13 poems that anticipate what would become the larger collection of poetic animals in *Album de zoología. Desde entonces* (*Since Then*), from 1980, depicts "a parade of animals, to mankind's discredit. The theme of ecological balance, an implied ethical environmentalism, is intensified in this collection" (Doudoroff 270). *Miro la tierra* (*I Look at the Earth*), published in 1986, with the devastating 1985 Mexico City earthquake as the central metaphor, features the "attribution of prophecy to animals" (Doudoroff 273). In the mode of *An Ark for the Next Millennium*, the poems of *Miro la tierra* explore a panorama of animals that inhabit our world, arrayed in their ecosystemic intricacy and integrity, interspersed with our society and our consciousness: "The omnipresent rats of Mexico City pursue the speaker in a sardonic nightmare *memento mori*. Bluebottles replace the sparrows and pigeons. A mock dithyramb to the flies leads into a lesson on the food chain at the insect level, the great chain of being degraded and inverted" (273). *Miro la tierra* presents what Doudoroff calls "moral lessons drawn from the observations of animals" (273).

Cynthia Steele reads *An Ark for the Next Millennium* as predominantly allegorical: the animals' main function, she suggests, is to offer a platform for the examination of people. Her summary of the collection focuses on the human context that she sees implicit in these poems: for example, "Many of the sea and river creatures have been endangered by man. . . . As for the creatures of the air, some are man's faithful companions and helpful harbingers of disaster. . . . Like people, animals react differently to the prison of this world and the void beyond. . . . In short, this ark's passengers share the beastly human condition" (91–2). Her reading, while not incorrect, is reductionist: it is assumptively, conventionally anthropocentric and understates the degree to which Pacheco's poetry depicts animals not *just* as a meditation on our own condition, but also to explore human–animal interaction and animals on their own terms, absent humanity altogether. Henry Beston reminds us that animals "are not brethren, they are not underlings; they are other nations" (25); Pacheco's poetry acknowledges such an ethic of independent identity for animals and transcends the implicit monodimensionality that underlies Steele's analysis, and that is, indeed, the default condition of much animal poetry.

Poetry like Pacheco's honors animals without implicating them (and thus positioning them as subaltern) in human cultural models. It attempts to confront animals as they are, instead of as they appear to us, or as they suit and flatter our habits. His subjects are unconstrained by the politically oppressive subtexts that tend to infuse animal poetry. A human presence in any poetry—as mediator, artist—is unavoidable, but Pacheco minimizes this as much as possible. He declines to play the control freak, as is usually the inclination of our species when we regard and represent animals.

I align Pacheco's poetry with animal souls for two reasons. First, he is keenly attuned to the poetic animals themselves, with a deep appreciation for a dignity they possess that is independent of humanity. ("The animal shall not be measured by man," as Beston writes [25].) Second, Pacheco's poetry examines how animals and people *share* the world, how our own species is inextricably connected with all the others. Pacheco tells us, as Mesoamerican spirituality holds, that our fates are connected with those of the animals—sometimes manifestly and rationally, and sometimes, as it seems to us, accidentally or coincidentally or ironically, although this sense of accident probably reflects our imperfect understanding of the larger logic at work in the ecosystem; what we conceive as an accidental human–animal relationship likely embodies a larger rationality in nature that eludes our perspective.

Sometimes Pacheco's poetic animals are pointedly in their own world: in their natural habitats apart from people or simply in an unspecific setting—but importantly, lacking any human presence—where they can be themselves. In poems without people, Pacheco celebrates the consequent freedom animals enjoy. He explains in "Forest Clearing" how human intrusion would undermine the tableau:

> Year after year the deer come
>   to this forest clearing
>   to mate.
> No one has ever seen their sacred ceremony.
>   Should someone
> somehow interrupt it, the next year
>   there would be no deer. (79)

The animals' world outside the forest, beyond the clearing, "is called death, / a word that to them means hounds / and high-powered rifles" (79). People are dangerous, and even in our absence from this poem Pacheco cannot repress the image, the potential, of our predatory violence. (Remember Yeats's poem to the squirrel, discussed in part 1, where the literal absence of a gun does not make the poem any less lethal.) The guns and dogs suggest that people's predatory style is unnaturally obsessive: unfairly stacked against the deer; overpowerful, with the fancy weapons and the other animals we co-opt and corrupt in our quest to destroy the deer. When Pacheco writes of "a word that to them means . . ." he broaches the possibility of inter-species communication, but to the extent that these deer *understand* people or that we *communicate* with them, Pacheco ironically asserts, what we express with our words and our guns is the failure of any real connection. When an animal encounters a person, humanness becomes the signifier for which the signified is the animal's death. In Mesoamerican terms, such a construct would be, literally, suicidal, as well as ecocidal. In *An Ark for the Next Millennium*, I believe, such a suicidal tenor resonates beneath Pacheco's account of people's relation to animals. The most basic ecological analysis of the human cultural behavior and attitudes depicted in Pacheco's poetry would confirm that when we destroy enough of "them," we will have destroyed ourselves as well.

"No one has ever seen their sacred ceremony," the poem asserts, infusing the world of "Forest Clearing" with a spiritual potentiality. Does Pacheco imply that if people happened to see this "ceremony"—this mating ritual, this gathering of deer—it would cease to be sacred, because our mere presence would profane it? Or because guns and dogs would presumably accompany our presence? The poem suggests that Pacheco envisions the animal ceremony as encompassing some experience or sensibility on the part of the deer that *must* remain separatist, within the realm of animals alone—and thus apparently antithetical to the shared sacredness that Mesoamericans believe connects people and animals. It seems finally impossible for the reader, within the terms of this poem, to perceive precisely what is sacred about the ceremony at the forest clearing—we cannot know, if we observe an event, that it would happen identically if we were not there: our observation somehow changes it. From Pacheco's assertion that people do not see the deer's sacred ceremony, we can extrapolate a larger point about not knowing animals: preserving the animals' essence and sanctity is contingent upon people's accepting limited omniscience. This exemplifies the epistemological consciousness I described at the end of part 1 about the intrusive dangers that accompany people's knowledge of animals.

By Pacheco's definition, we cannot experience the sacredness of which the animals partake. Yet the invocation of sacredness here in "Forest Clearing," despite its elusiveness to people, is a trope that locates Pacheco's poetry, whether intentionally or coincidentally, in the same realm as the spirituality of Mesoamerican animal souls. Although the poem forestalls people from participating in the sacredness of the forest ceremony firsthand, perhaps the contact zone of the poem per se, the ground that Pacheco stakes out and "clears" for us, is indeed a safe vantage point from which people *can* watch what is going on—what these animals are doing, what their sacred ceremony comprises. Just as Pacheco is telling his readers that we can't share in the animals' sacredness, he is actually, paradoxically, simultaneously offering at least a glimmer of something—something that people have always known animals did (mating), but probably not something we had consciously perceived as cloaked in spirituality.

This sacred, albeit tenuous, shared experience that occurs as we read "Forest Clearing" is less extensive than what Mesoamericans enjoy in their belief system. Certainly we must accept that any inkling we may find in poetic animals of the connection that Mesoamerican culture posits between people and animals will be more nebulous and more paltry than the full-blown system of animal souls. It is perfectly fitting—as a consequence of the ecological hauteur pervading Pacheco's industrial-world culture—that we merit no more than the tiniest whiff of a natural, interspecies spirituality that Mesoamericans perceive so much more acutely. But if we did find a vision, attenuated, of the spiritual potential lurking at the margins of our culture, I suggest that it would look exactly like what Pacheco presents in moments of sacredness that we are forbidden to see as we find in "Forest Clearing."

Pacheco repeatedly describes how animals, when they interact with people, end up the worse for the encounter. The poem "Octopus" reiterates the theme from "Forest Clearing" of animals' sublimity in the world away from people, contrasted with the dangerous degradations they suffer when in proximity to us. At the opening the octopus, distant from human environs, is "Dark god of the deep, / fern, mushroom, hyacinth / among rocks unseen by man, hidden in the abyss"; a "Radiant, nocturnal beauty." Contact with people triggers the poem's peripateia:

> But on the beach contaminated by plastic garbage
> that fleshy jewel of viscous vertigo
> is a monster... and people are killing it,
> clubbing the beached, defenseless creature.
> Someone hurls a harpoon and the octopus breathes death
> through the wound, a second suffocation. (23; ellipses in text)

The description of the animal as "a monster" is in the poet's ironic, rather than authentic, voice: among people, the animal becomes that. We distort the octopus, calumniate it as a monster, and treat it accordingly—attacking with pollution and spears.

A few of Pacheco's poems posit a possible, if unremarkable, coexistence between people and animals—a symbiosis along the lines of *tonalismo*, although in a starkly pedestrian mode. The poem "3:05" describes a bird who "comes to our patio" every afternoon at the same time,

> Looking for... what? No one knows.
> Not food: it rejects

> the slightest crumb.
> Not a mate:
> it always is alone.
> Maybe from simple inertia, from watching us
> at the table, always at the exact same time,
> it gradually has become, like us,
> a creature of habit. (33; ellipses in text)

Although the poem connects the lives of people and animals, in the spirit of animal souls, it does so in a resigned, uninspired way—lacking the brand of spirituality that Mesoamericans would bring to such a connection. Rarely does Pacheco portray people having the necessary appreciation of animals to embrace the sort of co-essential relationship betokened by bona fide *tonalismo*. When, as in "3:05," he situates the animal as the initiator of such a relationship, the poem challenges whether we are deserving of such a bond. If, like the bird in this poem, an animal has sought out a link with a person, Pacheco drily suggests that it is an indication of the animal's having somehow sunk to our level, where it deserves no more than it gets.

Another manifestation of anthrozoological relations depicted in Pacheco's collection is manifestly parodic: the poem "Lions," for example, begins,

> Like the courtiers of Louis XV
> they smell bad
> but revere appearance.
>
> They live on their past glory, the roar
> given a forum on MGM's
> movie screens. (75)

Lions *don't* smell bad, at least not for lions—they smell as they are supposed to smell. They are *not* like Louis XV's courtiers, although they do revere appearance. The cinematic reference point,[1] while embodying an icon of the animal that is potent to millions of human beings, is obviously meaningless to the lions themselves, so it is a curious image to use in describing their lives. Pacheco is playing here with the relationship between people and lions. There are lions, and then there are *our* lions—caricatures of lions, human cultural constructs. While "Lions" does testify to a kind of coexistence between people and animals, it suggests that that coexistence is not genuinely informed. The ways we choose to represent lions may move us farther away from actually knowing them. But at the same time, the reality of our cultural situation is that we do in fact know lions primarily as Pacheco depicts. Taking the MGM icon and the extremely strained courtier simile as emblems of human epistemologies of animals, Pacheco's poetry forces his readers to acknowledge that, for better or worse, these are the sorts of cultural processes and appropriations that mediate our relationships with animals. Our conceits and prejudices, applications of our own sensibilities that overlie the animals' real selves, make it likely that we will not know them well—will not recognize them, appreciate them, or understand them on their own terms.

Our figures of language, far-fetched and imprecise, betray our deficits of natural appreciation and our abilities to interact with animals in some way *beyond* the human cultural contrivances in which we have entrapped them (movie logos, zoos, circuses, and so forth). If we are to know animals better, we must attempt to remain keenly aware of this built-in degree of error in our representations of them. Even Pacheco himself, despite his devout appreciation of the natures of animals, seems aware that he cannot escape his implication in the human tendency to impose our own standards on animals. A self-deprecating tone—wry, or cavalier, or deflationary, laden with the assumption of irony bespeaking the impossibility of Pacheco's ever really commanding this "ark"—resonates throughout the collection.

Yet, Pacheco pragmatically acknowledges that however ludicrous or anthropocentric our sensibilities with respect to animals, this is where we must start from: if our predominant association with a lion is from a movie opening or if our imaginative tendency is to mull an animal by comparing it to an irrelevant human social milieu, then this is where Pacheco, too, will begin, presenting his animals in the ways we know them. Perhaps his triumph will be to commence with his cultural audience at our present, uninspired, level of coexistence with animals and then, over the course of the collection, take us at least a bit beyond this, making us aware of the limitations of our interactions. When Pacheco says the things he does about lions in this poem—"Show business is in their blood. / They are gluttons, / gigolos, entrepreneurs / that eat / proletarian horsemeat" (75)—he describes them ridiculously but at the same time, he does the best that he can, trapped in our culture, of attempting to understand them.

Pacheco attempts to situate "Lions" in a space common to both animals and people—the same space that gives rise to the greater enterprise of Mesoamerican spirituality. The meeting ground Pacheco discovers is mutually unsatisfactory, strange, silly; the two camps are worlds apart—a direct consequence of which is the tenor of ecological failure, the retrograde consciousness, that pervades *An Ark for the Next Millennium*. In *tonalismo*, the relationship between people and animals is closer and more natural, although still not perfect: in that system, too, there is a cultural gap between people's perception of animals and the animals themselves; indeterminacies, mistakes, and prejudices plague people's interaction with animals in animal souls as in our own culture. But finally, Pacheco's poetry—as strongly as Mesoamerican spirituality—asserts that however difficult or inauspicious the terms of the relationship between people and animals may seem, the bottom line is that we must accept its existence, one way or another. People and lions coexist in this world, in ways that MGM movie logos barely begin to tap, but if that is our entrée, our common ground, so be it: some of Pacheco's poetic animals, like his malodorous lions here, must be content to exist there.

Many of Pacheco's poetic animals resist the world of people. The first line of "Investigation on the Subject of the Bat," for example, depicts animals as glibly oblivious to their situation amid our culture: "Bats know not a word of their literary reputation" (49). (Lions, of course, similarly, know nothing of their star presence at MGM—but Pacheco doesn't need to make every point in every poem.) "Fragment of a Poem Eaten by Mice," a seven-line work that trails off in ellipses at the ending, embodies animals' resistance/antipathy to human culture: their ability to devour and destroy, in the conduct of their natural behavior (eating paper), what people value as our crowning glory, a text. The poem reads:

> A community of primitive rituals,
> mice worship darkness.
> At night they seem
> fierce, always furtive.
> Incisive, hungry, confronting
> persecution, they need to hide.
> Forever spying on those who spy on them . . . (135; ellipses in text)

The poem evokes what Stanley Fish dubs the "self-consuming artifact" (something that "becomes the vehicle of its own abandonment. . . . A self-consuming artifact signifies most successfully when it fails, when it points *away* from itself to something its forms cannot capture" [3–4]). Its subject matter (it is about mice, as well as having been eaten by mice) consumes the human artifact, or all but seven lines. It points away from itself (as Fish's trope describes), and toward that which is no longer present, the poem that mice have destroyed.

This absence is frustrating—presuming that we enjoy Pacheco's poetry, we would like to have more of it, the putatively larger poem that has been partly devoured. But the absence also contributes to Pacheco's poetic, literally and physically making a key point that underlies the entire collection: the force of animals is somehow greater than we conventionally acknowledge, especially in contrast to the value we accord the human force. We had better watch out for these mice, which can hold their own against the poet and poetry. Do the mice realize what they've eaten? *Why* have they eaten the poem about themselves? How did they decide what to eat—where to stop, what to leave uneaten? What were their editorial principles? Such questions just begin to skim the surface of the issues Pacheco's poetry raises regarding how animals and people meet on the field of aesthetics. Pacheco and his poetry represent the human element here, and he willingly gives this over, allowing his presence to be usurped—nibbled—by the animal presence. He asks us to consider what animals in animal poetry may take from us, not just what they may give to us (or we may take from them). He thus evokes an equilibrium to which we must attune ourselves. If we want to engage with animals (poetic or real) *veritably*, we must realize that they will not lie there inert.

I regard the experience that the poem enacts as "self-consuming"—rather than, what might seem more literally the case, as "mouse-consuming"—in a testament to what I believe Pacheco thinks of as the "self" (the center, the ego, the consciousness, the voice) of this poem, and of all his poetry: it is a self jointly occupied, jointly comprised, of the human and animal elements. "Fragment of a Poem Eaten by Mice" is a meeting ground of the human soul (art) and the animal soul. One may, in this formulation, regard the animal soul as anti-art, since it has devoured the man-made artifact. Instead of what might be, say, a 14-line poem if it had been protected from hungry mice, we have only a 7-line remnant representing the engagement, the interaction, between people and mice. But I consider the rodential action as a vital contribution to the art. People and mice are, as Pacheco constructs it here, mutually engaged in cultural production. The title of the poem, of course, depends upon the animals' contribution to (not, I think, "subtraction from") it. The poem begins with and is predicated upon the inevitability that it will be eaten by mice. Pacheco seems to enjoy this circumstance and means for us to as well. He is perhaps flattered that mice might think his work worth the trouble to ingest; he may believe that this experience represents as much intercourse between our souls and theirs as we are likely to get. There is nothing tragic in his poem's consumption: there are lots more poems where this one came from. Pacheco is a poet, and the "food" he has to give animals, his offering to them, is poetry. It signifies his respect for animals, his desire to connect with them and delineate a common ground, when he offers (or concedes) his poem to them.

If Coleridge's frustration of alleged incompletion in "Kubla Khan" betokens the power of ephemerality that characterizes the Romantic imagination, then Pacheco's incompletion here is a comparable testimony to the power of his subject matter. These animals will not let themselves be restrained by people, and will not march to our marching songs; *that* insight—animals' unconsciousness of our hubristic self-adulation—trumps the plodding mechanics of human capturing, fixing, in art. The mice have eaten one poem, we are explicitly told. They would have no reason to stop with one, we might reason. The entire catalog we hold in our hands—Pacheco's poetry, *any* poetry—is written in what we should recognize as a kind of disappearing ink: the animals could eat it all. The world of rodents, bugs, birds, worms *et al.* is capable of eventually ingesting (devouring, destroying, heedless of the value with which we invest it) any text that we celebrate as a cultural treasure. Pacheco posits his textuality as neither superior to nor immune from the powers of animals. This ecologically balanced, humble perspective infuses Pacheco's poetry and, I believe, typifies the best model of how people can write animal poetry without exploiting (subjugating, co-opting, domesticating, aestheticizing, stylizing) the subjects. Instead, Pacheco looks at the animals—while they, in the poems, look back at us in tandem—on equal footing, eye to eye, as cohabitants of this planet.

Pacheco's short poem "Sparrow" explains animals' resistance to our world as a manifestation of a simple, classic dichotomy—the nature/culture clash:

> In our quiet garden, it alights
> but suddenly startled by your gaze
> takes wing, rising in unbounded flight
> preferring its liberty to our maze. (35)

Like countless animal poems, "Sparrow" contrasts animals' freedom to experience their own natural processes with the unnatural repressions that human society has created, which fetter and torment us. This rift is one source of the ecological dissonance—the incompatibility between people and animals—in *An Ark for the Next Millennium*, but it is not the only reason for our disharmony. Animals react with a range of complex behaviors, consciously or instinctually, to resist people, to escape our influence, and to preserve their own often-fragile integrity as they negotiate the biotas we desecrate. Animals may warn starkly, as in a jeremiad, of the dangerous encroachments that accompany our human processes. The prose poem "Augury," for example, recounts:

> Until just recently I was awakened by the sound of birds. Today I realized they're no longer there. Those signs of life are gone. Without them, things seem much drearier. I wonder what may have killed them—pollution? noise? starving city dwellers? Or maybe the birds realized that Mexico City is dying, and have flown away before the final ruin. (37)

Another poem, "The Buzzard," expresses the threat inherent in the loss of animals in the world around us: the unappreciated role they play in our ecosystem, and the cost of losing them. "Augury" depicts a world where animals have simply abandoned a human biota, shaming us implicitly by their refusal to coexist with us amid the conditions we have created. But "The Buzzard" is more ecologically explicit and adjudicatory about how people may fare when we have insulted these birds to extinction. The opening stanzas describe people's scorn for the bird's aesthetics, reflecting the speciesist prejudices that accompany our malfeasant ecological ethos. Then the poem offers a moralistic warning: rebutting the bird's bad reputation, Pacheco celebrates its ecological importance and exposes the short-sightedness of our failure to appreciate the importance of living codependently (the sensibility that comes easily to the Mesoamerican mindset) with buzzards:

> But without this regional variant
> of the vulture so defamed by rhetoric,
> without this "turkey buzzard" or "carrion eater"
> —with such names it is insulted—
> what would have become
>   of the accursed regions
> visited
>   by yellow fever
> and other plagues
>   of the *tristes tropiques?*
> Buzzards
>   were our recycling brigades
> And now that buzzards are extinct
> garbage is about to engulf the world. (47)

The last two lines convey Pacheco's bitter appraisal of human behavior, conjoined with a sense of revenge, justice, consequence, *contrapasso*: we will get what is coming to us, and it won't be pretty.

Most of Pacheco's animals are very much in and affected by our world, insistently intermixed with people, generally to their detriment, as in "Bitch on Earth," which begins:

> A pack of dogs is following a bitch
> through the uninhabitable streets of Mexico City.
> Extremely dirty dogs,
> half-lame and blind,
> knocked about,
> and covered with oozing sores.
> Condemned to death
> and, more immediately, to hunger and homelessness. (141)

The streets are equally uninhabitable for man and beast; the tableau happens to highlight the resident animals but could just as easily describe the human population of the city's underclass. Often, as here, Pacheco's account of the sad fate of animals in our society accompanies a report of people's corollary misfortunes. We are fellow sufferers with the animals, which is the condition that is fundamental to the Mesoamerican system of animal souls. The fate of people and animals that occupy the same space is linked, coincident, interdependent. And in Pacheco's poetry, this interdependence manifests itself most prominently in the depictions of a world commonly painful for people and animals. "Bitch on Earth" portrays people fouling their environs, creating a slum, and animals suffering concurrently. Another poem, "Equation to the First Degree, with Unknown Quantity," raises a similar vision of animals suffering in environs people have despoiled:

> In the city's last river, through error
> or spectral incongruity, suddenly
> I saw a dying fish. It was gasping,
> poisoned by filthy water as lethal as
> the air we breathe. (19)

The poem is not only about the dying fish, but also about the illness that the people who share this fouled ecosystem may expect: the people who breathe the poisoned air as the fish ingest the poisoned water (not that the lethal water alone isn't dangerous enough to us). Everything is connected to everything else, as Barry Commoner's ecological mantra asserts. The poem's first-person observer tries to hear the language, the moral, of the dying fish, but cannot penetrate through the sullied environment, the void of its impending death. "I will never know what it tried to tell me," the poem concludes, "that voiceless fish that spoke only the/omnipotent language of our mother, death" (19). As happens often in Pacheco's poems, inter-species communication fails, a casualty of the fouled medium of our commonality—the environment. But the remaining ur-language is extinction. If we fail at all other means of communication and interaction with animals, Pacheco promises, the default "language" that will fill the vacuum will be simply death.

A baboon in "Baboon Babble" offers another example of an animal ensconced, to its misfortune, in human culture. "Born here in this cage," in a zoo, completely circumscribed by the circumstances of human captivity, the first lesson it learned was that

> in every direction I look this world is
>   bars and more bars.
> Everything I see is striped
> like the bars of a tiger's pelt.
> They say somewhere there are free monkeys.
>   I have seen nothing
> but an infinity of kindred prisoners,
>   always behind bars. (69)

"The Well" depicts an instance of unfortunate interaction between people and animals. An epigraph describes an ironic human misperception of turtles' power: we have looked to them to safeguard our own health, but we are ecologically mistaken.

> The traditional method for purifying well water—keeping a turtle in the bottom—was instead an extremely efficient form of contamination. Ambrosio Ortega Paredes: *El agua, drama de México* (1955). (9)

Despite our best intentions in seeking a human–animal relationship that recognizes animals' power and tries to tap into that power, "The Well" portrays our failure. Perhaps Pacheco believes we deserve to fail, given our opportunistic exploitation of animals and our refusal to work towards nurturing inter-species relationships when there is no immediate payoff for us. Once again, the short-sightedness of Western industrial culture—the insincere and naive unsophistication of our relationship to the natural world as compared with Mesoamerican tribal cultures—arises as the definitive difference between their successful integration of animal souls into their lives and our much more halting, sloppy attempts. In the well is

> the gloomy turtle
>   we drop in
> as instrument or talisman or spell

to purify
water, or consciousness,
Never realizing
that our subterfuges are the traps
into which, invariably, we fall

It's clear:
the turtle
does not purify—
it fouls. (9, 11)

Pacheco's well symbolizes the unknown quantity in the relation between people and animals. "We will never know the extent of the well / how deep it is / or the substance / of its poisoned filterings" (11). Pacheco warns us not to take nature for granted—not to believe we have to have mastered all its tricks, at the risk of punishment for our overweening pride; we are hoist with our own petard.

In *An Ark for the Next Millennium*, as in Mesoamerican spirituality, our necessary coexistence with animals is ignored only at the cost of death. In "Whales," Pacheco describes the pathos surrounding the plight of that species amid human harvesting:

Through the sad night of the deep
resounds
their elegy and farewell
because the sea
has been dispossessed of its whales. (25)

Pacheco complements this abstract paean with a more concrete, literal indictment of human behavior toward the animals. "They must surface to breathe," the poem explains,

and then
the cruel, explosive harpoon
gluts itself on them

And all the sea becomes
a sea of blood
as they are towed to the factory ship
to make lipstick
soap oil
and dog food. (25–7)

So the poem's narrative ends: the whales are dead, and we have our lipstick and dog food. But of course, the story doesn't really end there.

An italicized coda to the poem celebrates the leviathan's power by reference to a passage from the end of the Book of Job. And the ecological story does not end with lipstick. It continues, more ominously, in the cycle of consumerism and consequent industrial/economic exploitation of the world and its creatures, its resources, its ecosystems. "A sea of blood," the simple image Pacheco tosses in before soap and dog food, portends the imminent repercussions of our polluting the repositories of life. It is as obvious to Pacheco as it is to the Mesoamericans what happens if we kill off the animals who are our co-essences to satiate our vanity with baubles.

The poem's conclusion, based on Job 41: 18–22, states,

> *His eyes [are] like the eyelids of the morning.*
> *Out of his nostrils goeth smoke,*
> *like that of a pot heated and boiling.*
> *In his neck strength shall dwell,*
> *and want goeth before his face.* (27; brackets in text)

In the Book of Job, this homage to the whale's strength is emblematic of God's omnipotence, his grandness of design; the Bible cites the glory of the most majestic of animals, the largest mammal, to remind Job of his own mortality and insignificance. But as Pacheco recycles this passage, it conveys a sad irony: humanity has humbled and vanquished this noble animal, which once seemed as omnipotent as the Creator. Modern humanity has subdued God's majesty. Job goes on to describe the impervious and sublime power of the whale:

> The sword of him that layeth at [the leviathan] cannot hold: the spear, the dart, nor the habergeon. He esteemeth iron as straw, and brass as rotten wood. The arrow cannot make him flee. . . . he laugheth at the shaking of a spear. (41: 26–9)

But the contemporary whale, as Pacheco's poem describes, falls easy prey to just these weapons that the biblical leviathan resists. In Job, the leviathan "maketh the deep to boil like a pot: he maketh the sea like a pot of ointment. He maketh a path to shine after him" (41: 31–2); this spectacular apotheosis contrasts ironically, pathetically, with the shining path, the "sea of blood," that is all Pacheco's modern whale can muster to mark his presence. "Whales" ends with the animal's impotent death, as opposed to the transcendent vitality of its existence that the Book of Job had celebrated in an earlier time. Pacheco suggests that we need to learn to respect the animals for their own inherent worth, and subdue our pretensions to omnipotence.

Pacheco's poems are, finally, more unlike than like the sympatico construction of the human and nonhuman world that characterizes Mesoamerican spirituality: as insistently as the poet strains to yoke people and animals, the final results of this attempted synthesis tend to be failures, or ironized beyond the range of any ecologically redemptive moral (other than a general "Repent O Man," which seems relatively feeble in terms of its ethical force). But in his depiction of the separateness of the human and animal realms and the danger people pose to animals, Pacheco suggests—however evanescently—an ideal condition, an ideal relationship, such as the sort embodied in animal souls. While his poetry depicts how far we often are from achieving this ideal, nevertheless it is not wholly pessimistic. It *does* succeed in introducing us to a world of shared connection, co-essence, between people and animals, if only, largely, by negation: by the connection that isn't there; that begins, but fails; that we repeatedly abrogate or betray. Pacheco repeats these overtures toward connection with his dozens of striking poems that—despite our unimpressive ecological record as a species—manage to imagine animals spectacularly, appreciate them diligently, respect them uncompromisingly, and empathize with them movingly. Pacheco's poetry leaves the reader with a powerfully sustained moment of insight: a shared existence between reader and subject, between person and animal.

Chapter 4
Marianne Moore: "flies in amber"

Marianne Moore wrote dozens of poems about animals, once referring to them as her "animiles" (which "means literally 'pertaining to animals,' " writes Margaret Holley, "but it is also loosely perhaps an echo of something like 'Anglophile,' the form of affinity" [79]). Composed throughout her career, the poems appear copiously amid her oeuvre with no particular ordering or arrangement.

Many of these poems identify the subject in the title ("The Wood-Weasel," "A Jellyfish," "To a Giraffe") and feature a polyvalent meditation on that animal: describing its attributes and powers (both physical and metaphysical, literal and figurative); its aesthetic allure; its regard by humankind, and its possible relationship to us. Moore is often rampantly anthropomorphic—typical is the expression from "To a Prize Bird": "Pride sits you well, so strut, colossal bird"[1](31). Her demeanor is unabashedly awestruck by her animal subjects; she unstintingly bestows admiring praise, perhaps in the service of illuminating readers who might have neglected to notice for themselves the intense fascination of these animals or the range of talents they possess. "The Pangolin" is an "impressive animal and toiler of whom we seldom hear" (117). The rust-backed mongoose is described in "The Jerboa": "Its restlessness was / its excellence; it was praised for its wit" (12–13). "An Octopus" receives this paean to its sublimity: "Neatness of finish! Neatness of finish! / Relentless accuracy is the nature of this octopus / with its capacity for fact" (76).

Moore's bestiary depicts a variegated spectrum of animal life: plumet basilisk, paper nautilus, porcupine, jellyfish, swan, arctic ox, chameleon, elephant, racehorse, ant, to name just some. I do not perceive any particular ethos or predilection governing Moore's selection of animal subjects.[2] Like José Emilio Pacheco, she simply aspires to compile a bounteous assembly that represents as many different types of animals as possible—big and small, wild and domesticated, local and exotic, common and rare—to generate a comprehensive catalog of animal life.

Always coyly elliptical, Moore's poetry seems especially prone to shift into a heightened state of elusive complexity when animals appear. Bruce Ross aptly illustrates the eclectic form and mechanics of Moore's work in his discussion of "An Octopus":

> In the two hundred odd lines of the poem a digressive strategy is established through metaphors within metaphors, dramatic shifts of narrative description and perspective, frequent interjections of philosophical commentary, and a plethora of diverse quoted materials. [While the first fifteen and the last twenty-two lines actually describe an octopus,] The remaining lines are devoted to descriptions of the area's weather, topographical features, animal and plant life, local lore, and vacationing tourists, as well as a long discussion of Greek metaphysical attitudes and a short comment on Henry James's sensibility. (333)

Moore's animals appear dazzling, overwhelming, enigmatic, somewhat unknowable[3]—or, knowable only with considerable difficulty, by the observer committed to intense examination of these creatures. Moore expects from her audience this rigorous determination—a kind of faith?—as a necessary prerequisite for reading her poetry; and this stance epitomizes, more broadly, an ideal perceptual ethos toward real animals as they come into our cognitive consciousness and as their lives intersect with ours. As we learn to understand and appreciate Moore's poetic animals, we may also learn by example how to understand and appreciate animals in the world around us. We might apply, in our thoughts about animals at large, many of the same skills we invoke when we grapple with a difficult and challenging poem: diligent, deliberate attention to detail and nuance; careful concentration; willingness to transcend pedestrian, conventional processes of cognition and representation and to engage in novel perspectives and sensibilities; and accompanying the ultimate comprehension and enjoyment of the formal object, perhaps an experience of rapture. Moore's poetry invites us as readers to interrogate our relationship with animals in a way that will lead us to recognize the importance of this interaction as an imaginative experience, as well as the difficulty of accurately and meaningfully knowing these animals. Her aesthetic thus has ecological implications beyond the confines of her text.

Away from Animals

The ideology of Pacheco's "Forest Clearing" (see chapter 3) resonates in Moore's poetry as well: a conviction that people should think about animals and how they live when they are out of our sight. We can guess at what animals' lives are like, and we can assume that these lives embody some "sacred ceremony," as Pacheco called it—in their own system of sacredness, not ours: an apotheosis we are not privy to. But people should not venture into the forest to find out. The syntax and perspective of Moore's poetry—idiosyncratic, contorted, confusing—ensure that we will not *fix* these animals that inhabit her poetry: we will not capture them in any way, even figuratively; we will not completely know them, in the Baconian sense of knowledge that implies mastery. We may come close to the animals, sometimes very close, but we will not fully *grasp* them (with both connotations of "grasp": "hold" and "understand").

Albrecht Dürer, an artist Moore admired greatly and who appears in several of her poems and essays, studied and drew animals from secondary sources. His famous *Rhinoceros*, for example, is adapted from a less famous print by an artist who actually saw a captive rhinoceros first-hand; but Dürer's art did not involve the direct capture, constraint, or exploitation of the animal subject.[4] Instead of literal, physical proximity to the animal subject, Dürer substituted a more visionary, aesthetic sense of closeness. Dürer, like Moore, could think about animals and create animals without degrading them. Unlike most artists, Moore and Dürer manifest no inclination to establish authority by conveying experiential proximity to the aesthetic subject. Typical of Moore's indifference to establishing a firsthand observing presence is the opening of "Rigorists":

> "We saw reindeer
> browsing," a friend who'd been in Lapland, said:
> "finding their own food..." (96)

The passage continues in quotation marks for 19 of the poem's 27 lines—in the words of this friend who had travelled to Lapland (at least that is Moore's construct; as Patricia Willis has discovered, her actual "friend," the source for this passage, was a newspaper photograph of two reindeer [14]). Moore has no qualms about abdicating the artist's conventional position of centrality with regard to voice, perspective, consciousness. Her secondhandedness quietly conveys her choice not to go to Lapland herself. She doesn't need to: she can imagine these animals with perfectly adequate detail, empathy, and insight from thousands of miles away. She leaves the animals alone, as they should be left alone: she doesn't intrude on them, or invade their habitat, or frighten them with her presence. I believe strongly that Moore feels, as I do, that

Brooklynites like herself are simply not meant to be in immediate proximity to reindeer, and that we do them (and ourselves and our art) a disservice when we glibly traipse through their habitats, or imprison them within our own, for the purposes of observing them or representing them aesthetically. Animals generally suffer whenever they come into contact with people, and I think this is why Moore, who wants to depict animals with as much integrity and dignity as possible, chooses a stance, like Dürer's, at a discreet remove. For both artists, precise naturalistic accuracy (which might demand observational proximity) was not a chief aspiration: more important was an imaginative connection.

Moore championed the importance of such imaginative—and only imaginative—connection with animals. In a 1927 essay from *The Dial*, Moore writes of "The death of our own two carnivorous dragons—brought last year from the Island of Komodo," which she calls "punitive possibly; in any case a victory, making emphatic to us our irrelevance to such creatures as these, and compulsory our mere right to snakes in stone and story" (*Prose* 188). The Bronx Zoo had acquired a pair of these giant lizards from the Dutch East Indies in 1926 following what the New York *Times* described as "one of the most romantic quests of science... Numerous expeditions had been sent out to bring them back, dead or alive, as true specimens of a dragon, and proof that a universal myth was based on reality" (Rich 5). The American team won the competition, but the animals soon perished in captivity. Moore's "punitive" reference suggests a judgment on humankind. In the death of these Komodo dragons, we are being punished for our overweening sense of entitlement to possess these animals. Explorers, zookeepers, and spectators conspired to remove the lizards from their natural habitats, exploiting and ultimately destroying them to satiate the popular appetite for diverting entertainment or lazy natural edification. Our punishment is, simply, the loss of these animals.

But we can sustain our experience of animals if we encounter them in "stone and story"—in sculpture, in poetry, in any form of human art. Such artistic representations, metaphysical and aesthetic as opposed to physical and literalistic, are our "mere right," Moore pronounces: that is, *merely* (i.e., only) in art may we *have* animals; beyond this we have no further claims on their bodies or souls. And when Moore paradoxically calls the deaths "punitive possibly" but "in any case a victory," the victory lies in the expectation that people may learn from this tragedy a more sophisticated cognitive orientation toward animals. Animals should not be captured and removed from where they belong simply so that people may gawk at them and experience them conveniently.

In all her poetry, Moore meshes the world of animals with the world of people. When I first began to read her poetry, I thought her poetic approach to animals seemed too heavily grounded in human culture and consciousness. Moore travelled little, never visiting firsthand the faraway climes where many of her animal subjects live. She learned about and "observed" animals mostly via books, magazines, and films, and the texture of her poetry is rife with indications of how these sources have mediated her perspective on animals: quotations from *National Geographic* or *Natural History* articles, endnote citations of reference books and films. A note to "Elephants" typifies such citation, announcing Moore's distance from the animal itself and her reliance instead upon various secondary sources: "Data utilized in these stanzas, from a lecture-film entitled *Ceylon, the Wondrous Isle* by Charles Brooke Elliott. And Cicero, deploring the sacrifice of elephants in the Roman Games, said they 'aroused both pity and a feeling that the elephant was somehow allied with man.' George Jennison, *Animals for Show and Pleasure in Ancient Rome*, p. 52" (281). (The quotation from Cicero exemplifies what Moore always sought in her research and in her poetry: examination of the connection, the alliance, between people and animals.)

"The materials of Moore's poems are rarely drawn straight from nature or direct experience," writes Guy Rotella. "Usually, her subjects have been subjects before and trail a digest of sources: newspapers and magazines; anecdotes, biographies, and memoirs; encyclopedias and handbooks; . . . histories and natural histories; . . . drawings and photographs; nature films; museum exhibits and catalogues" (154). Moore's "emphasis on materials previously interpreted, depicted and described accents our separation from the original," Rotella continues (154). Her "cobbled" poetry, the collage of a *bricoleur*, represents a "surrender [of] her own authority to the multiple perspectives of other voices and views"; a pervasive sense of imitation, indebtedness; a tension between originality and belatedness (155). "She employs without distress the subjective cultural 'filters' that protect us from the threat of wholly wild nature and that are essential to representation. She does so in ways that never presume completely to control or possess nature and that expose repeatedly but without anxiety the illusions of art" (183).

Moore's habitual secondhandedness might seem to argue against her inclusion in this study, which celebrates the potential intimacy in cultural representations of animals. But Moore acknowledges the limitations of her perspective and departs from that point to present a panorama of animals and animal experience that compares favorably, in its sincerity and intensity, with the Mesoamerican belief in animal souls. And she does so without apologies and without conceding any diminution in the validity of her sensations. Indeed, her acceptance of limitations in the human epistemological consciousness of animals is, I believe, a necessary stance for the ideal account that we may render of animals in human art. People cannot, finally, see or know animals from anything other than the vantage point of human culture, so one might as well make the best of this. As Rotella puts it, "the realms of art and nature meet, mingle, and separate" in Moore's poems, and the "conflicting claims [of art and nature] cannot be reconciled but, at best, can coexist" (183). Poetry is artifice and construct; uncomplainingly accepting this, Moore exuberantly plunges, armed with her secondary sources, into the sphere of animals. The paradox of her enterprise—finding pure animals while thickly ensconced in the trappings of human culture—is best illustrated in her famous description, from "Poetry," of the poet's onus to present "imaginary gardens with real toads in them" (267). The medium of poetry itself is the imaginary garden, but there may still be real animals lurking herein.

In "When I Buy Pictures," Moore addresses the problem of aesthetic and experiential distance. The first two lines, following on from the title, mitigate the title's implication of the control/ownership of art, a possessive sensibility that is anathema to Moore's aesthetic; after "When I buy pictures," the poem continues: "or what is closer to the truth, / when I look at that of which I may regard myself as the imaginary possessor" (48). Moore (initially) situates the viewer of art as a smug, imperialistic consumer of cultural fodder, characterizing the process of artistic reception in blasé, unmomentous terms. When she confronts art, she writes,

> I fix upon what would give me pleasure in my average moments:
> . . . the old thing, the medieval decorated hat-box,
> in which there are hounds with waists diminishing like the waist of
> the hour-glass,
> and deer and birds and seated people. (48)

The simple, prosaic details do not invite any particular intimacy with the subjects. The specific genres and artifacts suggested by "the old thing, the medieval decorated hatbox" seem arbitrary, whimsical; and the catalog of subjects throughout the poem seems pedestrian, lacking any manifest aesthetic power.

At the end of the poem, however, Moore augments the initial description of the experience of regarding art (and it is not insignificant that this art includes numerous animal representations: hounds, deer, birds) with a more satisfying and more powerful ethos. Indeed, the process of the poem exemplifies the process of experiencing art, as Moore would have it. At the beginning of the poem we see the things, the artifacts, in simple and unremarkable literal detail. Only after a while, after some reflection, do we perceive a deeper resonance. Just before Moore's moral denouement at the end of the poem, she warns how *not* to process art: we should resist "Too stern an intellectual emphasis upon this quality or that," which "detracts from one's enjoyment," and we should not appraise the art competitively: not affirm, that is, that something in the art "is great because something else is small." Ultimately, she concludes,

> It comes to this: of whatever sort it is,
> it must be "lit with piercing glances into the life of things";
> it must acknowledge the spiritual forces which have made it. (48)

This explains and justifies an apparently derivative, distant mode of poetry. Something as flat as a dog or deer on an old hatbox can eventually trigger, in the mind of the astute viewer of art, something much deeper: "piercing glances into the life of things" (quoted, Moore's notes inform, from A. R. Gordon's *The Poets of the Old Testament*). A cultural interaction may start out mechanically, unpromisingly, as one looks at an item in a museum (or in a poem), regarding the object, registering it, moving on to the next display. One may be in a calculated mode of consciousness, being spoon-fed cultural data as if on a conveyor belt. (Think of the end of a long day of museum-going in one of the world's cultural capitals: is there any space left to cram in one more insight from that last room in the Smithsonian?) But Moore's point is that even if one's cultural experience starts out constrained, mediated, secondhand, it *can* become valuable—"lit," "piercing": illuminated, energized, incisive—if we play our parts as a sentient and committed audience, determined to use the art-object at hand as a springboard to an epiphany. And this metaphorically encapsulates the power of Moore's own canon, and her poetic praxis: in her animal poems, Moore starts with a mere dog or deer, or pangolin or jerboa or octopus, and transmogrifies, alchemizes, our experience of these two-dimensional museum pieces or *National Geographic* subjects into something much deeper.

Germane to my juxtaposition of Moore's poetry with Mesoamerican spirituality, the end of "When I Buy Pictures" explicitly invokes, twice, an innate sense of spirituality linked to art: through the specific use of the word in the poem's final line, as Moore demands that the ideal experience of art must acknowledge the spiritual forces inherent in its genesis, and again through the quoted reference to Gordon's book that celebrates the conjunction of poetry and spirituality. Moore manifests a *spiritual* commitment—whatever that might mean: deep, intense, devotional—to her animiles. Her faith in the importance of animals resembles the affirmations embodied in Mesoamerican animal souls.

Mesoamerican spirituality presents a rich and intricate vision of animal potentiality, animal consciousness, yet one which is largely imagined on human terms—in our own voice: *people* have decided that animal souls and their own are linked and that a jaguar co-essence signifies a stronger and richer person, while a rabbit or squirrel betokens a weaker and more ordinary type. We don't know what, if anything, the animals that Mesoamericans consider spiritually entwined with them think of this arrangement; nor can we interrogate Moore's animal subjects to determine their feelings about her poetry. As I concede in chapter 2, *tonalismo* and *nagualismo* have an inherently anthropocentric bias; but given that, one may use animal souls and poetic animals as the foundation for a leap of faith into the animal world. Moore, like Mesoamericans, constructs an epistemology of animal-sensitive consciousness that, despite its speciesist limitations, extends to a degree that very few other human expressions do with regard to animals.

Moore infuses her animal portraits with a precise spiritual tint through her recurrent association of "grace" with animals. In conventional Christian discourse, grace signifies God's freely-given and unmerited love for people—the influence and the spirit of God as it operates in people. Moore appropriates the experience of grace for animals as well: she triangulates the relationship of grace between God and people to include the animals who figure, in her poetry, as fully and equally possessive of this spiritual favor. In "The Frigate Pelican," the bird is "A marvel of grace" (25); "To a Snail" begins, "If 'compression is the first grace of style,' / you have it" (85); in "The Pangolin," the animal has a "fragile grace" (117), Moore writes, the "creep of a thing / made graceful by adversities." She continues: "To explain grace requires / a curious hand" (118). And this curiosity inspires and impels Moore's hand, via her poetry, to explain (to an unaware human audience) the grace with which her animals are brimming: the inherent spirituality that resonates in animals, if we are willing to seek it out via the methods and perspectives she presents in her poetry.

Moore discussed the spirituality that may be associated with animals in the same 1927 essay that laments the death of the Komodo dragons. Paradoxically, she both rejects but also embraces such a spirituality.

The essay begins: "The usefulness, companionableness, and gentleness of snakes is sometimes alluded to in print by scientists and amateurs. Needless to say, we dissent from the serpent as deity; and enlightenment is preferable to superstition when plagues are to be combated—army-worms, locusts, a mouse army, tree or vegetable blights, diseases of cattle, earthquakes, fires, tornadoes, and floods" (*Prose* 187).

Moore contrasts an *enlightened* perspective on animals (exemplified by scientists or amateurs who study the biological nature of snakes and observe such behavioral attributes as "companionableness," "gentleness") with the *superstitious* belief that animals are deities. In real-world situations involving challenging interactions with animals—as when an "army" of mice threatens human habitation—Moore suggests that we need to regard animals accurately and not superstitiously. A spiritual conception of animals (as connoted via Old Testament plagues) seems, Moore implies, primitive; foolish; unrealistic. But the essay continues: "A certain ritual of awe—animistic and animalistic—need not, however, be effaced from our literary consciousness. The serpent as a motive in art, as an idea, as beauty, is surely not beneath us, as we see it in the stone and the gold hamadryads of Egypt; in the turtle zoomorphs, feathered serpent columns, and coiled rattlesnakes of Yucatan; in the silver-white snakes, 'chameleon lizards,' and stone dragons of Northern Siam" (187).

Moore's historical evocation of animals in art is also self-reflexive: she broaches here an aesthetic mode of spirituality for her own poetry, "A certain ritual of awe," that will not go by the names or forms of conventional/institutional spirituality. This ritual of awe, in which the animal image embodies highly charged metaphorical currency, is ensconced not in scripture or dogma but in art and beauty.

Moore's earlier caveat—"we dissent from the serpent as deity"—cautions against a too-easy, absolute, formulaic idolatry of the animal. Her sense of animal spirituality, as I see it, eschews such conventional modes and tropes of spiritual practice. Instead, as an artist, Moore sets out in this essay a more nuanced spiritual sensibility (nuanced, specifically, by *art*—mediated by the workings and the consciousness of aesthetics). The vocabulary she invokes for her spiritual terminology—art, ideas, beauty, rituals of awe—points precisely toward her own poetry as a sacred text for this "animistic and animalistic" spirituality. Moore's essay offers an elaborate catalog of extravagant animal art (gold hamadryads, zoomorphs, stone dragons, and so forth), in which she seems to perceive a transcendent apotheosis; and certainly, by implication, her own poetic animals belong in this tradition as well. Moore's animals, as celebrated in her poetry, have the potential to stand as lasting artifacts, infused with the fascination, the beauty, the compelling nobility, and the awe that have more traditionally been associated with the icons and rituals of institutional religion. In her own formulation here, Moore is explaining and justifying what I have characterized (in *my* formulation) as a strong affinity to the Mesoamerican spiritual veneration of animals.

A Panoply of Animals

Moore uses animals a great deal, in large and small ways, throughout her poetry: to illustrate points about behavior or culture or sensibility; to invoke a comparative analysis of people and other creatures; to convey a vivid, exotic sense of the array of life in the world at large; to construct ethical paradigms; to bear witness to human exploitation and ignorance. Of the 120 poems in her *Complete Poems*—an authorized collection of the poems Moore wished preserved and the text upon which I base my discussion of her poetry—I place 36 firmly in the category of poetic animals;[5] but in fact, only 17 out of these 120 make no mention at all of animals.

"Critics and Connoisseurs," for example, like most of Moore's poems, addresses multiple topics simultaneously: art (both its creation and reception); conscious vs. unconscious behavior; ambition and understanding; instinctual determination and dedication to a cause ("unconscious fastidiousness," as Moore calls it). One might categorize this poem in a number of different ways, but it seems obvious to me that it deserves to be included with her poetic animals simply because the first stanza describes a pup, the second a swan, and the other two an ant. Moore uses the animals—their attributes and behavior, as she has observed them—to carry the burden of what she has to say in this poem.

Many critics consider this poem predominantly allegorical, as if they believe that it is reductionist to consider it as an animal poem; I would respond that it is perverse and obscurantist to regard it otherwise. Perhaps some readers (and Moore would disdain such readers) feel that the subjects of this poem are more important than what one would expect from animal poetry. Some scholars acknowledge the presence of the animals and the keen poetic attention paid to them, but believe that the poem more fundamentally concerns *human* cultural and intellectual attitudes and that the animals serve merely as a metaphoric vehicle. Linda Leavell suggests that Moore, in her early poetry, "adopt[ed] animals as subjects instead of persons" so that "the moral critic could go disguised as animal lover" (155). Such an argument misses the point that Moore posits so fiercely throughout her canon: animals and people are inextricably, for better and worse, connected with each other. Animals pervade our culture, and we cannot write about ourselves without including them, inviting them into our poesis, which is exactly what Moore does so enthusiastically. She doesn't use animals as fronts or disguises or symbols for other, more important things; they *are* the important things.

Mesoamericans recounting stories about animals feel, just as Moore does, that in speaking of the animals they are speaking simultaneously of themselves. Certainly, Moore is always writing about herself when she writes about animals. As a girl, she was an animal in a family of animals: she signed her letters with such nicknames as Weaz, Rat, Fish, Gator, and Rusty Mongoose, while other members of her family were Toad, Turtle, Fawn, Mouse, Bunny, and Beaver (*Letters* 4–5); so from her youth, she inscribed herself in the animal. Biographer Charles Molesworth writes of the animals in her poetry: "Such animals are interpretable as versions of herself, of course" (xiii). And Moore writes not just about herself in her animal portraits and scenes, but also, more broadly, about *our*selves, our aesthetics and our cultural processes. Animals are intimately involved in Moore's enterprise of appraising our lives, not merely adjunct: they are part of the fabric of our existence on this planet.

In an interview, Moore was asked, "As a poet what distinguishes you, do you think, from an ordinary man [sic]?" Her response testifies to the importance of animals in her poetic practice: "Nothing; unless it is an exaggerated tendency to visualize; and on encountering manifestations of life—insects, lower animals, or human beings—to wonder if they are happy, and what will become of them" (*Prose* 674). Her defining characteristic as a poet, she says here, is her attention to the spectrum of living creatures, from bugs to people. A 1936 review she wrote of Wallace Stevens' *Ideas of Order* begins with Moore's explanation that, in her view, "Poetry is an unintelligible unmistakable vernacular like the language of animals" (*Prose* 329), and she praises Stevens' poetry because his "Serenity in sophistication is a triumph, like the behavior of birds" (330). Moore's accolade to a triumphant poet is that he is like an animal, and we might repay this compliment to Moore herself.

In characterizing her poetic career, Moore often invokes animals. In the foreword to *A Marianne Moore Reader* (1961), she asks, "Why an inordinate interest in animals and athletes?" and answers her own question: "They are subjects for art and exemplars of it, are they not? minding their own business. Pangolins, hornbills, pitchers, catchers, do not pry or prey—or prolong the conversation; do not make us selfconscious; look their best when caring least" (552). In the same foreword, Moore addresses the question she was often asked about the frequent use of quotations in her poetry and explains: "When a thing has been said so well that it could not be said better, why paraphrase it? Hence my writing is, if not a cabinet of fossils, a kind of collection of flies in amber" (*Prose* 551). The fragments of quotations, which represent Moore's most pervasive poetic device, her trademark, are here analogized by reference to animals: if not fossils, then flies in amber.

Both these images testify to the importance of animals in Moore's poetic and also to the indirectness that characterizes her poetic animals. A fossil marks the shape of a long-dead animal, and amber preserves and allows one to see a fly which is, again, long dead. But even though these animals are past life, they still captivate our attention and appear, perhaps, all the more fascinating in their present condition: as the *remnant* (the shape, the form, the memory, the approximation) of the living organism that endures in our time.

Moore would like her poetry to captivate her audience with the same sense of allure and naturalistic importance as the amber-fly or the fossil. And if her poetry is, metaphorically, an artifact like a fossil, then we must realize that this poetry emanates from intimate contact with an animal subject just as the prehistoric mud that turned into a fossil-stone did with the animal whose shape it preserves and represents. This metaphorical construct is, of course, only figurative: Moore's contact with the animal is not as physically proximate as that of the fossil medium and its animal model. But we are induced to see in Moore's art a poetic that works via the splendors of the aesthetic and perceptual imagination *as if* Moore had touched and cradled her animals as closely as the mud had done to its future fossil. And amber, like the fossil mold, symbolizes the medium and the process of preservation: the record, and the beauty, that have accreted around the animal. This perfectly represents what Moore herself is doing: think how closely the amber wraps around the fly, and then imagine Moore's poetry doing the same. In both cases, there is a formal, elemental, compositional intimacy.

Tropes

Four main tropes recur in Moore's poetic animals. These categories overlap significantly: usually several—if not all—of these things are going on at once when Moore writes of animals. These tropes bring her reader as close as possible to an intimate understanding, via aesthetic experience, of what Mesoamericans would recognize as animal souls.

Observing Animals

Moore indulges copiously in resplendent observation of animals. Her observations are inflected by what Linda Leavell calls organic functionalism, a major theme of Moore's poetry that "is not limited to animals but her animal poems show it most characteristically": a belief that "beauty inheres in . . . things created honestly and for honest purposes" and that "animals are the most obvious exemplars of this morality" (190).

When Moore observes animals, she describes their physical appearance, their deportment, their movement, their daily routines, their personalities: all the attributes that conjure up an ample sense of their living vitality. "Peter" begins:

> Strong and slippery,
> built for the midnight grass-party
> confronted by four cats, he sleeps his time away—
> the detached first claw on the foreleg corresponding
> to the thumb, retracted to its tip; the small tuft of fronds
> or katydid-legs above each eye numbering all units
> in each group; the shadbones regularly set about the mouth
> to droop or rise in unison like porcupine-quills. (43)

In "Elephants,"

> One, sleeping with the calm of youth,
>
> at full length in the half-dry sun-flecked stream-bed,
> rests his hunting-horn-curled trunk on shallowed stone. (128)

In "An Octopus," we see the title animal:

> Deceptively reserved and flat,
> it lies "in grandeur and in mass"
> beneath a sea of shifting snow-dunes;
> dots of cyclamen-red and maroon on its clearly defined pseudo-podia
> made of glass that will bend. (71)

In "The Wood-Weasel," Moore characterizes the animal as

> the skunk—
> don't laugh—in sylvan black and white chipmunk
> regalia. The inky thing
> adaptively whited with glistening
> goat-fur, is wood-warden. In his
> ermined well-cuttlefish-inked wool, he is
> determination's totem. (127)

"Rigorists" begins with simple behavioral and physical descriptions of reindeer:

> they are adapted
> to scant *reino*

or pasture, yet they can run eleven
miles in fifty minutes; the feet spread when
the snow is soft,
and act as snow-shoes. (96)

"A Jellyfish" (quoted here in full) illustrates many of the things that happen when Moore looks at an animal:

Visible, invisible,
a fluctuating charm
an amber-tinctured amethyst
inhabits it, your arm
approaches and it opens
and it closes; you had meant
to catch it and it quivers;
you abandon your intent. (180)

The terms of description are carefully selected: brief, yet fully adequate. The sensory palette presents, first, visual color. The explicit reference to pure color is amber; remember Moore's reference to the physical embodiment of this color, the amber fossil resin, in the analogy she offers of her poetry as being like "flies in amber." Moore regards amber not just as an abstract hue, but as a graspable material entity. This concreteness, this extension of pure color into three-dimensional form (or even four-dimensional, if one considers the paleologic history of amber and the time span it embodies), resonates in "A Jellyfish." The amber here denotes the color of a different organic element and form, amethyst. The effect is loosely synesthetic (and typical of Moore's idiosyncratic extension of visual imagery): the first image of amber, a resin, is then transformed into a different state, the mineral quartz—which is itself only loosely, figuratively descriptive of the organism under observation. The squishy, amorphous jellyfish is actually strikingly unlike the crystalline amethyst or the solid hard amber. Moore often plays with antitheses, paradoxes, and figurative imprecisions, which ring true in an imaginative/aesthetic sense, if not literally. A poet attempts, as Moore does here, to wean readers from our dependence on literality and physical scientific fact as we know it, to allow our transcendence into a world of unfettered fabrication: poesis. The modifier attached to amber, "tinctured" ("a slight infusion, as of some element or quality; a trace, a smack or smattering; tinge; a dye or pigment" [Webster's]), suggests the presence of a delicate artist's hand—the tincturer—that chooses just the right, subtle degree of pigment to infuse the amethyst with amber, generating the precise color desired to paint the jellyfish (with words).

Around this physical sensory detail, Moore crafts a more complex set of observational dynamics. The jellyfish is also a "charm": a magical human trinket, something people invest with superstitious or supernatural power; something that might charm (cajole, coerce, trick) another person. Perhaps Moore feels it is dangerous to regard animals this way—to expect them to carry the burden of our superstitions; or, perhaps she believes it is inevitable.

The animal appears, in the opening line, "visible, invisible." First one and then the other? Both at the same time? Visible to some (people? animals?) but invisible to others? Moore's resonant ambiguity should be preserved rather than resolved. As she writes, the jellyfish *fluctuates*, both physically, and imagistically: in just the first three lines—nine words!—of the poem, it is an animal, and a gem, and a fossil resin, and an amulet... We can see the jellyfish (sometimes), but we also can't (at other times). We may see the animal washed up on the shore, for example, but not when it swims in the sea. We may see it in one moment of its life, featured frozen as in a magazine picture (as in amber), but not in the other moments. Or we may see it in the space of Moore's poem, but not when we're done with the poem. We might appreciate *some* of its attributes, its colors, its movements, but we might be oblivious to its other qualities. We might see its color and shape, but see these figuratively aestheticized, transmogrified: there isn't *really* a stone in the jellyfish. The amethyst provides simply a starting reference point for color and form emanating from nature, suggesting that the jellyfish, too, exhibits a naturalistic beauty via its color, shape, mass. The statement that the amethyst "inhabits" the animal is imprecise—a deception, strictly speaking, or more indulgently, poetic license. The amethyst actually inhabits Moore's aesthetic vision, and ours; it is invoked here for the sake of metaphor: to allow us to sense and to see, more crisply, the *impression* of the animal.

The dualism suggested in the opening line is fundamental to Moore's observational aesthetic; or, it might be, the dualism is a kind of dialectic suggesting a trinity: with visible/invisible representing thesis/antithesis, and the poem demonstrating the burden of the synthesis: perhaps, say, a poetic visibility, or a transcendent visibility. This dualistic (or dialectical) trope recurs twice more in the poem. The effect is to convey the idea that an animal is not *one* thing, not positivistically fixable, but polymorphously multiple, for an animal may be a thing and its opposite: accessible to us—visible—and also, not. Animals are vast and varied; they may be, simultaneously, mushy soft and rock hard.

Moore first reiterates this dualism as she depicts the jellyfish opening and closing. The description explains, simply, how the jellyfish moves in water, contracting and relaxing muscles to force water out of the bottom of its bell, thus pushing itself forward. And her second reiteration describes the human presence in this poem: "your arm" grabs for the animal and then abandons this grasp. There is a parallelism here, as these passages relate the movements of, first, the nonhuman animal, and then the human animal. Moore presents a representative depiction of the animation, the life force, of a jellyfish and a person, showing both how people fit into the animal modes of our biosphere, and also how we don't fit.

When the human being appears in the second person voice, Moore assumes that people—*you*, the reader—will want to catch, touch, experience this jellyfish, which, needless to say, will not reciprocate in this desire for physicality. The animal would naturally fear us, flee from us. But people want to catch and hold animals, especially when something about their appearance strikes us as exotic. We want them. We want to touch them (though we shouldn't—we might hurt them, and also, we might hurt ourselves: many jellyfish sting). "A Jellyfish" sets up the poles of desire, acquisitiveness, the human proclivity to try to possess whatever catches our fancy... and, set in opposition to this, elusiveness, ephemerality, loss, escape. Visible, invisible: Moore titillates us, but also hides, withdraws, the object of fascination. We approach it, but in this poem we also back off. We had meant to catch it—to constrain it, and perhaps consequently to destroy it (not that this would trouble us unduly: we just *want* it, regardless of its feelings), but finally, we abandon our intent.

Why do we abandon our intent? This question embodies the poem's ethical dilemma, the fulcrum that balances Moore's dualistic construction; and the moment when the jellyfish "quivers" represents the peripateia. Perhaps the quiver scares us away: an animal's profoundly unhuman movement, like the weird trajectory of a bat in flight or the eerie feeling of an ant climbing up one's leg, can highly unsettle a person. Perhaps the quiver demonstrates our inability to catch the jellyfish: it will quiver away; it is more at home in the sea than we are, and presumably it has some powers of self-protection, escape; catching a jellyfish is probably as difficult as getting a solid grasp on... jelly. When, at the end of the poem, "you abandon your intent" to catch the jellyfish, there are two distinct possible readings. First, Moore may be suggesting that we want and try, but simply fail, to catch the animal: out of fear or inability. We wish we could, but we can't, and there are other fish in the sea, so we admit defeat. Or, more felicitously (in Moore's ethos), perhaps the quiver triggers some recognition of the animal's specialness, its difference, its essence, that makes us decide to forsake our attempts to catch it. If so, then this physiological quiver might metaphorically accompany a kind of intellectual, and ecological "quiver"—spiritual believers may experience a comparable quiver of insight, epiphany, ecstasy, at the moment of their perception of the pure, spiritual experience. Maybe, for some readers, this quiver signifies the realization that we just shouldn't grab: it's inconsiderate to touch these things, no matter how colorful, charmed, and alluring they may be. Better just to look: to enjoy the show, the animal, the poem. Pure observation itself, with no consequent physical contact or possession, is sublime.

The explicit observational perspective of "A Jellyfish" does not figure in all Moore's poetic animals. There are many different ways of looking at animals. It may take several readings of "The Fish," a vividly descriptive poem of colors, movement, and energy, to notice that fish are actually hardly described at all, hardly seen at all in this observationally-rich poem: instead, the poem is chiefly about their habitat. The title deceives, if one expects that a poem called "The Fish" will depict fish. But in a sense the poem *does* give us fish, even as it doesn't. Moore takes us where the fish go, and part of the point of seeing an animal is seeing where it lives. "The Fish" depicts the animals' habitat in such profuse detail that we hardly realize we haven't gotten what we thought we were bargaining for. Here is a way of seeing an animal without seeing the animal: these fish, like the subject of "A Jellyfish," are also "Visible, invisible." Moore's lesson for people is that we shouldn't be too confident, when we look at animals, that we will see exactly what we want in the way we want. Animals do not appear in full and clear view, on demand, to suit our convenience (except in zoos, and this is precisely the problem with zoos: they distort the terms of people's experience of animals). How many people have gone out on, say, a buffalo-spotting tour at a bison range or a whale-watching boat trip and come home disappointed because they didn't see what they paid for? This is silly, of course, because they simply saw (whether or not they realized it) something else instead.

Cultural Surveys of How People Regard Animals

In "He 'Digesteth Harde Yron,'" Moore lambastes people's treatment of animals. (The odd title quotes Lyly's observation in *Euphues* that the ostrich "digesteth harde yron to preserve his health" [Moore 277].) She recounts the cultural fetishes with which we have encumbered animals and our consequent heedlessness of their well-being as we wantonly reap whatever "harvest" their physical corpus may offer. How could the ostrich, Moore asks,

> respect men
> hiding actor-like in ostrich skins, with the right hand
> making the neck move as if alive
> and from a bag the left hand strewing grain, that ostriches
>
> might be decoyed and killed! (99)

Moore decries the deception and the violence that accompany people's exploitation of animals. Most perverse about her account of human venality is the fact that the person depicted in this passage is, on some level, so close to an ostrich—*inside* an ostrich skin, and acting as if he were an ostrich—and yet at the same time, obviously, so far away from valuing ostrichness. Moore's challenge is for us to get inside an ostrich *imaginatively* and to learn that we should behave toward them in exactly the opposite way people have traditionally acted. In one horrifying stanza, "He 'Digesteth Harde Yron' " illustrates the sort of treatment the ostrich has suffered amid human culture:

> Six hundred ostrich-brains served
> at one banquet, the ostrich-plume-tipped tent
> and desert spear, jewel-
> gorgeous ugly egg-shell
> goblets, eight pairs of ostriches
> in harness, dramatize a meaning
> always missed by the externalist. (100)

Moore's "externalist" signifies a person who sees only the external facades and appearances, as opposed to the essences, with their potential to afford us ethical and imaginative insights, that inhere *internally* within a creature. The "meaning" that the externalist misses, and that this stanza dramatizes, is the misappreciation, oppression, consumption, and general destruction of the animal to suit our whims. What the animal means when it is ensconced in Western culture is merely (as Moore might put it) "externalistic": it is an object of currency, a source of exotic plunder; but so much about the animal is being missed. In contrast, Mesoamerican culture, which does not treat its animals in these ways, misses much less about animals.

Odd things happen to Moore's animals when they enter the realm of human culture. Several of her animal poems relate uses of animals in relatively harmless ways (at least compared to bashing out the brains of

600 ostriches), which perhaps preserve the possibility of generating some internal appreciation of the animal. Some of these poems convey a cautious or skeptical curiosity about how people interact with animals, but they do not provoke explicit outrage as in "He 'Digesteth Harde Yron.'" In "Tom Fool at Jamaica," the race horse's involvement in a human spectacle, a contest of chance, seems not to trouble Moore; she appreciatively observes the animal as it plays its role in this cultural exercise:

> You've the beat
> of a dancer to a measure or harmonious rush
> of a porpoise at the prow where the racers all win easily—
> like centaurs' legs in tune, as when kettledrums compete;
> nose rigid and suede nostrils spread. (162–3)

"No Swan So Fine" and "An Egyptian Pulled Glass Bottle in the Shape of a Fish" depict consummately artificial—artificed—animals. In these poems, Moore depicts some of the things craftspeople do with animals and invites her readers to consider the implications of these cultural constructions: what these animals mean, how we are using them, how much (if any) of the original, live animals resonates in these artifacts. Whenever Moore introduces a poetic animal in any context whatsoever, a real, internal, animal is always straining to emerge; sometimes it does and sometimes not. Poems like these direct our attention to the vast number of "animals"—whether live or representational—that inhabit our culture; poems with crafted animals provoke us to consider how these culturally attenuated subjects help or hinder our overall understanding of and relationship with real animals.

"No Swan So Fine" describes the animal as follows:

> No swan,
> with swart blind look askance
> and gondoliering legs, so fine
> as the chintz china one with fawn-
> brown eyes and toothed gold
> collar on to show whose bird it was. (19)

It is not only the collar that shows whose bird this was: the entire cultural fabrication demonstrates that this is *our* bird (as opposed to nature's bird, i.e., the bird's own bird). The issue of possessing animals, which arises throughout Moore's poetic animals, is foreign to the

Mesoamerican sensibility in which one can no more possess an animal than one can determine one's own fate. The second stanza accentuates the swan's aestheticized artificiality, its profound mediation by the styles and forms of human culture and history:

> Lodged in the Louis Fifteenth
>   candelabrum-tree of cockscomb-
> tinted buttons, dahlias,
> sea-urchins, and everlastings,
>   it perches on the branching foam
> of polished sculptured
> flowers—at ease and tall. The king is dead. (19)

The poem, writes Charles Molesworth, "was sparked by reading about the estate of Lord Balfour being auctioned off, with two swans part of the sale. . . . The poem is an extremely subtle interweaving of the realms of nature and culture, as the 'real' swans are aestheticized by having 'gondoliering legs' while the china swan is energized by perching on 'branching foam.' The ending sees the china swan as alive and its original owner as not" (259). This poem's power inheres precisely in what Molesworth calls its "subtle interweaving," and Moore's reader faces the task of unweaving: figuring out what all this signifies and how we might finally regard the animal at the core. The tableau described here does not seem terribly dangerous, in Moore's view, but nonetheless, it is skewed by human prejudices and by the self-flattering blinders that accompany our cultural productions. Moore's rendering is sarcastic. The ideal reader will respond to the trinkets (however regal) that Moore presents here by countering that, in fact, there *are* other swans so fine as, and even *finer* than, this chintz china one; real ones are better. French kings, English lords, and decorative styles come and go, but swans transcend cultural fashions.

And yet, a degree of ennobling dignity endures in this chintz swan—it is "at ease and tall," and as Molesworth notes, it has a life force that outlasts that of its human cultural frame, testifying to the power of even an artificial representation of an animal. One cannot efface the resonant forces that emanate from an animal, both the life and the aesthetic forces, however hard human cultural artificers might, in their perversity, try to co-opt the allure of a real swan with an ornately crafted simulacrum. There is, perhaps, nothing too insidious about admiring this gold and china concoction, but we should remember, in paying tribute to its beauty, where its inspiration originated; and we should not allow culture to attenuate too drastically our proximity to, or our memory of, the original animal.

The title "An Egyptian Pulled Glass Bottle in the Shape of a Fish"—intentionally awkward, and not much shorter than the entire poem that follows—directs our attention to the polyvalent issues surrounding a cultural artifact generated from an animal and the nature of the relationship between the representation and the original. The title, indeed, says it all: it identifies the cultural provenance ("Egyptian"), the process ("Pulled"), the medium ("Glass"), the artistic genre ("Bottle"), the animal being represented ("Fish"), and the consciousness of aesthetic artificing, representational *approximation* but not mimesis ("in the Shape of"). The poem begins: "Here we have thirst / and patience, from the first, / and art" (83). The thirst denotes what one might use the bottle for (the quenching thereof), and thus what would have induced an ancient artisan to make a bottle in the first place: thirst is, on one level, the motivation that lead to the creation of this object. But, of course, a bottle doesn't *have* to be in the shape of a fish: this detail points toward a higher motive inherent in this cultural artifact. The patience and art that follow the thirst indicate Moore's sense that the Egyptian craftsperson had more in mind than just the alleviation of thirst. Functionality may initiate, but does not wholly encapsulate, the *quidditas* of this object. This bottle in the shape of a fish is

> not brittle but
> intense—the spectrum, that
> spectacular and nimble animal the fish,
> whose scales turn aside the sun's sword by their polish. (83)

Here, as in "No Swan So Fine" when the swan is "at ease and tall," we see the animal *through* (behind, or underneath) the art: we see a creature that is "spectacular and nimble." In Moore's greatest expression of homage to the potential of an aesthetic representation, the last lines present an ambiguity about the nature of the beauty it describes: the glistening polished scales may be those of a real fish, or they may belong to the bottle-fish. Moore suggests here that, at times, we may receive a burst of splendor and beauty equally from art and nature; or, *either* (indeterminately) from art or nature. And if this intense mini-ecstasy that Moore offers at the end of the poem does, indeed, emanate from the Egyptian bottle rather than from the fish itself, then Moore would want us to remember (as we are not prone to do amid the sarcasm of the swan poem) the necessary proximity, in the source of this beauty, between the animal and the art.

"Tippoo's Tiger" describes a bizarre cultural representation of a tiger. One might be surprised at Moore's titular suggestion that a tiger can belong to a person, but the artifact this poem features, a kitschy mechanical contrivance representing a large tiger standing ferociously upon its hapless human victim, is not subordinate to humankind. Tippoo, an eighteenth-century Indian sultan, inscribed himself in the tiger: "The tiger was his prototype. / The forefeet of his throne were tiger's feet. / . . . The jackets of his infantry and palace guard / bore little woven stripes incurved like buttonholes" (241). When Tippoo died, the British captured, and subsequently displayed in the Victoria and Albert Museum (where it resides today, in various states of operability),

> a vast toy, a curious automaton—
> a man killed by a tiger; with organ pipes inside
> from which blood-curdling cries merged with inhuman groans.
> The tiger moved its tail as the man moved his arm. (241)

Moore may envision the moral suggested by this curiosity as man's comeuppance: the tiger has the final victory, as it is depicted perpetually mauling the victim, perhaps in repayment for the Sultan's appropriation of its power for his own iconography of dominion. Perhaps she sees in this vast toy the revenge of the tiger. Or, perhaps the point is how people, in our perverse representational relationships with animals, show ourselves to be—like the decoy in ostrich skins from "He 'Digesteth Harde Yron' "—so close (as the tiger and man are in a kind of eternal embrace) and yet so far from appreciating and connecting with real animals.

The tiger and man here, the ostrich and ostrich-killers in the other poem, seem such near, yet sad and hopelessly ironized approximations of the Mesoamerican model of closeness to animals and recognition of the common ground that links our lives and theirs. And compare the jointly choreographed movement of man and tiger in the line "The tiger moved its tail as the man moved his arm" with another iteration of human–animal mirrored movement, the one discussed earlier in "A Jellyfish." In that poem, we saw the jellyfish's dual motions (as it opens and closes) and the person's (arm approaching, then abandoning its intent) as if on a kind of split screen; Moore, in a comparatist mode, showed the potential harmony and disharmony between the movements, and the lives, of a person and a jellyfish. In "Tippoo's Tiger," though, with a tableau that evokes a *danse macabre*, Moore is more cynical about the possibility of human–animal harmony, or equilibrium, or (in the terminology of animal souls) co-essence.

When Mesoamericans envision animal–human proximity, a spiritual harmony flourishes; when people attempt it, as Moore depicts in these poems, we just look ridiculous: isolated from the animals that we strive so pathetically to embrace. The sensory dissonance, the cacophony Moore presents in this poem—"blood-curdling cries merged with inhuman groans"—represents a sound, a dysfunctional music that is as far as one could imagine from the poetry of spiritual concord—prayer, sympathy, unity. If we wish to approach the kind of communality with animals that the Mesoamericans have achieved, we will have to stop imagining animals in the ways described by "Tippoo's Tiger." This poem offers the diverting token of an unusual historical plaything, but it also taunts us with the absence of a more deeply meaningful human–animal connection that might exist.

"The Jerboa" chides people for undervaluing the worth of animals and demonstrates a more fitting way of envisioning the way they exist and coexist in our world. The poem begins with a seemingly arbitrary and irrelevant (to jerboas) account, a kind of imagist survey of ancient Roman art and culture that blends into European Catholicism. It is a history of human consciousness in miniature:

> A Roman had an
> artist, a freedman,
> contrive a cone—pine-cone
> or fir-cone—with holes for a fountain. Placed on
> the Prison of St. Angelo, this cone
> of the Pompeys which is known
>
> now as the Popes', passed
> for art. A huge cast
> bronze, dwarfing the peacock
> statue in the garden of the Vatican,
> it looks like a work of art made to give
> to a Pompey, or native
>
> of Thebes. (10)

At the outset, Moore yokes together three important concepts: art, nature, and the power dynamics (which we would now characterize as Foucauldian) underlying the process of art. The ancient artist takes an object from nature as his subject and *contrives* it. The word is accusatory: it suggests, however delicately, a falsification or prettification: a lack of fidelity to the original, a lack of appreciation for a cone in nature. The real cone perpetuates the plant species; the false cone contrives to domesticate nature for our vanities. A fountain, where this contrived cone sits, fetishizes water in a garden, distancing it from its real function, the perpetuation of life. This water "recirculates" endlessly and mechanically inside a stone apparatus without nourishing the ecosystem as it is supposed to do in nature. Water and cones are both natural elements, but in the poem's contrived context they appear inauthentic, bastardized. Moore accentuates a sense of disrespect for natural artifacts by suggesting that the artist does not even know what sort of a cone he is contriving, pine or fir; the accurate and authentic nature of the cone seems irrelevant to his art.

The artist is subordinate to "A Roman," the character who opens this poem and who has ordered the contriving by commissioning the work. This Roman is implicated in the networks of social power, along with the Thebans and Pompeys, aristocrats whose social power was later absorbed by the Popes; and, as if in anticipation of Foucault, Moore contextualizes the art as ornamentation on a prison, testifying to the power of the socially empowered to impose their aesthetic upon civic architecture and, at the same time, to imprison within such architecture those who have transgressed their laws.

What does any of this have to do with nature, animals, jerboas? Moore begins this animal poem by setting up, in condensed and stylized images, the praxis of the human society that *uses* nature, plants, and animals: that contrives to celebrate them in our culture, but does so in a way that dissociates them from their authentic existence. A cone (which is naturally small) becomes contrived into a different medium (bronze) and a very different size and perspective so that it dwarfs a peacock statue, despite the fact that a peacock is actually much larger than a cone. Things are out of kilter. Plants and animals are turned into stone, bronze, statues, fountains, and in this process they are appropriated and defamed. "The Jerboa" begins with Moore's critique of people's orientation toward nature. Imbalance characterizes our cultural representations of nature: a failure to achieve a balanced, integrated relationship among all nature's creatures. The poem's first part—subtitled "*Too Much*"—indicts our proclivity toward decadent excess. The second part, where the title character will appear resplendently at center stage, away from the trappings of human aesthetic contrivance, is titled "*Abundance.*" The jerboa has abundance: abundant beauty, elegance, fascination. People have too much: more than we deserve; overweening; and some of what we have has been appropriated from peacocks and waterways and cones. Nature has abundance for all, but people, with our greedy, imperialist co-optation of the fruits of nature, throw the whole ecosystem out of whack.

"The Jerboa" continues from the opening cone-and-peacock tableau to address more directly the ways our cultural processes affect animals.

Others could
build, and understood
making colossi and
how to use slaves, and kept crocodiles and put
baboons on the necks of giraffes to pick
fruit, and used serpent magic.

They had their men tie
hippopotami
and bring out dappled dog-
cats to course antelopes, dikdik, and ibex;
or used small eagles. They looked on as theirs,
impalas and onigers,

the wild ostrich herd
with hard feet and bird
necks rearing back in the
dust like a serpent preparing to strike, cranes,
mongooses, storks, anoas, Nile geese;
and there were gardens for these—

combining planes, dates,
limes, and pomegranates,
in avenues—with square
pools of pink flowers, tame fish, and small frogs. (10–11)

In these concentrated images, Moore presents a profoundly intricate ecological logic and ethos. If it seems too haphazardly far-reaching and not obviously unified, remember Barry Commoner's rallying cry, which I believe Moore would endorse enthusiastically: "Everything is connected to everything else." While it may not be *explicitly* clear how all the poem's elements are related, one might look to the earth itself to demonstrate the logic that underlies Moore's schema. After people have ignorantly contrived cones without even knowing their species, "others" extend this ethic and make things: colossi (*big* things, as in "too much": representations of people many times our own already-abundant size). And we use slaves: we abrogate freedom, the fundamental standard of human integrity, as we embark upon this colossally self-aggrandizing sensibility. And we keep animals. "Keep" is ambiguous: it can mean benevolently caring for; protecting (albeit with an inescapable dominionist subtext). Or, more bluntly, it can mean simply to possess, to have. The builders of colossi and users of slaves certainly *possessed* rather than protected their crocodiles. They kept crocodiles for their amusement, perhaps: as a rarity, to testify to their own wealth and the exotic, spectacular vastness of their estates. Semiotically, they strove to co-opt and symbolically to embody the fierce power of the crocodile. Moore's subtle connections show how our power fetishes, as embodied in prisons and slavery, also infuse and infect our relationship with animals.

This is the link between the world of human foibles and the world of animals, and this is where people begin to get dangerous. Moore is didactic: culturally and historically, we have used animals badly. The poem launches into illustrations of various human uses/appropriations of animals: some more insidious than others; some (like serpent magic) evoking a genuine human amazement with the power of animals and the spiritual aura they evoke, but even this is ultimately selfish. The human beings in "The Jerboa," representatives of Western culture from Roman through Christian imperialist hegemony, oppress animals (tying hippopotami) and incite one animal to attack another (dogcats coursing antelopes). People are excessively possessive: "They looked on as theirs . . ." And once people have possessed, tied, coursed, sculpted, and done whatever else we choose to do with these animals, we put them in a pretty garden—reiterating the trope of contrived, domesticated nature (the fountain) that opened the poem. In this garden, natural elements are divorced from nature: caged, isolated, for people's aesthetic amusement. (Michael Pollan proposes in *Second Nature* that "Nature abhors a garden," a sentiment Moore would probably affirm.) The artifacts in the garden are ranged and regulated by human rather than natural geometries of landscaping: there are "avenues" of trees and "square pools." At the end of Moore's account of how people use and shape nature, we are left with a trivially diminished sense of animals—"tame fish, and small frogs"—in contrast to we "colossi" who have created and who survey all of this from a position of power.

This is the wrong way to situate ourselves with respect to animals: us in several-times life size, them in cute miniature. It is diametrically opposed to the Mesoamerican sense of co-essence. "*Too Much*" continues to enumerate exploitative desecrations of the world of plants and animals: nests of eggs are given to boys as playthings; "Lords and ladies put goose-grease / paint in round bone boxes"; and on and on, creating

> a fantasy
> and a verisimilitude that were
> right to those with, everywhere,
>
> power over the poor.
> The bees' food is your
> food. (12)

Moore characterizes this entire scenario as a shameless display of human power played off against the powerlessness of the subaltern nonhuman world. We can take honey and eggs and goosefat, so they are ours.

We use animals trivially: for baubles, fashion, toys; we co-opt the image of animals. The poem critiques the dominionist mindset (as codified in the book of Genesis) that leads us to believe, as David Hancocks writes, that "everything exists for humans' sake." Hancocks offers several historical illustrations of this conviction: "An English preacher in 1696 observed that God had most wisely located very dangerous animals in uninhabited regions 'where they may do less harm.' . . . A sixteenth-century bishop, James Pilkington, believed savage beasts were put on earth as useful sparring partners for warriors. . . . A Virginia gentleman, William Byrd, in 1728 guessed that horse flies had been created 'so that men should exercise their wits and industry to guard themselves against them,' and an English reverend decided that the louse's role was to encourage humans to keep clean. . . . singing birds were devised 'to entertain and delight mankind' " (19).

Moore condemns the ways in which people imagine animals and import animal images into our world: her poetry asks us to contemplate the aesthetic as well as the physical tolls of this behavior. Recall "A Jellyfish," where Moore instructs people about how not to approach animals. We are not meant to catch them, to touch them, to possess them. "A Jellyfish" ends with the abandonment of a human, possessive intent: we need to learn to look at animals and think of the ideal endpoint of this experience as letting go rather than capturing and harvesting. We should learn other, metaphysical, modes of experiencing animals (such as the imaginative experience of a poem).

After castigating human cultural exploitation of animals, "The Jerboa" has a peripateia that embodies an ethical response to the condition it has portrayed. Following the historical orgy of animal abuse, Moore begins to approach the jerboa, a humble animal perhaps overlooked by the exploitative hordes because of its apparent uselessness to the enterprises of human cultural contrivance. On her way to the jerboa, Moore introduces a near relative:

> Pharoah's rat, the rust-
> backed mongoose. No bust
> of it was made, but there
> was pleasure for the rat. Its restlessness was
> its excellence; it was praised for its wit. (12–13)

In the mongoose Moore shows an animal that has begun to escape the tyranny of human transformation and aesthetic control. The animal was (the previous stanza indicates) tamed, which is a diminishment, and it carries the same sort of human-possessive moniker ("Pharoah's rat") as

Tippoo's tiger. But the mongoose was not the subject of a bust, which suggests at least a partial escape from the ken of the master species. The animal's "pleasure" and "excellence" indicate a sublime consciousness antithetical to that of the animals degraded by human culture. The plain-spoken simplicity of its condition indicates a tenor that arises out of the mist of Moore's often-convoluted prosody and diction to signify an epiphany, an entelechy.

The mongoose has emotions (pleasure), drives (restlessness), talents (excellence, wit). All animals, of course, have such virtues, but we mostly don't see these in the catalog of animals that have passed by our eyes up to this point in "The Jerboa," as they have been obscured or stripped away by human excessiveness. We begin to see these virtues only when we come upon one animal, the rust-backed mongoose, which has somewhat eluded the vicissitudes of human culture. The mongoose's cousin, the jerboa, is even more obscure and even freer to exult in its own nature away from human contrivance. Moore employs a precise periphrasis in her approach to the title animal by way of a dozen others. She does the same thing in another poem, "The Monkeys," which is not at all about monkeys, but rather, features a large cat protesting its exploitation in the zoo; the monkeys are merely the first animal the reader confronts in the poem, and we wander past numerous other animals before the poem finally settles on its protagonist, the cat. In "Critics and Connoisseurs," Moore meanders for half the poem before she arrives at her star character, the fastidious ant. We have to approach these animals cautiously, indirectly: if we just bluster right up upon them, we will scare them away or otherwise fail to appreciate the essence of their existence. Birdwatchers will appreciate the importance of a cautious approach.

The poem offers its payoff, its rewarding insight, as we poetically ramble away from people's animals—animals that we possess and treat as suits our imperial pleasure, like Yeats with his squirrel at Kyle-na-no—and find an animal that hasn't been spoiled. The mongoose, Moore writes,

> was praised for its wit;
> and the jerboa, like it,
>
> a small desert rat,
> and not famous, that
> lives without water, has
> happiness. (13)

The transition is sly, casual: "the jerboa, like it . . ." The jerboa is small (but not in the same way that the small frogs in the square pools are small), and, most important for its self-preservation and integrity, it is "not famous." People don't know about it, or else they would try to find a way to exploit it. Of course, people who didn't know about the jerboa before do now—people who are introduced to the animal, as I have been, by reading Moore's poem. But I think Moore believes, and I think she is right in this belief, that those who read and like this poem will not reveal to the world at large the secret of this unfamous and happy animal. If a mainstream human gaze did light on the jerboa, the gazer might be jealous of its happiness and want to take from it whatever makes it happy, to make himself happy, leaving the animal sad. This, at least, is the model, the trajectory of everything else we have done with animals, as described in this poem: the bees' food is your food.

But we who have made it to this point in the poem, and in Moore's ethical indoctrination, will not look at the jerboa's happiness with an eye to harvesting it; rather, we will attempt to see it and understand it without destroying it. Perhaps we indeed could be happy, or become happier, by looking at the jerboa, as we are about to do, but we must not abrogate its happiness, for the experience here is not meant to be (as so many other human–animal interchanges are) a zero-sum game, winner take all. We must not take too much, but rather, appreciate the abundance the jerboa possesses and try to find, in ourselves, our own abundance. This is how to become co-essences of the animals around us, as Moore constructs it. She brings us through the human history of various kinds of appropriations and exploitations of animals and finally leaves us, thus chastened, prepared to meet the animal (as the Mesoamericans would have it) eye to eye and on equal footing. And what a show she presents once we attain this perspective: everything you ever wanted to know about a jerboa but were afraid to ask.

We begin at the beginning, with a thumbnail sketch of the jerboa's habits and habitat.

> Abroad seeking food, or at home
> in its burrow, the Sahara field-mouse
> has a shining silver house
>
> of sand.

So much for literal observation: next, Moore ascends to rapture, in an ecstatic spiritual exuberance:

> O rest and
> joy, the boundless sand,
> the stupendous sand-spout,
> no water, no palm-trees, no ivory bed,
> tiny cactus. (13)

Moore conveys the joy, the boundlessness, the stupendous aura that emanates from this animal just because it is being what it is, where it is, where it belongs, untrammeled by contrivers of any stripe.

The poem celebrates, as Moore and her reader watch from the sidelines in humble fascination, the processes of the jerboa in its desert, with a devout attention (the attention of a consummate artist, and of a worshipper) to its movements and energies, its rhythms, its physical and biological detail, its life force. She records a few traits in detail, offered in a fashion that is picaresque rather than encyclopedic; she means us to infer from these images what this animal means—how it lives, what it feels—as it scampers quickly past our line of vision.

> The translucent mistake
> of the desert, does not make
>
> hardship for one who
> can rest and then do
> the opposite—launching
> as if on wings, from its match-thin hind legs, in
> daytime or at night; with the tail as a weight,
> undulated out by speed, straight.
>
> Looked at by daylight,
> the underside's white,
> though the fur on the back
> is buff-brown like the breast of the fawn-breasted
> bower-bird. It hops like the fawn-breast, but has
> chipmunk contours—perceived as
>
> it turns its bird head—
> the nap directed
> neatly back and blending
> with the ear which reiterates the slimness
> of the body. The fine hairs on the tail,
> repeating the other pale
>
> markings, lengthen until
> at the tip they fill
> out in a tuft—black and
> white; strange detail of the simplified creature,
> fish-shaped and silvered to steel by the force
> of the large desert moon. (13–14)

The descriptions are largely literal and naturalistic, though with the comparatively metaphorical, figurative touch of the artist thrown in occasionally for effect ("launching as if on wings"; "fish-shaped and silvered to steel"): indeed, for a very important effect. Such passages undercut or transgress a natural literalism—the jerboa has no wings; its desert existence bears no relation to that of the fish; it has no steel in its constitution (as the jellyfish has no stones)—to convince the reader of the desirability of going beyond literality to appreciate the animal's essence. The jerboa, after all, is obviously not at all present, except imaginatively, as we read this poem, so Moore embraces the imaginative tropes as a necessary vehicle for our perception of the animal. She does this only after ensuring that the poem, the representation, has a solid foundation of biological and ecological authenticity; the figurative tropes come after this, on top of it. Moore attributes to the animal properties and characteristics that it does not literally have—avian, amphibian, mineral—just as Mesoamericans construe their animal-soul animals as more than they literally are. And this is not to say, by the way, that animals don't possess the powers that Mesoamericans believe them to have, nor to say that jerboas aren't in some sense avian and amphibian. These apparent contradictions (in literalist terms) are reconciled in a spiritual/metaphysical faith.

This is how poetry brings us to the same place as Mesoamerican animal souls: both require us to extend beyond the obvious, the sensible, the biological, into a realm of trust in things unproven. Both poetic animals and animal souls enable our embrace of animal powers that elude most people who encounter animals, and both expand the ways we have been acculturated to regard animals. Both systems are richly imaginative, which does not mean they are not real, but only that their reality deflects positivistic scrutiny.

Moore concludes her poem with a concise, sharp warning to any predators—human or otherwise, she does not specify—to respect this animal's integrity, its existence:

Course
the jerboa, or
plunder its food store,
and you will be cursed. (14)

The curse, a conventional ramification of transgression against a spiritual power, quietly advances the religious perspective of Moore's worship before the jerboa. She offers one last physical observation:

It
honors the sand by assuming its color;
closed upper paws seeming one with the fur
in its flight from a danger. (14)

And finally, Moore pays homage to the musical geometry of the jerboa's movement. The terms she uses are those of art, pattern, instrument: she concludes in the vocabulary of her spiritual experience of the animal, the art and music of her poetry:

> By fifths and sevenths,
> in leaps of two lengths,
> like the uneven notes
> of the Bedouin flute, it stops its gleaning
> on little wheel castors, and makes fern-seed
> foot-prints with kangaroo speed.
>
> Its leaps should be set
> to the flageolet;
> pillar body erect
> on a three-cornered smooth-working Chippendale
> claw—propped on hind legs, and tail as third toe,
> between leaps to its burrow. (14–15)

What Moore finally shows us about the jerboa is profound: having dispensed with the world of honey owners and ibex coursers, she brings us to the realm of this animal. She advocates the importance of seeing how an animal lives in its own world, rather than how it is contrived in ours. Her observations of the jerboa become transcendentally evocative as a result of her idiosyncratic force of worship, which initiates of her faith (i.e., readers of her poetry) experience as intensely as do worshippers in any institutional religion responding to the incantation of the sacred formulations of their faith. "The Jerboa" resonates with Moore's belief in the nobility of the animal—how expansively (in Moore's guiding hands) it claims our attention, our consciousness, our respect.

Names and Misnomers

In her poetry, Moore grapples with the problem of language as it relates to animals: the words we must use are human words—how can they be used to approach and to depict the animal? To make her readers conscious of this problem, she reminds us often that our very names for animals are plagued with inaccuracies. These errors highlight our proclivity to misrecognize animals—to see them as they serve our purposes or as they function within our constructs, rather than as they actually exist. In her quest to inculcate, through her poetry, a keener recognition of animals, Moore strips away faulty perceptions and appraisals as she points out the distortions in our vocabulary and in our aesthetic.

In "The Buffalo," Moore writes: "The modern / ox does not look like the Augsburg ox's / portrait" (27), and she also criticizes a "freakishly / Over-Drove ox drawn by / Rowlandson" (28). Although not exactly failures of language, these are similar enough: failures of representationality. Our cultural depictions of animals, Moore indicates, are prone to inaccuracy, and her blunt rejection here of Augsburg's and Rowlandson's representations implies that her own poetry will serve as a corrective. She will tell us what others have gotten wrong about animals, and presumably she will get it right.

In "The Pangolin," Moore refers to the title animal as "a true anteater" (117), and Bernetta Quinn explains: "Actually, the pangolin is the world's only creature living on ants, the others (misnamed anteaters) preferring the less ferocious termites" (291). Moore subtly directs our attention to the issue of misnamed animals, "anteaters" who do not eat ants, via her observation of the one—not commonly known as an anteater—that does.

The title of "The Arctic Ox (Or Goat)," suggests a variant name, or correction, for the featured animal. In the poem, Moore reveals an erroneous appellation given to that animal and mocks those who have so named it: "The musk ox / has no musk and it is not an ox— / illiterate epithet" (193). She goes on to illustrate its true properties:

> Bury your nose in one when wet.
>
> It smells of water, nothing else,
> and browses goatlike on
>   hind legs. Its great distinction
> is not egocentric scent
> but that it is intelligent. (193)

We should not rely on unfounded names that others have given to animals, Moore counsels; these may be obfuscatory. Instead, she shows us a better way to know an animal: get up close to it, bury your nose in its fleece, watch its behavior—note how it browses; try to appreciate its personality, its virtues, its intelligence. The seminal point here, as in all Moore's poetic animals, is her suggestion that we get as close as possible to animals so that we may see them more clearly. And if the cognitive process Moore describes here seems like an assault or encroachment upon these animals, remember that the poem only figuratively asks us to nuzzle up to a so-called musk ox. Moore herself has not done this— the poem's headnote announces that what follows is "*Derived from 'Golden Fleece of the Arctic,' by John J. Teal, Jr., who rears musk oxen on his farm in Vermont, as set forth by him in the March 1958 issue of the Atlantic Monthly*" (193). It would be undesirably invasive to suggest that everyone do what Moore's poem suggests: it is enough that one person, John J. Teal, Jr., who knows whereof he speaks, has done so. Moore conveys the experience to the rest of us in the poem so that we undertake a sensory intimacy with these animals as we bury our noses in them *imaginatively*, without actually presuming to do so firsthand. The appeal to/detachment from an animal that this passage embodies—as we are invited to smell one but also reminded that Moore herself has not done so—reiterates the dynamics in "A Jellyfish," where the human arm approaches to grab the animal, but then abandons its intent.

The title animal in the poem "Blue Bug" is a pony bearing the unusual name of a very different kind of animal. "I don't know how you got your name," Moore writes,

> and don't like to inquire.
> Nothing more punitive than the pest
> who says, "I'm trespassing," and
> does it just the same.
> I've guessed, I think. (218)

Perhaps she doesn't like to inquire because she is embarrassed to discover what sort of peculiar reasoning people are capable of when we name animals. (I often wince when I learn the names that friends have chosen for their cats.) Or more charitably, perhaps Moore cherishes the pony's alliterative name, with its idiosyncratic evocative resonance, as pure language, so she doesn't want to discover what might be a prosaic derivation. Probing the mystery of the pony's name is like trespassing—intruding on some private aspect of the animal's being. Moore finally hazards a guess at what the name might mean, but she keeps it to herself, refusing to announce her surmise publicly or explore further to determine whether she is right or wrong. Blue Bug, with the inexplicable name that Moore tells us she might (or might not) have figured out, resonates with an air of unknowability and thus self-control over its image, its presence, its integrity. Moore shows here the power of naming, the importance of a name in affecting how people come to regard and appraise an animal. And Moore's own process here—guessing the name without knowing it for certain and without "trespassing"—signifies the sensitive respect for the animal's integrity that infuses her poetry. The animal has greater allure when we don't definitively know or understand its name than when we do. Nominalistic positivism—a name that fixes, frames, defines the animal—would reiterate the dominionist tradition of God's arrogating to Adam the right to name the animals in Genesis. Moore, instead, leaves us to savor the unknown.

At the beginning of "His Shield," Moore describes several armored animals:

> The pin-swin or spine-swine
> (the edgehog miscalled hedgehog) with all his edges out,
> echidna and echinoderm in distressed-
> pin-cushion thorn-fur coats, the spiny pig or porcupine,
> the rhino with horned snout—
> everything is battle-dressed. (144)

An echidna is an Australian toothless burrowing mammal resembling the hedgehog, sometimes called a porcupine anteater (though it is different from either of those two animals); an echinoderm is a class of animals that includes sea-urchins and sea-cucumbers—the name refers to the sharp-pointed spines that stud the skin. Moore seems to find these scientific names acceptable references, but she criticizes a misnomer as she draws our attention to "the edgehog miscalled hedgehog." The *OED* explains that the hedgehog is "named from its frequenting hedgerows and from its pig-like snout." "Edgehog" may be Moore's neologism: I can find no reference to it elsewhere; apparently she calls the animal an edgehog because, as the line continues, all his edges are out. Neither are pin-swin or spine-swine listed in any source I consulted; they, too, may be inventions, though they have the ring of folk or fable appellations. Both of those names have an enchanting mellifluity, and this is certainly something that, Moore would believe, enhances our understanding of animals: they should be infused with rhyme, poetry, felicitous sound, as Moore's poetry bestows this aesthetic on them.

In trying to determine precisely Moore's criteria for adjudicating the (h)edgehog's correct and incorrect names, one uncovers a good deal of terminological confusion and imprecision. The *Dictionary of American Regional English* lists, as a reference for the common usage of "hedgehog," porcupine and woodchuck (two similar, but different animals—the porcupine, like the hedgehog, is covered with spines, and the woodchuck, like the hedgehog, burrows in the ground). In *Speaking of Animals*, Robert Palmatier notes that both "hedgehog" and "porcupine" are misnomers: they "are both named for swine, but they are actually large rodents... and look nothing like hogs or pigs. Like the hog, however, they are both 'rooters'" (188). Perhaps Moore finds "edgehog" preferable to "hedgehog" because it is poetically descriptive: given that the animal begins, in our consciousness, as a nominalistic muddle, "edgehog" represents an improvement because, as it rejects/revises the received wisdom, it directs our attention to the animal's interesting, striking edges. A misnomer, "hedgehog," is redeemed by three possible alternates that are all more poetic. Moore does not, finally, correctly or definitively rename the animal—as with Blue Bug, a degree of indeterminacy about the name remains—but the mistake is mitigated by poetry. This is a potent indicator of the power of poesis, as Moore sees it, in reorienting our visions of animals. As we dispense with one wrong name, we get three new poetic names.

Clearly, there is some cultural confusion between porcupines, anteaters, hedgehogs *et al.* Moore's intent is not to castigate our terminological mistakes. She points out nominative and representational inaccuracies, but at the same time she contributes some new coinages and images that may well include inaccuracies of her own. Her point is that if we are going to make things up (which are bound to be laden with the inaccuracies, prejudices, and limitations of understanding that are unavoidable when one species looks at another), then we should be sure that we realize what we're doing. Our inaccuracies should make poetry, as opposed to an "illiterate epithet" (her complaint in "The Arctic Ox (or Goat)"). If we are going to distort these animals, we should distort them in the right way: a way that helps subvert the tyranny of literality (tyrannical in part because seemingly objective literality nevertheless embodies its own errors: a hedgehog, the literally accepted name, is not a hog, and a musk ox is not an ox). Poetry, on the other hand, embodies "mistakes"—what we call poetic license—that help induce us to imagine animals more resplendently and more vitally than we conventionally do. Edgehog, pin-swin, and spine-swine all do this in some way. And, for all the confusions of names and identities that are invoked in "His Shield," Moore has clever and insightful things to say about animals' armored exteriors.

As in many of Moore's poems, the animals appearing in focus at the beginning shift to a different topic as the poem develops. "His Shield" goes on to profile Presbyter John, a legendary medieval Christian king (more commonly known as Prester John—like the edgehog, his name has multiple variants). "I'll wrap / myself in salamander-skin like Presbyter John," Moore writes (144), alluding to "a detail from the legend, in which this king is said to wear the fire-proof skin of the salamander" (Costello 120). Like the ostrich decoys in "He 'Digesteth Harde Yron,'" though without the insidious intentions of those men, Prester John wraps himself up in the skin of an animal, literally getting inside the animal. This enables him, as Moore presents it in the poem, to accomplish superhuman (and animal-inspired) feats: he is "A lizard in the midst of flames, a firebrand / that is life. . . . he can withstand / fire and won't drown" (144). She writes of him admiringly, "His shield / was his humility." The point of invoking the earlier array of those other armored animals was to educe, or synthesize, a characteristic that ennobles the honorable man (or animal). Those other armored animals are literally, physiologically "battle-dressed," while Prester John, in his *metaphorical* shield (of humility), "rules by restraining his power," according to Bonnie Costello, with the elusive powers Moore attributes to all her lizards (120). With his strong faith, he doesn't need the literal armor that the other animals from the beginning of the poem have. But this does not lessen the significance of Moore's initial recourse to animals to characterize their armored qualities, their edges, and the importance of transcending the misrecognition of these animals so that we may perceive and appreciate their essential nature (their shields, their strength): and, what for Moore is identical with this, their poetic nature.

The issue of names and misnaming is a way of showing people's clumsy inability to know animals, literally and precisely, amid our cultural proclivities to manipulate things and despite our fantasies of omniscience. Moore's emphasis on our failure to contain and denote animals within our linguistic boundaries serves to accentuate the metaphysical resonances inherent in these creatures.

Seeking a More Harmonious Coexistence

In "The Pangolin," Moore sees "Sun and moon and day and night and man and beast / each with a splendor / which man in all his vileness cannot / set aside" (118). She implies that "man" would *want* to set aside the splendor of what we (competitively, arbitrarily) would characterize as subordinate: "moon," and "night," and "beast." Threatened by parity, people tend to array dualistic terms as dominant/subaltern. But Moore castigates this habit: we are vile for wanting to "set aside" animals' "splendor." In any case, Moore announces, we *cannot* sublimate their splendor, however much we aspire, in our vileness, to do so. The animals will endure (with Moore's assistance) to show us our true selves: we are not masters, nor uniquely splendid, but as Mesoamericans have long known, we all coexist as peers. Moore's poetic animals compel readers to consider how we comparatively appraise people and animals, and ask us to revisit received ideas: to contemplate how this relationship has traditionally existed and to imagine what it might be.

Moore has two basic modes of depicting the relationship between people and animals: we may interact badly or admirably. Linda Leavall summarizes the first of these:

> The moral aspects of Moore's aesthetic . . . are especially evident in those poems, such as "Peter," "The Jerboa," and "He 'Digesteth Harde Yron,'" that contrast the moral purity of the animal with the often impure motives of human beings. (160)

And Bruce Ross explains the more appealing mode:

> The Indian buffalo in "The Buffalo," the Alaskan reindeer in "Rigorists," the elephants in "Elephants," and the oxen in "The Arctic Ox (or Goat)," as well as the figurative encounter of the unicorn and the virgin in "Sea Unicorns and Land Unicorns," serve as vehicles for portraying the nature of positive accord between man, animal, and nature. Each of these poems dramatizes an exchange of respectful sympathy from man to the domesticated creatures. (331)

I have already discussed what Leavall characterizes as "impure motives" in two of the poems she invokes: the violent barbarity and wanton appropriation of animal essences undertaken by the "externalist" in "He 'Digesteth Harde Yron'" and the excessive taming, stylizing, and artificing of nature in "The Jerboa." The third poem she mentions, "Peter," more subtly castigates human motives. This paean to a carefree cat celebrates an animal who sleeps when he wants, plays exuberantly when the mood hits him, and ceases his activity as soon as "it shows signs of being no longer a pleasure" (43). What Leavall characterizes as the motivational contrast between the cat and people suggests that people are too calculating and hypocritical—unwilling to act on impulses and innate desires. The critique of our species comes through, by implied antithesis, as Moore praises Peter's character:

> It is clear that he can see the virtue of naturalness,
> that he does not regard the published fact as a surrender. (44)

People, on the other hand, fail to appreciate the virtue of naturalness, and we *do* regard the published fact as a surrender. That is to say, if something has been "published"—studied, announced, put forth, by someone who is accepted (perhaps erroneously, uncritically) as an authority—we surrender: we do not challenge the fact; we accept and act upon it as a certainty, a *fait accompli*, instead of, as a cat might do, trusting our own instinctual sense of what we feel like doing. At the end of the poem, Moore depicts Peter's varied and quizzical life and passes laudatory judgment on the cat's existence:

> To leap, to lengthen out, divide the air, to purloin, to pursue.
> To tell the hen: fly over the fence, go in the wrong way
> in your perturbation—this is life;
> to do less would be nothing but dishonesty. (44)

But people "do less," and are, thus, dishonest. We live, and act, too timidly: lacking immediacy and follow-through; overconcerned about what others might think about us, or what published facts constrain our individual expressions. The point here, simply, is that we could learn a thing or two from these animals; indeed, this insight (at the risk of seeming too facile, or too obvious) might serve well as the overall moral emanating from Moore's entire assembly of poetic animals.

Moore's poems seem about evenly split in terms of castigating people who pale in comparison to the animals, as above, and testifying to the possibility of harmonious coexistence. Many of the poems do both at once. Ross's formulation of the poems that characterize Moore's most sublime mode—"vehicles for portraying the nature of positive accord between man, animal, and nature . . . dramatiz[ing] an exchange of respectful sympathy from man to the domesticated creatures"—seems to me a fully adequate approximation of the equivalence I have been seeking between poetry and Mesoamerican spirituality: this is, perhaps, as close as one can get to defining a trope that exemplifies in poetry what Mesoamericans embody in their religion. I conclude my discussion of Moore by examining a few instances (among very many throughout her canon) where her poetry achieves this plateau.

"Dock Rats" begins in the title animal's narrative voice: "There are human beings who seem to regard the place as craftily / as we do" (53). The poem that follows depicts a vibrant and dazzling panorama of the New York riverfront with its bustling ferry boats and cargo ships and the sensory profusion of the port's exotic sounds, smells, and sights. Moore's readers are granted an entrée to observe this scene only if we agree, from the outset, to experience it as if we were dock rats—to regard the place as craftily as they do, seeing it through their eyes. Only those who affirm the keenness of the animals' point of view may pass the threshold into Moore's poetry. A "dock rat" may refer either to a person or a rodent, and Moore probably cherishes the polyvalent term. For both rodents and people, the conventional connotation of dock rat is pejorative: Robert Palmatier defines the human dock rat as "A homeless person who finds food and shelter on the docks. . . . The original dock rat was probably the Norway rat, or brown rat, which is partial to water. . . It is the rat that boards ships and carries plague and typhus to other countries. The homeless person is regarded as much a pest on the docks as is the brown rat" (113).

But Moore celebrates, rather than denigrates, both the human and nonhuman dock rats as she revels in the allure of urban nautical color. The egalitarian human–animal coexistence that this poem promotes on two levels—asking people to see as animals and titling/framing the encounter with an appellation that people and animals share—seems to efface, in Moore's consciousness, any lingering distasteful associations; we see anew, specifically because the "dock rat" perspective offers such a valuable common ground. Throughout her oeuvre, Moore provokes her readers to discover and celebrate such (sometimes subversive) moments of synchronicity, coexistence, shared consciousness between human and nonhuman animals.

In "The Arctic Ox (or Goat)," Moore begins by characterizing exploitative relations between people and the animals we harvest for our comforts, in contrast with more harmonious, sustainable, ways of obtaining animal fur:

> To wear the arctic fox
> you have to kill it. Wear
>   *qiviut*—the underwool of the arctic ox—
> pulled off it like a sweater;
> your coat is warm; your conscience, better.
>
> . . .
>
> Chinchillas, otters, water-rats,
> and beavers, keep us warm
>   but think! a "musk ox" grows six pounds
> of *qiviut*; the cashmere ram,
> three ounces—that is all—of pashm. (193–4)

The poem's final stanza uncompromisingly expresses the need for people to live in symbiosis with animals (as Moore indulges in some mild self-mockery):

> If you fear that you are
> reading an advertisement,
>   you are. If we can't be cordial
> to these creatures' fleece,
> I think that we deserve to freeze. (195)

"These creatures" refers to all the animals from which we take fur—gently or violently. Moore's conclusion reiterates the Mesoamerican conception of the relationship between people and animals: if we are not cordial to them—if we trap, hurt, kill them—then we deserve to die. Our moral fates are intimately bound up with our ecological behavior, good or evil. If we honor animals, then we deserve sustenance, protection from the elements, and if not, then we should suffer the consequences—which is exactly the point of the Mesoamerican animal tale.

"In 'Rigorists,' the introduction of Siberian reindeer into the Eskimo culture is seen as a miraculous event," Bruce Ross explains. "In reality these animals, as the poem notes, saved the Eskimos from extinction.... The introduction of the reindeer was an ecologically sound act that allowed the Eskimos to preserve their indigenous natures as dependents upon animals" (331–2). Moore describes this vital connection between people and reindeer only briefly in the final lines of "Rigorists." The animal,

sent
to Alaska,
was a gift preventing the extinction
of the Eskimo. The battle was won

by a quiet man,
Sheldon Jackson, evangel to that race
whose reprieve he read in the reindeer's face. (96)

Moore's endnote explains that Jackson, a General Agent of Education in Alaska in the late nineteenth century, "felt that to feed the Eskimo at government expense was not advisable, that whales having been almost exterminated, the ocean could not be restocked as a river can be with fish, and having prevailed on the government to authorize the importing of reindeer from Siberia, he made an expedition during the summer of 1891, procured sixteen reindeer—by barter—and later brought others" (276).

"The biblical coloring of the language," Ross writes, "underscores the miraculous nature of the Eskimos' survival. ... What Jackson saw in the reindeer's gaze was the possibility of insuring the cultural as well as the material survival of the Eskimo. And implicit in his description of the animal... is a respectful sympathy for the creature's beauty and the benevolent service that it could render in its new found home" (332). ("For Moore, these animals are 'rigorists,'" writes Charles Molesworth, "in part because they adapt so well to adverse surroundings" [305].)

As Ross notes, the spiritual language is not incidental: Jackson's establishment of ecological harmony between people and reindeer signifies what Moore characterizes as an "evangelical" salvation in Lapland. The poem's last line is typically compact, powerful. In this freeze-frame tableau, we see the "evangel" seeing the Eskimo, saved from destruction, by reading the animal's face. The human being (the Eskimo) is reflected in the reindeer's eyes, its gaze, its consciousness. It is hard to imagine any more intimate assertion of connection between people and animals than this one that Moore depicts, mediated by a man who had the insight that human and nonhuman animals can and *must* be envisioned as living in a mutually supportive ecosystem. If we accept the importance of linking our lives with theirs, we can survive together.

"Elephants," like "Rigorists," invokes explicit spiritual language to describe the connection between people and animals. Moore describes the animals:

> Elephant-ear-witnesses-to-be of hymns
> and glorias, these ministrants all gray or
> gray with white on legs or trunk, are a pilgrims'
>
> pattern of revery not reverence—a
> religious procession without any priests,
> the centuries-old carefullest unrehearsed
> play. Blessed by Buddha's Tooth, the obedient beasts
>
> themselves as toothed temples blessing the street, see
> the white elephant carry the cushion that
> carries the casket that carries the Tooth. (128–9)

The poem interweaves the elephants with two major spiritual systems, Christianity and Buddhism. Moore depicts the elephants, somewhat improbably, as intimately involved with the rituals and relics of these religions, as the animals witness hymns, figure as ministrants and pilgrims, and so forth. Moore's initial, far-fetched contrivance—and we are meant to be conscious of its awkwardness—casts these animals as Christian or Buddhist. But she goes on to *supplant* the conventions of established human religions: the elephants' religious procession is "without any priests," and the animals are not just subaltern accompanists in the homage to a relic from the Buddha, but are "themselves . . . toothed temples."

Moore shows (at first, when the elephants are "ministrants") how animals can be linked with people in our own spiritual discourse, but then she raises the animals above this: they do not need to adapt themselves to our established anthropocentric models of spirituality. We may start with these, as her poem does, but we then move on to a consciousness where the elephants no longer need Christian priests or Buddhist temples to experience spirituality or to justify their spiritual potentiality. Moore comes to perceive, and shows her readers, the elephants' own realm of spiritual power, which we may share with them, and which does not demand their conversion to—or subordination within—a human-centered piety. It is a moment, once again, in which Moore brings her readers to a point uncannily evocative of Mesoamerican spirituality in its assertion of a faith that is not speciesist, but instead betokens an egalitarian communion between people and animals. This epiphany is consecrated at the end of the poem with an intimate physical proximity between people and animals; the intimacy here counters the ironizing perversity of some of these depictions, as in "He 'Digesteth Harde Yron' " or "Tippoo's Tiger." The elephant's

> held-up fore-leg for use
> as a stair, to be climbed or descended with
> the aid of his ear, expounds the brotherhood
> of creatures to man the encroacher, by the
> small word with the dot, meaning know—the verb bűd.
>
> These knowers "arouse the feeling that they are
> allied to man" and can change roles with their trustees. (129–30)

As the person and the elephant touch and embrace—body to foreleg, hand to ear—the tableau depicts brotherhood (though without sanitizing humankind's unfortunate track record as "the encroacher") between people and elephants; acknowledges the intelligent sentience of the animals; celebrates the alliance between us and them; and simply, but powerfully, bespeaks a two-way evenness, symbiosis, between species, as the animals *know*, with the ancient wisdom evoked by the Buddhist terminology ("Buddha" is the past participle of the Sanskrit word budh or bűd, which means to awake, know, perceive), that they "can change roles with their trustees." Sometimes people are in charge, and sometimes elephants are: they take turns. The reciprocal equilibrium, the radical equity of this relationship between people and animals, is virtually inconceivable amid the mainstream cultural *zeitgeist* that surrounded Marianne Moore. I am thus compelled to invoke something far outside the commonalitics of Moore's culture, something like the Mesoamerican belief system, in order to approach and understand her ideas about animals.

"These knowers," as Moore characterizes the elephants, present a resolution to the quandary I expressed in part 1 about knowing animals. Here are knowing animals, with "knowing" as an adjectival modifier of the animal rather than a gerund expressing a human verb, a human action. The problem of knowing animals is ultimately settled only when we discover, as Moore has here, knowing animals.

Chapter 5

Smith, Larkin, Snyder, Heaney, Rogers: "we should be kind"

Gratitude to Wild Beings, our brothers, teaching secrets,
freedoms, and ways; who share with us their milk;
self-complete, brave, and aware
in our minds so be it.
(Gary Snyder, "Prayer for the Great Family")

I believe each nonhuman life is an expression somehow of an aspect of myself, if I were only clever enough to decipher all of those messages.
(Pattiann Rogers, *The Dream of the Marsh Wren*)

Marianne Moore's and José Emilio Pacheco's poetry embody extensive evocations of animal souls; their systematic considerations of how animals and people relate offer sustained parallels to Mesoamerican spiritual ideals. The poets in this chapter—Stevie Smith, Philip Larkin, Gary Snyder, Seamus Heaney, and Pattiann Rogers—do not address anthrozoological concerns as exhaustively as Moore and Pacheco, or present in their poetry as comprehensive a platform for celebrating and intensifying human–animal interactions. Still, their works offer a range of significant poetic animals that advance my examination in a varied assembly of texts. Several examples of poetic animals from such different writers will help illustrate, as diversely as possible, how one may apply the ecocritical ethics I am formulating.

My enterprise here, probably like all ventures in literary criticism, is tinged with the subjective quirks of personal taste. As I illustrate my theories about cultural representations of animals with two poets in-depth and five more in briefer detail, I don't mean to argue that these writers have some exclusive and exhaustive claim on ecocritical insights about animals. Of course every reader will have his or her own favorite poets, not to mention artists in other genres and media, whose work can be interrogated according to the general principles I propose. As I examine several different poets in this chapter, I hope to encourage readers to evaluate even others beyond these. (W. S. Merwin, Elizabeth

Bishop, Wendell Berry, Ted Hughes, and Edward Thomas, e.g., spring immediately to mind—had I but world enough and time...) The poetic animals in this chapter expand the stylistic and cultural scope beyond what appears in chapters 3 and 4. These poets, of course, are not necessarily doing similar things with their poetic animals, or creating them for similar reasons; the different sets of poetic animals I examine here are distinct in their manifestations and their purposes. No single cultural orientation is inherently more conducive to poetic animals than another: the poetry can be English, American, Mexican—or from any of countless other languages and cultures. It can be complex or simple; characterized by gutsy naturalism, or more sedately and intellectually distanced; detailed and sensorily intense, or stylized and idiosyncratic.

Style is an important issue here, as always in art: in earlier discussions of Mary Oliver and Ogden Nash (part 1) I criticized stylistic demeanors that seemed egocentric/anthropocentric and hostile to the depiction of poetic animals. Style can keep a poet out of this club, although it won't get anyone into it. (I have never, incidentally, felt especially enamored of Marianne Moore's style, which I find choppy and difficult; it's not the form *I* would have chosen for such outstanding poetic animals—but, obviously, it's not up to me: I take them where I find them.) The important thing about style for my purposes here is that it not overwhelm the spirit of these works. Moore and Smith are highly stylized poets; Pacheco, Rogers, Larkin, and Heaney somewhat less so—it can work either way. Perhaps, ideally, the imaginative texts that springboard readers to a range of metaphysical relationships with animals would be unencumbered by any stylistic mediation at all, eliminating the need to "psyche out" and come to terms with the language, the imagery, the voice... and this would be "ideal" in a certain sense, but only a very limited one: where would be the fun in it? the art? I don't want to get fixated on style, and I don't want it to be a barrier to what I want to get out of this poetry—style should, of course, actually be of some help in terms of seducing readers: engaging us in the world of human–animal relationships that these poets present. My examination of several different styles, voices, schools, and approaches to animals begins with Smith.

Stevie Smith

If Marianne Moore's poetic animals reverberate with intense and enigmatic complexities, Stevie Smith writes in a considerably less ornate mode. Her poetry is commonly (and unfairly) undervalued because of what seems at first a contrived childlike tenor—although it resonates more deeply as one sounds its lurking depths.

Two elements characterize Smith's poetry about animals: a strident, righteous tenor, resounding with unabashed, sometimes impolite, and always fiercely polemical advocacy for animals; and a broad diversity of sub-topics concerning animals' existence in human culture. Smith addresses the ways in which people interact with animals in many different facets of our lives, and doesn't give us a pass on any of them. We always need to consider how we are treating animals, how they are doing in the world around us. We mistreat animals in a range of different ways, Smith asserts, and so her poems recount not just one cognitive fault, but a series of interrelated transgressions and blind spots.

Smith's poems correspond with animal souls, first of all, antithetically: human attitudes, as she depicts them, reflect the absence of a co-essential consciousness toward animals. If Smith's culture believed in the parity and relevance of animals as Mesoamericans do, there would be no need for her screeds about people's abusive behavior. But without such an understanding about our connections with animals, Smith believes we need to be rebuked—copiously. Her reproofs, if heeded, might encourage her audience to reform and to appreciate more keenly our relationship with animals. Yet, Smith's readers may not respond en masse to her hectoring in the ways she would wish; often idiosyncratic and sanctimonious, she does not inspire unilateral allegiance. I admire Smith's poetry, eccentricities and all, because I value what I perceive as her underlying goodness of spirit. More commonly, readers are somewhat put off by her animal scoldings, and also by the other extensive theme that pervades her poetry: lonely isolation, wariness of social engagement with people, tinged with a bit of suicidal despair. Reading Smith calls to mind the apothegm variously attributed to Pascal and Charles de Gaulle among others: The more I know people, the more I like cats (sometimes, dogs). It seems as though Smith would subscribe heartily to that sentiment.

In "Parrot," Smith castigates people's oppression of pets and our heedlessness of their needs and desires, their nature:

> The old sick green parrot
> High in a dingy cage
> Sick with malevolent rage
> Beadily glutted his furious eye
> On the old dark
> Chimneys of Noel Park
>
> Far from his jungle green
> Over the seas he came
> To the yellow skies, to the dripping rain,

To the night of his despair.
And the pavements of his street
Are shining beneath the lamp
With a beauty that's not for one
Born under a tropic sun.

He has croup. His feathered chest
Knows no minute of rest.
High on his perch he sits
And coughs and spits,
Waiting for death to come.
Pray heaven it wont be long. (18)

She pulls no punches: there is no fancy language, no elaborate figurative construction; just a stark, incontrovertible description of a parrot's displacement and constraint. People condemn parrots to misery when we bring them into our sitting rooms in order to enjoy their exotic presence. The poem attributes powerful and precise emotion to the animal: malevolent rage. One may perceive Smith's characterization as an anthropomorphic fallacy—but it doesn't seem that she worries about such criticism, about expressing how an animal might experience (and how the poet might depict) some manifestation of the emotion of rage; she just calls it as she sees it. People pull animals out of their worlds, away from where they belong, and resituate them, however uncomfortably, in our world (Noel Park is a London neighborhood near where Smith herself lived). This proclivity to displace parrots *et al.* represents a *faulty* sort of correlation or connection between people and animals. Smith wants her readers to recognize this disjunction and to honor animals as equals instead of using them as playthings. People shouldn't keep animals in cages, Smith believes, and shouldn't transplant tropical creatures into England's dripping rain.

References to death, heaven, and prayer at the end of "Parrot" invoke a sense of spirituality, albeit ironized. Smith doesn't suggest that people and parrots share a common heaven or afterlife: but nevertheless, her forced, awkward invocation of spirituality here is not accidental or insignificant. A lame appeal to a hopeful spiritual transcendence in the poem's last two lines is all that Smith can conjure up to try to mitigate the awful treatment animals experience in this life, in their (and our) daily existence. If, instead, Smith's culture had a spiritual system like the Mesoamericans' and animals were somehow equal with people, the speaker wouldn't need to "pray heaven" for the parrot's respite at the end of the poem, and the parrot wouldn't have only death to anticipate as a release from its torment, but instead would have the prospect of a meaningful *life* (as would be the entitlement of every living creature, one would hope). Mesoamericans do not conceive separate worlds for animals and people, but rather, see all living creatures as equally resident in one unified place. The dichotomies that plague the title character in "Parrot"—tropics vs. England, cage vs. freedom, healthy environment vs. sickly prison—are endemic to the situations that the Western industrial world imposes upon animals.

Mesoamericans believe that there's an animal out there sharing a person's experiences, our fate, our sense of the world, and so does Smith—a belief that she expresses through her poetic animals. Humanity, as a species, appears throughout her poetry as bitter, crimped, metaphorically caged. Her poetic animals, like the parrot, reflect the fact that we have brought them down to our level, tainted them with our stinted spirits. People are relatively miserable in our world, as Smith depicts it, and so are animals; and this correlation is fundamentally *causal*, rather than coincidental—this is the crucial synthesis that comes from reading Smith's poetry through the lens of animal souls. Human misery causes animals' misery, and animals' misery causes human misery; the malaise that pervades Smith's poetry is contagious, and this contagion spans across species. We are all in this together—or, in light of Smith's trope of displacement, we are all out of it together.

"The Zoo" also depicts the suffering animals experience as a result of being displaced from their habitats for human convenience and amusement. Like the parrot in a cage, Smith informs, the zoo animal is angry at his lot:

> The lion sits within his cage,
> Weeping tears of ruby rage,
> He licks his snout, the tears fall down
> And water dusty London town.
>
> He does not like you, little boy,
> It's no use making up to him,
> He does not like you any more
> Than he likes Nurse, or Baby Jim. (29)

As in "Parrot," the climate to which this lion has been relocated is pointedly unpleasant, unsuitable. And like the pet bird in a cage, the lion in the zoo is explicitly angry that he is being used, being put on display: he simply doesn't like being there. Smith contrasts the parrot's sad English fate with its intended life in "the jungle green," and in "The Zoo," too, she ironically and painfully juxtaposes the lion's present captivity against his natural life. The lion

> knows the hot sun slants
> Between the rancid jungle-grass,
> Which never more shall part to let him pass
> Down to the jungle drinking-hole,
> Whither the zebra comes with her sleek foal. (30)

Instead, his London life is, like the parrot's, unmitigatedly bleak as he devolves toward decrepitude at the end of the poem:

> His claws are blunt, his teeth fall out,
> No victim's flesh consoles his snout,
> And that is why his eyes are red
> Considering his talents are misusèd. (30)

Both "Parrot" and "The Zoo" highlight something crucial about how we conceive of animals and what we do to them in our culture. Our cultural appetites demand the importation of animals from the four corners of the earth, while animal connections in Mesoamerican spirituality draw upon creatures that naturally live around the people in their world: coyotes, weasels, foxes. The anguish that Smith's animals suffer when they are abducted from *their* world and badly resettled in ours does not occur in Mesoamerican culture simply because the animals they worship, and worship with, are *already* in the world they share together. The animals that Mesoamericans worship are easier for them to relate to, compared to the animals that the people in Smith's poetry interact with, precisely *because* the coyotes and foxes are happier, better situated, than our zoo lions and caged parrots. If we want to establish better relations with animals in our own culture, we would do well to start with (and end with) the animals that are proximate to us.

Among the numerous other anthrozoological topics Smith broaches are carnivory: in a short poem with a long-winded title, "Death Bereaves our Common Mother, Nature Grieves for my Dead Brother," Smith writes:

> Lamb dead, dead lamb,
> He was, I am,
> Separation by a tense
> Baulks my eyes' indifference.
> Can I see the lately dead
> And not bend a sympathetic head?
> Can I see lamb dead as mutton
> And not care a solitary button? (9)

A single word, "mutton," subtly but definitively informs that this poem concerns not just an animal's demise but, more specifically, the transformation of a living animal into a meal. The language Smith uses suggests parity, coexistence, a sense of connectedness between people and animals—or rather, she describes what *should be* a condition of parity, except that it's ironized, as we kill and eat the lambs. The near- (but not exact) parallel in grammatical construction—"He was, I am"—shows that human and ovine existence are comparable, except for that "separation by a tense." People and lambs are similar in our tenses, as in our lives, except when we kill them and relegate them, grammatically and poetically, to "was" instead of "is." The terms of filiation in the title—common mother, dead brother—evoke a sense of relationship, as all living creatures are in some sense related, though carnivorous human society undercuts the mutuality of this relationship. One doesn't eat one's relatives—so, if we do eat these lambs, we must be giving the lie to the relationship that the title posits. Animals can't really be our brothers, and we don't have a common mother—the poetic conceit is a nice one, and the reinforcement of prominent rhyme words, mother/brother, advances this conceit, but the denouement of our relationship with the lamb-cum-mutton finally destroys this. Could the words mother/brother, rather than mutton, have defined our relationship to each other? In Mesoamerica, yes, but not in Smith's England.

Several of Smith's poems invoke God and animals' spiritual condition in oddly backhanded and unexpected ways, as with the bitter interjection, "pray heaven," at the end of "Parrot." "Sunt Leones" concerns the early Christian martyrs who were thrown to the lions, but unlike other accounts, this one takes the lions' point of view. Smith lightly underplays the significance of the human martyrdom, which would normally figure centrally ("And if the Christians felt a little blue / Well people being eaten often do"), before she gets to the crux of the poem:

> My point which up to this has been obscured
> Is that it was the lions who procured
> By chewing up blood gristle flesh and bone
> The martyrdoms on which the Church has grown.
> I only write this poem because I thought it rather looked
> As if the part the lions played was being overlooked.
> By lions' jaws great benefits and blessings were begotten
> And so our debt to Lionhood must never be forgotten. (11)

Smith emphasizes the significance of nonhuman actors in what is arguably the most species-exclusive human cultural institution, religion.

Animals in Western sacred texts, religious parables, foundation myths, and moral exempla rarely appear as more than foils, or two-dimensional bit players: the ur-story for animals, in the Garden of Eden, frames their creation story with their destiny to be dominated by man, and adds, as a kicker, an illustration of the chaos that ensues when one uppity animal, the serpent, aspires above its station and tries to exert its own independent consciousness; that animal is condemned for eternity to brutality at the hands (feet, actually) of people.

But Smith believes our spirituality should include animals. Highlighting the lions' central role as martyrs in early Christian history seems, at first, perhaps playfully sacrilegious—but it reflects Smith's sincere and serious intention to promote animals as meaningful participants in religious culture. Spirituality was an important topic for Smith: she wrote a great deal of Christian poetry that was basically devotional, albeit flavored with a hefty dose of cynicism and institutional deflation. It seems likely that one reason for her skepticism was that Christianity does not incorporate a strong, clear presence of animals. Smith believes, as Mesoamericans do, that animals must be at the heart of our spiritual expressions. Animals and animal images appear, of course, pervasively throughout the Bible: in the stories of Noah's Ark, Jonah and the whale, Abraham's sacrifice of the ram instead of Isaac, the golden calf, and on and on—but as Smith reminds us, our real debts to these animals tend to be neglected. Our spiritual histories and practices do not substantially acknowledge their importance; "Sunt Leones" argues for a revisionist recognition that animals deserve inclusion in our spirituality.

Smith sometimes wrote in the voice of God; one such poem, "Nature and Free Animals," again addresses the intersection of people, animals, and spirituality. The poem begins with God chastising humankind:

> I will forgive you everything,
> But what you have done to my Dogs
> I will not forgive.
> You have taught them the sicknesses of your mind
> And the sicknesses of your body
> You have taught them to be servile
> To hang servilely upon your countenance
> To be dependent touching and entertaining
> To have rights to be wronged
> And wrongs to be righted.
> You have taught them to be protected by a Society.
> This I will not forgive,
> Saith the Lord. (8)

The God that Smith believes in cares about animals and values their integrity in a way that most people do not. People distort animals and pollute them with our own faults, which makes Smith's God intensely angry. The poem's human speaker responds to God's admonishments with a wilting ambivalence that reflects Smith's discomfort in a world where people diminish animals:

> Well, God, it's all very well to talk like this
> And I dare say it's all very fine
> And Nature and Free Animals
> Are all very fine,
> Well all I can say is
> If you wanted it like that
> You shouldn't have created me
> Not that I like it very much
> And now that I'm on the subject I'll say,
> What with Nature and Free Animals on the one side
> And you on the other,
> I hardly know I'm alive. (8)

Smith's recurrent life-weary, vaguely suicidal tenor appears here—"You shouldn't have created me / Not that I like it very much." The speaker is frustratingly caught—paralyzed—between two forces, God and animals. Smith regards both of these as awesomely important, although she also believes that neither manifests itself in our lives as perfectly as it might—both are flawed, amid our flawed world. "Nature and Free Animals" laments the imperfections in the two entities that could be such an important source of sustenance to Smith. And once again, animals and religion are provocatively entwined. People would benefit from a better God as well as a better nature (with "Free Animals," as opposed to caged parrots and zoo lions and mutton), if we did a better job of understanding and respecting God and animals. And people would better understand and respect God and animals if animals and spirituality were unified, as they are in Mesoamerica. If something like animal souls existed in Smith's own culture, she might be considerably less existentially angst-ridden than she is here. Each force, God and free animals, stands on a different side of her, and both are far away. God and animals are hard for her to see, hard to grasp; the potential value they might offer is thus highly attenuated, if not (at times) completely inaccessible. And the result of this quandary is a human vacancy, a sense of dulled and deadened distance from the endpoints, the ideals of God and animals, as Smith wallows in the middle: "I hardly know I'm alive."

A vital and satisfying spirituality, Smith suggests, wouldn't situate God and animals on different sides, tantalizingly inaccessible to the person isolated in the middle. God wouldn't have to chastise us about how we treat animals, and the person wouldn't suffer the dissonance, the alienation from a meaningful value system, that "Nature and Free Animals" describes.

Another topic on Smith's spectrum is the environmental danger people pose to animals, addressed in "Friends of the River Trent."

> A dwindling body of ageing fish
> Is all we can present
> Because of water pollution
> In the River Trent
> Because of water pollution, my boys,
> And a lack of concerted action,
> These fish of what they used to be
> Is only a measly fraction. (117)

In her exhortation against our dirty ecological habits Smith reminds us, just as the central tenet of animal souls posits, that the fates of people and animals are interrelated. In the poem's final lines, the fish in their polluted depths ingest enough tainted water and food

> To carry 'em to a natural death,
> And may we do the same, my boys,
> And carry us to a natural death. (117)

This reiterates the deluge of contemporary ecological warnings that Western industrial society is inclined to ignore: the survival of animals and people is mutually codependent. As Tom Lehrer sang, "We will all go together when we go."

Many of Smith's poetic animals are depicted in unassuming and pleasant ditties that celebrate their subjects' jouissance, their otherworldliness, as in "My Cat Major": "Oh Major is a fine cat / He walks cleverly / And what is he at, my fine cat? / No one can see" (84). (Perhaps Smith thinks that we *could* see more clearly what the fine cat is at if we were not so alienated from animals, as her other poems posit.) Some of Smith's poems depict people just having innocent fun with animals, as in "My Cats": "I like to toss him up and down / A heavy cat weighs half a Crown / With a hey do diddle my cat Brown" (57). Consciousness of animals frequently provokes guilty or angry jeremiads in Smith's poetic, but sometimes generates less troubled moments of play and intimacy. For Smith, playing with animals, being with animals—animals that aren't sick with croup or dead as mutton—may result in poems that are pure textual expressions of an animal experience, and this experience is always tinged with a consciousness of animals' spiritual aura.

Philip Larkin

Unlike the other poets I discuss, Philip Larkin wrote only a handful of animal poems, and these are not generally regarded as central to his oeuvre. His cranky misanthropic persona somewhat resembles Stevie Smith's, but while Smith's distrust of people was in a sense offset by her embrace of animals, Larkin does not seem motivated to cast his sights beyond (as he sees it) the cesspool of humanity, and his poetry wallows in human inadequacies; loneliness and cynicism pervade his canon. In Smith's poetry, animals represent an alternative life-form to humanity, and the poet finds in animals a respite from tawdry human foibles. Smith's poetic animals, morally elevated, elicit our sympathies due to the victimization they have suffered at human hands. Larkin's scattershot animals experience no special dispensations: they are part of the same gray world as his human characters and topoi.

But one of Larkin's short poems about animals raises the prospect that it and a few others might present, in an understated but meaningful way, some of the same insights found more prominently in other writers' poetic animals. "Pigeons" suggests Larkin's attunement to animals:

> On shallow slates the pigeons shift together,
> Backing against a thin rain from the west
> Blown across each sunk head and settled feather.
> Huddling round the warm stack suits them best,
> Till winter daylight weakens, and they grow
> Hardly defined against the brickwork. Soon,
> Light from a small intense lopsided moon
> Shows them, black as their shadows, sleeping so. (109)

It is brief, simple, unmomentous. One might almost consider it a still life: still lifes generally depict insensate subjects, although these faint, stationary creatures seem "still" enough to qualify.

"Pigeons" quintessentially evokes Larkin's mood, his energies, his self-image; indeed, I am inclined to read it as one of the most intimately autobiographical poems in Larkin's oeuvre. This might seem unlikely given that Larkin was largely a "confessional poet," highly self-referential, often self-obsessive—so many of his other compositions would appear to be more likely candidates for autobiographical insight. Yet I would argue that none of his many poems about mildly neurotic, introspective, and sexually frustrated bachelors who have squandered their opportunities captures as incisive a portrait of Larkin's essential character as "Pigeons."

The poem presents creatures set amid a compact urban habitat (shallow slates). Their minimal animation (shifting, backing, huddling) amid dreary weather (the unrelenting thin rain that makes the English, man and beast, what they are) evokes a sense of mild, persistent depression of spirit (in the sunk heads) and acquiescent resignation (in the settled feathers) to the inescapable permanence of this narrow, dusky, damp, and dreary life. A reader ferreting for anthropomorphic fallacies would counter that I cannot know, or presume, that the scene is as dreary and depressing for the birds as it would be for me or for Larkin. But I believe that it is, and that the poem's triumph is that it demonstrates this. Larkin has observed these birds, carefully and sensitively, empathetically, and has come to understand them. The poem is effective and moving to the extent that Larkin depicts these pigeons' gloom—vicariously, as he voices his own. This simultaneity, this depiction of the pigeons' bleak tableau executed in tandem with an evocation of the poet's own parallel consciousness, qualifies "Pigeons" as an iteration of animal souls.

Larkin depicts in his pigeon scene a necessary social grouping that is biophysically motivated—animals huddled together around a warm stack for mutual self-preservation—though we see little of the consequent reward or nurture that one might desire from such a grouping. Larkin saw himself as part of a social group by necessity, figuratively huddled together with other human beings, but his proximity to others rarely produced any succor apart from a literal (and minimally-fulfilling) physical sense of body warmth. Larkin found in pigeons via "Pigeons"—plural—the figure to express the sense of social relationship, stinted and ironized albeit necessary, that underlies his human poems. Deleuze and Guattari assert that the animal, in becoming-animal, is always multiple, and Larkin's perception of multiple animals in "Pigeons," I believe, trumps the copious plaints of solipsistic protagonists in his other poems. Most of Larkin's poetry calls to mind, for me, Gloucester's tragically misguided assertion from the end of *3 Henry VI*: "I am myself alone." But I think Larkin is ultimately as wrong about his isolation as Gloucester was. In his self-portrait as pigeon, however subtly (so subtly, indeed, that I believe I am the only critic who has remarked upon this, though I am convinced of its accuracy), Larkin grudgingly accepts this multiplicity, this sense of membership in a social mass, however tenuous and imperfect.

I am usually wary of the poetic device of inscribing oneself in an animal as a valid, authentic way of imagining and connecting with animals: it is prone to co-opt the animal as a figure, a metaphor, for what the poet believes to be the much more profound human character that the animal temporarily represents, thus obviating the animal's essence. In the case of "Pigeons," however, I do not find the poet's animal inscription infelicitous: perhaps because Larkin's pigeon-ness is so obliquely drawn here (as evidenced by the fact that no one else has remarked upon the autobiographical resonance). Although I think Larkin *is* being metaphorical in his appropriation of the pigeons as himself here, he engages in this metaphor so quietly as to leave the images of the pigeons unexploited, unmanipulated—as Ezra Pound would say, *echt*. Larkin looks at birds, thinking about his life and his environment, but he is able to do this without trampling or overwriting the birds. This, to me, epitomizes the ideal achievement of co-essentiality in poetic animals. It's difficult to explicate formulaic guidelines for how a poet can use an animal as a metaphor, a figure, a vehicle, without crossing the line and co-opting the animal's spirit: as noted earlier, there is a subjective element to this, but I hope to define by example when this co-essential sensibility works most eloquently, and Larkin's "Pigeons" is such a case.

As the poem/portrait matures to apotheosis, we see (ironically) a blurring of definition. Regularly in Larkin's poetry, the culmination depicts the central character fading into a blur, a sad and mildly bitter little man, hardly defined and barely visible against the backdrop of his similarly blurry, indistinct habitat. For a human analog to the pigeons' shallow slate, Larkin's poem "Home is So Sad" depicts an environment with a comparably minimalist yet keen detail: "You can see how it was: / Look at the pictures and the cutlery. / The music in the piano stool. That vase" (119). At the end of "Pigeons," we finally see the title characters, or stop seeing them—losing them in the dark and sleepy atmosphere—as they vanish into the art, the tableau, the environment.

"Pigeons" shows the poet (and prompts readers to emulate the poet) looking at pigeons, and thinking about pigeons, without disturbing them, which is unusual. The customary human response to pigeons is to shoo them away, somehow denigrating them either physically or imaginatively. For contrasting literary pigeons, Zadie Smith's novel *White Teeth* presents a more common expression of the reception those birds expect in our world: "Overhead, a gang of the local flying vermin took off from some unseen perch, swooped, and seemed to be zeroing in on Archie's car roof—only to perform, at the last moment, an impressive U-turn, moving as one with the elegance of a curve ball and landing on the Hussein-Ishmael, a celebrated halal butchers." Smith initially notes, grudgingly, the impressive elegance of the birds' flight, but then goes on to undercut this. Archie (who is in the midst of a suicide attempt)

> watched them with a warm internal smile as they deposited their load, streaking white walls purple. He watched them stretch their peering bird heads over the Hussein-Ishmael gutter. . . . The Hussein-Ishmael was owned by Mo Hussein-Ishmael . . . Mo believed that with pigeons you have to get to the root of the problem: not the excretions but the pigeon itself. *The shit is* not *the shit* (this was Mo's mantra), *the* pigeon *is the shit.* So the morning of Archie's almost-death began as every morning in the Hussein-Ishmael, with Mo resting his huge belly on the windowsill, leaning out and swinging a meat cleaver in an attempt to halt the flow of dribbling purple.
>
> "Get out of it! Get away, you shit-making bastards! Yes! SIX!"
>
> It was cricket, basically—the Englishman's game adapted by the immigrant, and six was the most pigeons you could get at one swipe.
>
> "Varin!" said Mo, calling down to the street, holding the bloodied cleaver up in triumph. "You're in to bat, my boy. Ready?"
>
> Below him on the pavement stood Varin . . . It was Varin's job to struggle up a ladder and gather spliced bits of pigeon into a small Kwik-Save shopping bag, tie the bag up, and dispose of it in the bins at the other end of the street.
>
> . . . One day, so Mo believed, Cricklewood and its residents would have cause to thank him for his daily massacre; one day no man, woman, or child on the Broadway would ever again have to mix one part detergent to four parts vinegar to clean up the crap that falls on the world. *The shit is* not *the shit*, he repeated solemnly, *the* pigeon *is the shit.* Mo was the only man in the community who truly understood. (4–5)

Larkin, instead, lets the birds be, respecting their quiet, unmomentous dignity. There are not many poems about pigeons: Wallace Stevens has a few fluttering around in "Le Monocle de Mon Oncle," and also in "Sunday Morning" where

> At evening, casual flocks of pigeons make
> Ambiguous undulations as they sink,
> Downward to darkness, on extended wings. (8)

And Marianne Moore, in "Pigeons," treats the birds with her customarily intricate homage. Her poem begins:

> Older than the ancient Greeks, than
> Solomon, the pigeon family is a

ramifying one, a
banyan of banyans; to begin
with, bluish slate,
but with ability. Modesty cannot dull
the lustre of the pigeon
swift and sure, coming quickest and
straightest just after a storm. (61)

Moore's paean to the bird's history includes an account of its role as a homing bird, a messenger:

Mysterious animal with a magnetic
feel by which he traces back-
ward his transportation outward,
even in a fog at sea, though glad
to be tossed near enough the loft
or coop to get back the same day.
"Home on time without
his message." (62)

And the poem concludes with an appreciation of the pigeon as breathlessly rapturous as that accorded to any of Moore's poetic animals:

a slender Cinderella deliberately
pied, so she on each side is
the same, an all-feather piebald,
cuckoo-marked on a titanic scale
taking perhaps sixteen birds to
show the whole design, as in chess
played with men and hors-
es. Yes, the thus medievally
two-colored sea-pie-patterned semi-swan-
necked magpie-pigeon, gamecock-legged
with long-clawed toes, and all
extremes—head neck back tail
and feet—coal black, the
rest snow white, has a surprising modernness and fanciness
and stateliness and. . . . Yes indeed;
developed by and humbly dedicated to
the Gentlemen of the
Feather Club, this is a dainty breed.
(65; ellipses in text)

(Like Larkin's pigeons and Deleuze and Guattari's becoming-animal, Moore's, too, are ideally multiple: one must conceive of them as a group—perhaps 16 of them, as she writes—to appreciate their essence.)

But unlike Larkin, Moore, and Stevens, most poets who feature pigeons tend to assault them. Fiona Pitt-Kethley's "Pigeons" evokes Yeats and his squirrel (discussed in chapter 1). Perhaps a pigeon is an avian analog to a squirrel: too common to be conceived as a really interesting animal—mainly a pest; perhaps amusing for a minute or two, but only as a plaything in the consummate power of the person, the poet, who deigns to toy with the animal briefly. In Pitt-Kethley's poem a lame pigeon hobbles into her house. She tends to the bird for a while, but then grows bored: "Close up, I decided, birds weren't so nice. / She pecked our hands for food and glared at us / with her red eyes. I never liked her much" (21). Finally, the family takes the bird to the vet, who breaks her neck.

Zadie Smith and Pitt-Kethley presume that the pigeons exist, ultimately, to kill: either within the text, or, as in Yeats's "To a Squirrel at Kyle-na-no," in a space hovering outside the text, just offstage. A pigeon's best shot at literary stardom is to pass as a dove, the nearly-identical bird (except for differences in coloration) that benefits from cultural prejudices favoring whiteness over darkness. Doves feature in myriad symbolic traditions arising out of religious iconography: pure, gentle, and peaceful; deified by Sumerians and Greeks as well as Christians (for whom the bird may be an incarnation of the holy spirit, as in *Paradise Lost*); foretelling renewal after the flood in Genesis; auguring love: lovey-dovey. In *Four Saints in Three Acts* Gertrude Stein writes, "Pigeons on the grass alas." The pigeons might have received a more exuberant reception if they were birds of another feather: Leonard Lutwack writes that Stein's line "is a reference to the doves seen by the saint as she is seated in a garden. Saint Ignatius questions whether they are pigeons: 'If they were not pigeons on the grass alas what were they. He had heard of a third and he asked about it it was a magpie in the sky. . . . He asked for a distant magpie' " (102). No pigeons need apply.

In contrast with the more common cultural images of pigeons, Larkin's account is surprisingly sensitive, nonviolent, open-minded. Pigeons are pigeonholed as the kind of bird that is not usually dignified in poetry—common, dirty, gray. They don't do the things that people like birds, especially poetic birds, to do: they don't fly like eagles, or preen elegantly like swans, or display lush feathers like peacocks, or swoop like vultures, or perform like parrots; they are stale and bothersome. Larkin transcends delimiting stereotypes to choose as his subjects the birds that other poets ignore or mock. "Pigeons" is the type of self-portrait he couldn't completely paint with human characters and scenes because, perhaps, he was always so cynical of his fellow creatures; his poetry about people resonates with detachment, irony, contrivance. Larkin's many poems that are clearly *somewhat* autobiographical are finally unconvincing as self-portraits: too skittish, clever, evasive, constructed. It is with animals that Larkin is best poised to define himself. Larkin reinvented the wheel in terms of conceiving what Mesoamericans know as animal souls—he found, in animals, a correlation that helped explain his own fate, his own existence.

Three other poems by Larkin explore connections between people and animals. "Myxomatosis" portrays a suffering animal whose experience parallels Larkin's in spirit if not in literal detail, along the lines of Larkin's relation to the pigeons on the shallow slate. (Myxomatosis, a fatal viral disease of rabbits characterized by erupting skin tumors, was intentionally introduced in Great Britain to reduce the rabbit population.)

> Caught in the centre of a soundless field
> While hot inexplicable hours go by
> *What trap is this? Where were its teeth concealed?*
> You seem to ask.
> I make a sharp reply,
> Then clean my stick. I'm glad I can't explain
> Just in what jaws you were to suppurate:
> You may have thought things would come right again
> If you could only keep quite still and wait. (100)

There is much that the rabbit cannot understand during its last hot hours: its disease, the trap, the nature of life. And like the rabbit, Larkin—throughout his poetry—finds much of what goes on around him inexplicable. He often professes bafflement at the scene in which he finds himself as he generates a poem and frequently admits his incomprehension forthrightly, a stunning concession for a poet: "I can't explain." (A poem is *supposed* to explain; the poet's comprehension of the subject would seem to be a prerequisite for *poesis*, the imposition of aesthetic order.) Not only does Larkin acknowledge his inability to explain, but he revels in it—"I'm *glad*..."—associating himself closely with the rabbit (perversely, given the rabbit's lot) in his ignorance of the world's complexities. Why does Larkin want to be allied with this rabbit, or the stinted birds in "Pigeons"? Is it just a depraved, self-pitying association with unlucky animals? Or is he somehow working to discover a kindred animal spirit in the mold of animal souls?

In "Myxomatosis," the speaker kills the animal—presumably to put it out of its pain and perhaps also from a sense of identification with the rabbit. I can imagine Larkin as being almost jealous of the animal who is fortunate enough to have someone to end its life; would that there was someone to repay the favor and—being certain (as the suffering subject himself is not) that the dismal status quo will only worsen—act decisively to end his own pain. As the speaker plays God to the rabbit, he must perceive the absence of any comparable force of guidance and fate in his own life. He kills the animal with a silly, uncomfortable pun—"I make a sharp reply"—poetically accentuating the awkwardness. Continuing in his omnipotent and omniscient role, the speaker suggests to the rabbit, posthumously, that its optimism was naive. Larkin struggles with a delusion similar to what the rabbit experienced, the hope that things might eventually come right again, throughout his poetry. Many of his poems end with a resolution, in one form or another, to "keep quite still and wait"—to bide one's time, in the hope that the immediate pain will pass; but Larkin seems to know that this is an unlikely fantasy. The pain won't dissipate, and this poem acknowledges the falsity of any pretense that it might. As "Pigeons" signifies an autobiographical breakthrough, "Myxomatosis" presents an entelechy in Larkin's philosophical understanding of the world: an acceptance of the ultimate eventuality of defeat, the inevitability of incomprehensible and terrible suffering.

In the rabbit's pain Larkin tries to see his own, and this is a striking approximation of co-essence. The second-person voice is unusual in animal poetry: poets rarely address animals explicitly because that would suggest an equality between poet and subject that the Parnassian denizens are loathe to admit. Larkin, however, establishes an evenhanded relationship between himself and the rabbit with the second-person pronoun ("you") indicating dialogue between the poem's two characters, man and rabbit. Larkin also allows the rabbit to speak, in italics, in its own voice: he makes the rabbit, for a line (of iambic pentameter, no less!), a poet like himself, or at least he conjectures ("... You *seem* to ask") what the rabbit's poetry would sound like. The mode of poetry, thus, serves as a meeting place, a common ground, for the poet and the animal.

Like "Pigeons," "Myxomatosis" is predicated upon a keen sense of connection—emotional, intellectual, physiological, eschatological. The speaker (whom I associate absolutely with the poet) and the rabbit are kindred spirits as they navigate the difficulties and the unknowns in their lives. The awkward titular term, starkly unpoetic, is, in a sense, the poet's answer to the rabbit's query (what trap was this?), but it's not really an answer, any more than "lowered T-cell count" *explains* why a person dies of AIDS. Myxomatosis is just scientific jargon to both Larkin and the rabbit. It is the poem's burden to grapple with life, and death, and the necessity of suffering, and the ironies of suffering. The rabbit, meant to die of the ironic disease (in that it was deliberately introduced), instead dies of the trap—or really, dies from the stick (that "saved" the rabbit from the trap, that "saved" it from the tumors) wielded by the man who, ironically, sympathetically understands and connects with the rabbit more than either creature has done with any other creature. Despite this connection, the poem nevertheless resonates with loss, pain, grief, betrayal, incomprehension. The association between people and animals as characterized by animal souls is by no means prone to be nurturing or pretty: it is intense and real, and it exists at the highest level of our emotional registers. It is just as likely, if not more so, to find an outlet in our lives amid moments of pain as it is amid moments of pleasant existence. While "Myxomatosis" is in no way an uplifting poem, nevertheless it is an important expression of how a person and an animal may conceive of their relationship to each other, and it is a remarkably clear, definite expression of this amid all the uncertainties and distress that surround the moment of the poem.

Two more of Larkin's poems deal with suffering animals—animals harmed by human actions, whose experiences (like the disease, the trap, and the sharp stick in "Myxomatosis") Larkin probably believes must be incomprehensible to the animals. "Ape Experiment Room" depicts an animal condemned to the indignities of scientific inquiry:

Buried among white rooms
Whose lights in clusters beam
Like suddenly-caused pain,
And where behind rows of mesh
Uneasy shifting resumes
As sterilisers steam
And the routine begins again
Of putting questions to flesh

That no one would think to ask
But a Ph.D. with a beard
And nympho wife who—

But

There, I was saying, are found
The bushy, T-shaped mask,
And below, the smaller, eared
Head like a grave nut,
And the arms folded round. (160)

While the poem is not quite an explicit animal-rights screed against scientific research on animals, still, it broaches the issues that a more activist polemic might address. The nuances of pain that nonhuman laboratory subjects suffer are present if not blatant—suggestively metaphorical: "... *Like* suddenly-caused pain." Larkin colors the scene with an uneasy atmosphere of insouciant sadism, as *questions* (not as literally violent as wires or scalpels, but still obviously assaultive) are put to flesh. The poem is all the more insidious for its muted evocations of what people do to animals. Larkin certainly aligns himself here, even if in an understated fashion, with the spirit of animal rights protest and exposé by detailing the tableau of torture: the relentlessly bright lights; the mesh cage of constraint; the sinister resonances of the steaming sterilisers and the "buried" laboratory setting, evoking death; and the elusively, politely brutal moment highlighted at the end of the stanza when the scientist puts questions to flesh.

The second stanza briefly raises an ethical dimension: who has thought to ask these questions—that is, to torture this ape? Why is this being done? A sketch of the torturer commences with a few skimpy character details, and then cuts off abruptly in a moment of (feigned) embarrassment, at the mention of a nympho wife. The poem protects a facade of human honor: we don't want to inquire too closely into the lives of the scientists, or puncture their intellectual respectability by imputing to them (or even their wives) such base drives as sexuality and nymphomania. Of course, even as the conspicuous dash halts the poem's exposition at that barrier, it simultaneously incites conjecture about what's beneath the facade. It's too late to put the cat back in the bag, and the bearded Ph.D. can never restore his dignity, or the fantasy of impersonal, detached scientific inquiry. If we kept digging (and of course we do, in our own extratextual extrapolations), what else would we find out about the motivations, the inner psyche of this scientist whose academic pedigree authorizes him to inflict pain on apes? As Larkin's dash asks the reader to turn away from examining human foibles too closely, we are also cajoled into abandoning an ethical investigation of what is going on in this experiment room (and thousands of others)—to fall back into a docile, unchallenging mode: Don't pry; don't ask questions. (But the canny reader will pursue the ethical question nonetheless, with the same lurid enthusiasm we bring to the salacious hint of the nympho wife.)

The final stanza presents the moment of co-essentiality, and, once again, as in "Pigeons" and "Myxomatosis," it links the murky anguish of people and animals. The ambiguous last image is a conundrum: to whom does the description refer? Who is wearing the bushy mask? It could be either the bearded Ph.D. or the ape. And in that ambiguity,

Larkin suggests that they are interchangeable. The torturer may suffer as much as the one he tortures: perhaps because he understands deep down the pain that his scientific investigation causes, and is tormented by a sublimated awareness of what he is doing. Perhaps he suffers, as Freud suggests in *Civilization and Its Discontents*, from the awareness of an artificially elevated sense of humanity, and the closeness of his experience with the animal in the buried white room (a womb image possibly: imagine the two creatures as twins) reminds him of his *hamartia*, his failure to empathize with his fellow creatures, his ethical dereliction. If the Ph.D. is the one with the bushy mask, then the image might be of a man with his arms folded in a stereotypical gesture of erudite scientific contemplation. If the stanza portrays the ape, then s/he might be cradling him/herself, as in a fetal position for self-protection against the scientist's incursions.

And if it is intentionally ambiguous, then that final image might be simultaneously ominous and sympathetic—indeed, there could be four arms folded together here instead of two. The scientist might be squeezing the ape, to restrain him, or, perhaps, holding tightly to the body of an anesthetized ape as he drags the animal over to the table where he will put questions to flesh. Alternately, a four-armed embrace might be somehow genuine, an acknowledgement of affiliation and connection. We don't know because, again, the whole scene is indeterminate (and willfully so: a consequence of looking away, failing to confront the situation head-on, as epitomized by the break-off at the nympho wife). There is a range of things that we might possibly be seeing here, a man or an ape (and remember there is minimal difference between the two, genetically and evolutionarily), or both, in a stance of aggression or compassion, or both. This continuum enables the potentiality—though not the certainty—for a connection of animal souls.

The human's and the animal's fate, here in this buried mesh-caged tableau, are inextricably linked; and the human suffers because/as the animal suffers. "But / There, I was saying, are found..." What *are* found there? A man and an ape in a bad place, resonating with pain. To deconstruct this place and this pain, and work to ameliorate it, we must realize that the two creatures are in this together: the ape who has been anthropocentrically construed as a guinea pig and the man operating the sterilisers who has been socio-intellectually construed as an experimenter, an inflicter of sudden pain. The Mesoamerican sense of interconnectedness, of shared fate, is the only way to transcend the division and opposition that have been enacted in this experiment room. The two animals in the final stanza look more than a little like each other, because they are. As Mesoamericans express via *nagualismo* and *tonalismo*, people and animals are interconnected.

Larkin's poem "The Mower" invokes the tradition of Andrew Marvell's "mower" poems, especially "The Mower Against Gardens," about human attempts to trim and control God's nature; the effort at domesticating and controlling natural beauty that Marvell's mower attempts is impotent, if not blasphemous. In Larkin's poem, the title describes a modern, mechanized version of Marvell's implement, which does correspondingly increased damage to nature, specifically to an animal:

> The mower stalled, twice; kneeling, I found
> A hedgehog jammed up against the blades,
> Killed. It had been in the long grass.
>
> I had seen it before, and even fed it, once.
> Now I had mauled its unobtrusive world
> Unmendably. Burial was no help:
>
> Next morning I got up and it did not.
> The first day after a death, the new absence
> Is always the same; we should be careful
>
> Of each other, we should be kind
> While there is still time. (214)

Without tendering any excuses, Larkin acknowledges the damage people may cause to the habitats and lives of animals with our large (compared to hedgehogs) and oblivious ways. People are powerless—enjambment highlights the word "Unmendably"—to rectify the damage we do. A neat construction of parallelism, or rather, disjointed, ironized parallelism ("Next morning I got up and it did not") reflects the disjunction of the killer and the killed. Ideally, absent the poem's violence, there *should have been* a parallel life-course here. The phrase recalls Stevie Smith's expression in "Death Bereaves our Common Mother, Nature Grieves for my Dead Brother": "Lamb dead, dead lamb, / He was, I am"— depicting parallelism between the lives of the person and the animal, except for the "separation by a tense" that derails the correspondence. Language, grammar, and poetic contrast comprise the discourse that Smith and Larkin use to express the relationship between people and animals. As a spiritual system uses prayer, faith, ritual, or exemplary ethical narratives to express its vision, we see how poets use their own poetic tools to do the same.

What is striking in "The Mower" is Larkin's sense of mourning for an event that most people in these circumstances would consider the accidental death of a trivial, expendable, irrelevant animal who got in the way of our human processes, the mowing and shaping of nature. Larkin's sense of lament leads to, at the end of the poem, a moral, "We should be careful of each other," which is an exact analog to the motivating spirit at the core of animal souls. We should be kind, Larkin continues, while there is still time. This sentiment reflects an ecological consciousness (not much time remains before we have mown down all the nature and animals in the world), as well as an eschatological one (there's not much time before our mortal hourglasses run out of sand, as the hedgehog's has already done).

The speaker's awareness of intertwined fates, and of mortality, results in a basic, obvious lesson: it is better not to mow down our co-essences—better to be kind. This is what one learns when one really attends to animals: feeding or otherwise caring for them now and then, and accounting their lives, and deaths, as meaningful. Larkin's attention to the dead hedgehog in "The Mower" typifies his rare attunement to animals. I have no explanation for why Larkin should have been so sensitively conscious of pigeons and hedgehogs and rabbits, and of how people relate to them. His poetic engagements with animals, and the valuable insights he seems to reap in the course of this interaction, seem an unexpected facet of a poet generally acknowledged as misogynistic, racist, and rude, whose most prominent legacy to twentieth-century poetry is probably consecrating the high poetic use of the f-word (along with a few other bon mots of similar ilk). Animals provide convenient poetic constructs, and Larkin was a master poet, always on the lookout for aesthetic devices and vehicles. But I cannot believe that Larkin's poetic animals were only fodder for his work. Something lurking in his treatment of these animals suggests a perspective that contributes importantly to the enterprise of envisioning and expressing human–animal relationships. Larkin's poetic animals show that we may find riches in the most unlikely places.

Gary Snyder

It would be hard to imagine a contemporary poet more different from Philip Larkin than Gary Snyder. Antithetical to Larkin's self-obsessed modernist neuroses, Snyder's poetry exudes the harmony and serenity of Zen (which he has studied extensively). Earthy, laid-back, and filled with worshipful homage to natural entities and schemas, Snyder conveys a refreshing faith in the biosystem. His poems are full of landscapes and animals, and even when some other immediate subject claims Snyder's attention, every poem is still conspicuously set in a world filled mainly with plants and birds and oceans—a world in which nature's immensity and dignity dwarf the artifacts of contemporary civilization. The title of a recent volume by Snyder, a long journal poem called *Mountains and Rivers Without End*, epitomizes his sense of nature's infinitude.

"What Happened Here Before" typifies Snyder's attention to the weight of nonhuman life: the resonances and the richness in the many layers of nature overshadow the relative novelty of human culture. At the top of each stanza, subtitles count off our planet's chronological history. In "300,000,000," Snyder describes the sea and the sands, the molten magma, crushing, lifting, submerging; in "80,000,000," "warm quiet centuries of rains" wear down two miles of granite to gravel and lay bare the veins of gold within. Three million years ago, "deer, coyote, bluejay, gray squirrel, / ground squirrel, fox, blacktail hare, / ringtail, bobcat, bear, / all came to live here" (78–9). Snyder goes on to characterize the earth 40,000 years ago, then 125 years ago and finally, "*now.*" One of the final images—"military jets head northeast, roaring, every dawn" (80)—portrays "now" as a time of powerful violence, disrupting the dawn's quiet natural peace. But then the poem's final line trumps the jet with another noise, an animal sound, that also breaks through the air: "Bluejay screeches from a pine" (81). Snyder's poetry reaches back, beyond the intrusions of human civilization, to uncover a larger picture. "Now" may blaspheme nature's sanctity, but Snyder's perspective transcends the immediate outrage of contemporaneity with the age-old sounds and energies of the animals who were here millions of years before the military jets. Presences like this bluejay's are not displaced by civilization, but endure at the center of Snyder's poetry. "What Happened Here Before" conceives nature as diametrically opposed to the conventional inscription propounded in Genesis, where natural habitats and animals function merely as a backdrop, and the quick, condensed narrative of their creation is just an opening act for the main plot starring Adam and Eve.

Snyder depicts animals, sometimes, suffering amid the forces of human encroachment and destruction; but his poetic animals more commonly appear as they prospered before people started boxing ourselves in and relegating animals to the outskirts of human culture. Snyder sees animals through, and beyond, and despite, our cultural maskings of them. "Raised in the Pacific Northwest, Snyder grew up close to the anthropomorphic richness of the local Native American mythology," writes Trevor Carolan, "the rainforest totems of eagle, bear, raven, and killer whale that continue to appear in school and community insignias as important elements of regional consciousness. It is unsurprising that they—and roustabout cousins like Coyote—have long been found at the core of Snyder's expansive vision."

"Coyote Valley Spring," a simple, quiet poem, typifies Snyder's vision of nature. It equates roughly to what "Pigeons" represented for Philip Larkin: a tableau in which the poet inscribes his consciousness; a place chosen by the poet as most amenable, most suitable for the aura of his voice.

> Cubs
> tumble in the damp leaves
> Deer, bear, squirrel.
> fresh winds scour the
> spring stars.
> rocks crumble
> deep mud hardens
> under heavy hills.
>
> shifting things
> birds, weeds,
> slip through the air
> through eyes and ears,
>
> Coyote Valley. *Olema*
> in the spring.
> white and solemn toloache flower
>
> and far out in the *tamal*
> a lost people
> float
>
> in tiny tule boats. (15)

To begin with, there are simply lots of animals here; this poem, like the world of Snyder's poetry as a whole, is prominently populated with animals. At the end there are people, too, but they are remote and do not very greatly affect the poem's mood. These people enter into this poem in terms of their relation to animals, their distance from animals; their presence in the poem's landscape is defined by reference to animals. Like Marianne Moore, Snyder populates his poetry with a rich animal presence simply by naming them and watching them for a while, gently, quietly, without disturbing them. The animals are set in their habitat, amid nature, illustrating the kindest things people can do to animals: leave them where they are, let them be, let them live; watch as they tumble and shift, and resist the temptation to acculturate them, to bring them somehow into the world of human civilization. The simple words that Snyder uses to connote nature—winds, stars, rocks, mud, hills—are inversely related to the splendor of what they signify, just as the poem's pedestrian catalog of animals—deer, bear, squirrel—barely broaches the magnificence of the creatures so named. A few less common details hint at the deeper intricacies of the poet's engagement with nature: toloache, a large, funnel-shaped flower considered sacred to some indigenous groups, with medicinal as well as hallucinogenic properties; tule, a large bulrush that grows in marshes. But the whole vision begins with and is comprised mainly of animals, portrayed with uncomplicated images and language—the most basic and eloquent tribute Snyder pays them.

Coyote Valley in Marin County, California, just south of San Jose, is in the process of becoming overrun by Silicon Valley development, which will, of course, obliterate most of its habitats and animals. (In "The Diary of Adam and Eve," Mark Twain wrote: "I have been off hunting and fishing a month, up in the region that [Eve] calls Buffalo. I don't know why, unless it is because there are not any buffaloes there" [58]. A latter-day incarnation of Twain might look out over Coyote Valley and observe, "I don't know why it's called that, unless it is because there are no coyotes there.") But before the most recent surge in Coyote Valley's human development, when Snyder wrote the poem in the 1970s, the animal place name that he chose for the title was meant to complement the prominence of animals in this poem: Snyder seems drawn to places that are named for animals. Olema, a nearby city, is also an animal-derived place name, and also taken from the word for coyote, òla, in the language of the Coast Miwok Indians who came from the region. Coyotes are thus twice inscribed in this poem, in two different languages, emphasizing their presence in—and even, Snyder suggests, their primary claim to—the land. The Tamal are another Indian tribe that once inhabited the Pacific coast. The only people in "Coyote Valley Spring" are from long ago—people who were less voracious inhabitants of the region than the current-day population. After watching animals for a while, Snyder reaches toward the *tamal* (again, as with Coyote Valley, naming the land for those who have long inhabited it). Why are the lost people from the past situated "far off?" What is the animals' connection to the Tamal? Are they lost because they're not here, with Snyder and his readers, watching the animals? Or because the indigenous human population has become lost, adrift, amid the transformed habitat? One senses a hope on Snyder's part that the lost people might somehow find themselves, and come back—which they might do by coming to the world of the poem. "Coyote Valley Spring" depicts what is primarily an animals' world—as it was thousands and millions of years ago—and people have "lost" this sensibility; Snyder tries here to return people to it. The foreground, as Snyder sees it, is animal-centered. If people want to get into this poem, and get back into the world, they need to paddle their tule boats through nature, to nature—back to nature, to where these animals will be waiting.

Another conspicuous animal-place name is Turtle Island, the title of Snyder's Pulitzer Prize winning volume of poetry (and the book that contains all the poems of his that I discuss here). An introductory note explains:

> Turtle Island—the old/new name for the continent, based on many creation myths of the people who have been living here for millennia, and reapplied by some of them to "North America" in recent years. Also, an idea found world-wide, of the earth, or cosmos even, sustained by a great turtle or serpent-of-eternity.
>
> A name: that we may see ourselves more accurately on this continent of watersheds and life-communities—plant zones, physiographic provinces, culture areas; following natural boundaries.

Calling the continent by a name that refers to an animal instead of an imperialist Italian cartographer signifies a vision of the land that connects people directly to its majority inhabitants: turtles, coyotes *et al.* Snyder strips away human accretions in his poetry: the very words and names he uses reach back to "what happened here before." More convincingly than "North America," "Turtle Island" invokes a world where people and animals are interrelated and share common habitats—all very much part of the same ecosystem. All living creatures can best prosper on Turtle Island by acknowledging and affirming each other—this is Snyder's version of animal souls. "Man is but a part of the fabric of life," he writes in a prose section following the poems in *Turtle Island*; "As the most highly developed tool-using animal, he must recognize that the unknown evolutionary destinies of other life forms are to be respected, and act as gentle steward of the earth's community of being" (91). Our fates are interconnected in this community. Snyder promotes the Buddhist belief of "respect for all life, and for wild systems. Man's life is totally dependent on an interpenetrating network of wild systems" (104). He notes approvingly how in some Native American societies "a kind of ultimate democracy is practiced. Plants and animals are also people, and, through certain rituals and dances, are given a place and a voice in the political discussions of the humans. They are 'represented' " (104). We must find a way to "incorporate the other people—what the Sioux Indians called the creeping people, and the standing people, and the flying people, and the swimming people—into the councils of government" (108). This conception of the parity of human and nonhuman life resonates with the essence of Mesoamerican spirituality. The failure of our civilization, Snyder writes, is the mistaken belief that nature is not as alive as man is, or as intelligent, that in a sense it is dead, and "that animals are of so low an order of intelligence and feeling, we need not take their feelings into account" (107).

Snyder clearly has a strong, idealistic confidence, like Mesoamericans, in the potential for and the necessity of intimate relationships between people and animals. But he also exhibits, like Pacheco and Moore, a pragmatic consciousness: an awareness of the disappointing reality of how we live our lives with respect to animals. Interestingly, even as he relates the failure to affirm animal souls, he still thinks in the terms of animal souls. "The Call of the Wild," for example, tells of how people perceive an animal, a coyote, in our world. People neglect the beauty in the coyote's song; an old man who hears the coyote howl "will call the Government / Trapper / Who uses iron leg-traps on Coyotes . . . And the Coyote singing / is shut away / for they fear / the call / of the wild" (21–2). Snyder yokes together America's Vietnam-era proclivity to global aggression and its home-front environmental negligence, finding them mutually symptomatic of a society blind to animals' sublimity. A society that practices political and ecological violence will also ignore animal souls. Americans are

> Dumping poisons and explosives
> Across Asia first,
> And next North America,
>
> A war against earth.
> When it's done there'll be
>   no place
>
> A Coyote could hide.
>
>   *envoy*
>
>   I would like to say
>
>   Coyote is forever
>   Inside you.
>   But it's not true. (23)

The last three words are Snyder's deflationary rebuke to our culture, his announcement of our failure. But balanced against this is his animal soul idealism—"I would like to say . . ." Even if it's not true, still, he would like to say "Coyote is forever / Inside you" (and, of course, he *does* actually say it, even if mitigated by the subjunctive tense).

Snyder presents, in three lines, the essence of animal souls, and then undercuts this in the poem's final line with the realistic revelation that we cannot lay claim to such a condition of co-essence with Coyote. Like many other progenitors of poetic animals, Snyder here approaches animal souls in the negative condition: he extols the value of such a sensibility in the same breath that he bemoans our distance from it.

Throughout his poetry, Snyder depicts animals' existence across a wide continuum. Animals are sometimes imbued with a transcendent spiritual potency, but at other times they suffer miserably. Two of his poems (discussed in chapter 2) illustrate these extremes: "Prayer for the Great Family," enacts a devout religious affirmation of animal spirits, while "Mother Earth: Her Whales," recounts the profound ecological abuse that afflicts animals. If the animals are so powerful and spiritual, as depicted in "Prayer for the Great Family," then how could they possibly suffer so desperately in the sea of methyl mercury, as they do in "Mother Earth: Her Whales?" Shouldn't they be able to transcend their toxic fate? Wouldn't every person recognize their sanctity, as Snyder does, and work to preserve instead of desecrate their habitats? The answer to both questions, obviously, is no: and it is in the warp of the resulting cognitive dissonance that Snyder situates much of his poetry. The animal soul power, while apparent to him, eludes most of his fellow citizens, and so he depicts the ways in which animals suffer our ignorance of their co-essentiality. And why can't the animals on their own—even in light of people's failure to recognize en masse their spiritual force—rise above the morass? Because "co-essentiality" fundamentally requires that both sides sign on; otherwise, it is the equivalent of one hand clapping.

A paradoxical, sacred-and-profane representation of animals colors "The Hudsonian Curlew," which describes both the beautiful power of the titular birds and the process of hunting and eating them. It resembles Larkin's "Myxomatosis" and "The Mower," which are about animals killed by the speaker, who then stands over their corpses and transmutes their demise into verse. The relationship between the animal-killer and the dead animal, while it would seem to be an inauspicious starting point for discovering animals souls, nevertheless evinces resonant connections. As Larkin's poems demonstrate, death need not necessarily negate poetic co-essentiality, any more than deaths of animals or other people in the real world negate our connections with them. Death only transforms the relationship from the realm of immediate, literal presence to that of memory, or history, or spirituality. Indeed, a spiritual relationship with a (once-)living creature could actually flourish more fully postmortem: with only metaphysical tropes to draw upon, one might embrace a spiritual relationship all the more fiercely.

At the opening of "The Hudsonian Curlew," Snyder depicts what he calls "the Mandala of Birds." ("An ecosystem resembles a mandala," Snyder has explained [Carolan]; "A big Tibetan mandala has many small figures as well as central figures, and each of them has a key role in the picture: they're all essential.") The Mandala is comprised of

> pelicans, seagulls, and terns,
> one curlew
> far at the end—
> they fly up as they see us
> and settle back down.
> tern keep coming
> —skies of wide seas—
> frigate birds keep swooping
>
> pelicans sit nearest the foam;
>
> tern bathing and fluttering
> in frothy wave-lapping
> between the round stones. (54)

Snyder's detailed observation is beautiful, elegant, simple, as he pays poetic homage just by letting the birds be birds—flying, swooping. It seems to embody quintessentially what Deleuze and Guattari call lines of flight to becoming-animal (see chapter 1). People are in this tableau, minimally, as the birds fly up and then settle down again in response to "us," but the human presence is only marginally significant here. That soon changes, however:

> Three shotgun shots as it gets dark;
> two birds.
> "*how come three shots?*"
> "*one went down on the water*
> *and started to swim. . . .*" (55)

Snyder proceeds to describe the harvesting of the birds with a poetic delicacy that may upset some animal lovers who would see this scene as inherently brutal and violent, and would expect that the murder would derail the tenor of aesthetic loveliness; perhaps perversely, it hasn't:

> The down
> i pluck from the

neck of the curlew
eddies and whirls at my knees
in the twilight wind
from sea.
kneeling in sand
warm in the hand. (55)

Snyder explains his views on hunting in the prose section of *Turtle Island*: "Don't shoot a deer if you don't know how to use all the meat and preserve that which you can't eat, to tan the hide and use the leather—to use it all, with gratitude, right down to the sinew and hooves" (98). But if one does know how to use all the parts of an animal, gratefully, then presumably Snyder approves of hunting, and "The Hudsonian Curlew" describes a hunter who knows what he's doing.

"*Do you want to do it right? I'll tell you.*"
he tells me.
at the edge of the water on the stones.
a transverse cut just below the sternum
the forefinger and middle finger
        forced in and up, following the
        curve of the rib cage.
then fingers arched, drawn slowly down and back,
forcing all the insides up and out,
toward the palm and heel of the hand.
firm organs, well-placed, hot.
save the liver;
finally scouring back, toward the vent, the last of the
        large intestine.
the insides string out, begin to wave, in the lapping
        waters of the bay.
the bird has no feathers, head, or feet;
        he is empty inside.
the rich body muscle that he moved by, the wing-beating
        muscle
anchored to the blade-like high breast bone,
is what you eat. (56)

The description of the dead bird—the body parts, the geography of the corpse, the energy that the poet sees in the carcass—is unchanged in style or voice from the representation of living birds at the poem's opening. Perhaps there's something beautiful and spiritual about this, but also, something unsettling. Hunters often defend hunting against animal-rights opposition by claiming that what they do is simply a more honest version of what most other people (who eat meat that has been killed and culturally neutralized by "invisible" processors) do, and that they are more prone than non-hunters to have a working awareness of the ethical relationship between people and animals.

People kill animals in various ways, all the time. Larkin writes powerfully about two he killed, accidentally or impulsively, raising potent philosophical and spiritual issues about life and death and human–animal relationships. Snyder addresses these issues head-on, even more intentionally than Larkin, hunting down the animals and then handling them intimately as he strips and dismembers their carcasses. While I, personally, would never do what Snyder's speaker here is doing, I think the expression nonetheless embodies a deep, nuanced, sincere way of connecting with an animal, even an animal that he has slaughtered. I don't think people should slaughter animals or should glamorize the act of slaughter (which this poem does). But "The Hudsonian Curlew" movingly explores the meaning and ramifications of that act on the deepest terms, and in ways that are not unrelated to animal souls.

The poem's two final sections describe, first, the cooking of the curlew, with unapologetic sensory and gustatory richness; and then, at the end, a vision of the curlews alive. The birds are perhaps reincarnated, in some sense, or have otherwise transcended the fate they earlier met at the hands of the hunter. Or, more likely, they are simply different birds that Snyder sees at the end, curlews who have not (yet) been slain by hunters. In any case, the poem affirms that even amid the death that characterizes the human–animal, hunter–curlew relationship here, there is also life: there is *finally* life.

> at dawn
> looking out from the dunes
> no birds at all but
> three curlew
>
> *ker-lew!*
>
> *ker-lew!*
>
> pacing and glancing around. (57)

People may kill the birds, but still they endure. At the end, they voice their name—the name by which we know them—asserting, as in Snyder's animal-place name poems, their profound claim on our consciousness. They exist all around us, and they will not be dispossessed, whatever we try to do to them. With regard to the basic philosophical question that I believe is in Snyder's mind and that is certainly in my mind—whether hunting is ethically defensible—I'm not sure what this poem has to say: probably, it says yes, and I disagree. But on another level the poem speaks about animals and people and our coexistence, and on that plane, it explores why and how we try to kill animals, and how they survive and sing themselves at dawn: at a time when most people (although not hunters) are asleep and birds have pretty much free run of the world. The animals' transcendence emanates from their powers: the swooping and fluttering shown at the beginning of the poem and the power of the "rich body muscle," enabling the fantastic power of flight, described in the dissection scene. Plucking the feathers, stripping back the intestines, stringing out the insides is a way, albeit macabre, of getting to know the animal: touching, connecting. This is finally what Snyder demands in his poetry: that we understand how we're connected to the animals, to *an* animal, even if it's one that we've killed.

Seamus Heaney

Again and again in Seamus Heaney's animal poems, the poet comes close to animals, resulting in at least a momentary epiphany, and then runs away: back into his own very civilized and politicized world, where animals are incidental. Heaney's poetic animals evince an appreciation of intimacies between people and animals, but also a hesitancy about actualizing the relationship. The encounter with animals is in some sense a kind of "excursion," as characterized by John Tallmadge (see chapter 1); perhaps Heaney values these experiences because they are a brief respite from the Irish Troubles that haunt his poetry. Heaney's flights away from animals may reflect an intentional decision to leave them alone despite their compelling power. Perhaps he feels unfit to enter into a sacrament with animals due to the fallen nature of humanity, as typified by the civil discord that surrounds him. Heaney may envision poetic interaction with animals as an unaffordable luxury in times of interminable conflict: people have to figure out how to live with each other before they can contemplate living with animals. But his hesitancy does not diminish, in my estimation, the sincerity or intensity of his connection with animals. If Heaney perceives the sanctity of animals and is less confident than Snyder about people's ability to tap into this, still, valuably, he knows it's there and points us toward this spiritual presence, even if he looks away at the last minute.

A moment in the *Squarings* sequence, poem xxv, epitomizes how Heaney sees-and-flees animals:

> Travelling south at dawn, going full out
> Through high-up stone-wall country, the rocks still cold,
> Rain water gleaming here and there ahead,
>
> I took a turn and met the fox stock-still,
> Face-to-face in the middle of the road.

The meeting is accidental, surprising. The encounter is, as in Mesoamerican spirituality, face-to-face: close, direct, and on equal terms. Without belaboring the obvious, I want to emphasize Heaney's poetic arrangement in this image: a fox has a face and a man has a face, and this way of characterizing their meeting highlights the momentary establishment of a common ground between the two creatures as opposed to the many grounds of difference that exist. In Heaney's simple, straightforward language of description, "Face-to-face" encapsulates the essence of *tonalismo*. And then comes the immediate separation. Usually in Heaney's poetry it is the person who first retreats, though here the fox initiates the departure, leaving the speaker to imitate the animal's flight soon afterwards in his car:

> Wildness tore through me as he dipped and wheeled
>
> In a level-running tawny breakaway.
> O neat head, fabled brush and astonished eye
> My blue Volkswagen flared into with morning! (79)

The encounter, however fleeting, is potent: "Wildness tore through me..." Heaney nurtures and savors the energy of the face-to-face contact: for a moment, the animal spirit, "wildness," inhabits the poet's soul—and not just inhabits, but tears through: rending, overwhelming. There is an instant of at least figurative *nagualismo*, the transformation of a person's soul into an animal's. And the poem retains little fragments of marvel from the encounter—images of the fox's head, brush, and eye seem imprinted upon the poet's consciousness—as man and fox "breakaway," dashing off back to their own worlds. But while some sense of the human–animal connection resonates here, the poem is more concerned with a *lost* connection with animals. Jonathan Bate writes that in *Squarings* Heaney "revisits Glanmore, the farm of his childhood, but he never fully gets back to nature. He... remains warily on guard as he crisscrosses between culture and nature" (202–3). In poem xxv, "at the heart of the poem the speaker is entered by 'wildness' but cannot return to the wild because he is contained within his car" (203). Yet even if the connection with animals is never fully consummated, still, I would not want to characterize this as a failure: more optimistically, it is a brief scenting of potential connection. The poet realizes the reality, the necessity, that the two animals remain in their separate spheres, which are largely mutually exclusive. But we may be grateful for even a moment of wildness tearing through; certainly, as the poem testifies, the speaker is affected greatly by this. And a moment, albeit only a brief moment, of animal souls connection is documented and sustained in the artifact of the poem, which endures in time even if the occasion itself dissipates.

Heaney's poems sometimes express a fear of animals—of the shocking sensations we may receive if we get too close. We may learn as children to be afraid of sounds, textures, smells that are unfamiliar; especially the more "civilized" our upbringing has been, people may feel threatened by many of the things that happen naturally around animals. The scary sound of the blunt farts and the feel of the slimy frogspawn in Heaney's "Death of a Naturalist" (see chapter 1) typify this reaction, and another work that depicts the animals' world as perilous and menacing to conventional human sensibilities is his prose poem "Nesting-Ground."

> The sandmartins' nests were loopholes of darkness in the riverbank. He could imagine his arm going in to the armpit, sleeved and straitened, but because he once felt the cold prick of a dead robin's claw and the surprising density of its tiny beak he only gazed.
>
> He heard cheeping far in but because the men had once shown him a rat's nest in the butt of a stack where chaff and powdered cornstalks adhered to the moist pink necks and backs he only listened.
>
> As he stood sentry, gazing, waiting, he thought of putting his ear to one of the abandoned holes and listening for the silence under the ground. (53)

The nesting-ground is *their world*, and hence, in Heaney's poetic, not the person's. Probably the prevalence of local combat in Ireland has hardened in Heaney a sense of the impermeability of boundaries. The speaker approaches nature with a demeanor characterized by poetry (where nests are "loopholes of darkness") and imaginative interaction with the birds in the nesting-ground ("He could imagine his arm going in . . ."). But previous experience, colored by fear of nature, arrests the poetic/imaginative impulse and prevents the human character from crossing the border into the nesting-ground. He "only gazed," and, in the encounter described in the next paragraph, he "only listened." I am fairly certain that Heaney's use of the modifier "only" is ironic: Throughout his oeuvre, Heaney *only* looks and *only* listens, and then *only* produces what is arguably the best English-language poetry of our generation. Heaney describes in "Nesting-Ground" how he has come to the aesthetic of distanced, detached watching, and it is an aesthetic that may facilitate a valuable relationship with animals. A sort of fear of animals leads the speaker to observe them rather than touch, disturb, mangle their habitats; this trepidation prevents him from encroaching onto their side of the boundary.

In *Every Creeping Thing: True Tales of Faintly Repulsive Wildlife*, Richard Conniff writes that "nature scares a lot of us silly," and admits his "gut feeling that fear of nature is normal—more normal, certainly, than the love of it. Or perhaps I should say that fear and love are thoroughly tangled together" (7). Conniff believes that "the fear of nature is not only normal; it can also be pleasurable" and that the horrifying aspects of nature can ensure that we "keep a respectful distance"; cool scientific attitudes toward aspects of the wild that instinctually strike us as fearful or a Romantic benevolence toward nature testify to a "wilderness [that] has been subdued" and "our urbanized distance from it" (8–9), he writes. Fear is generally conceived as emotional rather than intellectual, and as an irrelevance or distraction in the quest for rational enlightenment; it is not viewed as a useful element of an epistemology, but perhaps, as Conniff suggests, it should be. Fear is perceived as a weakness and therefore suppressed; but we might reexamine our received ideas, and embrace a sensibility that more honestly reflects the world—which would acknowledge that some aspects of it are fearful—rather than constructing epistemolgies predicated upon reassuring our sense of safety and omnipowerful supremacy.

Fear, though, doesn't fully explain the emotion that Heaney feels around animals. We may experience simple fear concerning possible physical dangers—a wasp sting or a snakebite, for example—or unusual sensory experiences as we come close to animals. But also in the mix is a sense of awe and confused wonderment at the lives and motions of animals as we see them in a way that we rarely do: up close and personal, face to face. The fear Heaney invokes is not unlike the sense of fear that infuses conventional conceptions of a divinity, whether mythological or theological—a God whose power we fear, even if we do not fully understand it, indeed, largely because we *cannot* understand it. A comparable emotion, I believe, surfaces as Heaney looks at animals.

In "The Badgers," the speaker describes his encounter with an animal as faint, somewhat supernatural or metaphysical, conducted at least as much in the realm of the imagination as in concrete reality. The effect is to evoke the animal's aura and the speaker's reluctance to come too close to it; a closer approach might puncture the poetic sense of an enchanted animal by dragging it down to the realm of literal observation:

> When the badger glimmered away
> into another garden
> you stood, half-lit with whiskey,
> sensing you had disturbed
> some soft returning.
>
> The murdered dead,
> you thought. (119)

The person watching the animal is a little tipsy, and the badger's motion is fuzzily described as glimmering. Such atmospheric characterizations that surround Heaney's animals accentuate their ethereal otherworldliness, their resistance to being pegged, pinned, literally (or figuratively) *captured*, by the poet or anyone else. Evoking *nagualismo*, Heaney wonders if the animal is a transmigration of a human spirit, although in the trope of reincarnation instead of as a living co-essence. He broaches a possible (ironized) relationship between the animal's innocence and the guilty violence of the human murders that plagues the society around him: he wonders whether the badger, if indeed an incarnation of the murdered dead, might be "some violent shattered boy / nosing out what got mislaid / between the cradle and the explosion" (119). Perhaps he feels that his culture, with its self-destructive violence, has squandered its claims to natural harmony. This suggests a beneficent reason for Heaney's insistence on the distance between people and animals in his poetry, the boundary between us and them: Heaney determines to let animals prosper on their side of the boundary, untroubled by us. But still, the people in his poetry look at the animals glimmering away and wonder if they suggest a redemptive vision of their own better lives. In Heaney's version of animal souls, the animal co-essence represents an idealistic hope of what a living creature can be.

As the poem continues, the speaker listens for more sounds from the badger—a consummately gifted listener, Heaney is habituated to turning his soundings into the sounds of his poems. "I listened / for duntings [thumps] under the laurels / and heard intimations whispered / about being vaguely honoured" (119). Once again, the experience that results from interacting with animals is fuzzy and indistinct: vague intimations are whispered, and the poet is left to decode the duntings. But a poet is, of course, well-suited to this task, as a master of duntings himself. Like the face-to-face moment with the fox in *Squarings*, there is a sort of ear-to-ear scene here, as Heaney brings the badger's rhythmic thumps into intimate interaction with his own poetic rhythms. Two creators of patterned sounds meet in this moment. Who is being "vaguely honoured"? The speaker, I think, by being privy to the distant sounds of the badgers and witnessing their nocturnal glimmering. His contact with the animals, albeit brief and attenuated, is an honor; Heaney values the sensory intimacy with the badgers, however indistinct. "Visitations are taken for signs," the poem says, again testifying to Heaney's sense of the animals as embodiments of metaphysical power.

Another fleeting moment of contact between a person and an animal occurs when Heaney, referring to badgers on the roadways, writes, "Last night one had me breaking / but more in fear than in honour" (119). Again we see the poet's fear of animals, but not simply fear—*more* fear than honour, Heaney writes, but thus still some honour: some sense of being in the presence of a creature that has powers of transcendence, and honours people by sharing even a glimmer of this. The moment of interaction is quick and almost (but apparently not quite) fatal—people can certainly harm animals with the violence that pervades our own lives, whether the intentional violence of civil war or the accidental violence of fast cars. Heaney's consciousness of this threat that people may pose to animals compels him to keep his moments of conjunction as brief as possible.

In the poem's final stanza the speaker muses:

> How perilous is it to choose
> not to love the life we're shown?
> His sturdy dirty body
> and interloping grovel.
> The intelligence in his bone.
> The unquestionable houseboy's shoulders
> that could have been my own. (120)

Here, the speaker substantially, if only imaginatively, interchanges himself and the animal—he fantasizes *nagualismo*. Contemplating badgers, honoured to be in contact with them even if only for a glimmering moment here and a fearful near-fatal moment there, makes the speaker question the life he has been shown—the life of people—and wonder what it would be like to be an animal. The badger's shoulders "could have been my own"—we *could* be animals; our souls could transmigrate. I could have been him, the speaker thinks, but he leaves the thought safely in the grammar of hypothetical possibility rather than actuality. The peril of associating too closely with animals, interchanging with them, is that we may taint them with our proven failure to live harmoniously. While Heaney extols the animal as intelligent and sturdy, he also resigns himself to his lot as a person. Mesoamericans believe that every person has an animal somewhere out there who shares his or her fate; Heaney resists burdening any animal with the sorry fates to which his countrypeople have consigned themselves. In many ways throughout his poetry, Heaney flirts with, though he ultimately refuses to embrace, a fantasy of escapism: escapism from being Irish and suffering the lot of the Irish. In his animal poems, Heaney seems to flirt with escapism from the condition of being human.

The badger Heaney contemplates is also, besides being a real animal, partly symbolic/representative of people—a displaced evocation of the murdered shattered boy Heaney earlier perceived in the animal's soul (and it is that boy as well, along with the badger, whom Heaney wonders about switching places with). In another poem, too, an animal has a vivid symbolic presence, as a stand-in for a person. Such symbolic use of animals, animals-as-people, often undercuts the essence of animal souls; but in Heaney's poems the animal symbol is extensively enough sustained so that the person really is, in part, the animal. In "The Otter," the animal represents (in part) Heaney's wife, Marie. The poet watches a figure that is simultaneously an otter and his wife:

> When you plunged
> The light of Tuscany wavered
> And swung through the pool
> From top to bottom.
>
> I loved your wet head and smashing crawl,
> Your fine swimmer's back and shoulders
> Surfacing and surfacing again
> This year and every year since. (135)

Eventually, it becomes clear that the subject is a beloved woman rather than an otter, or at least, more lover than otter, as Heaney becomes emotionally and sensually intimate with the figure:

> When I hold you now
> We are close and deep...
>
> My two hands are plumbed water.
> You are palpable, lithe
> Otter of memory
> In the pool of the moment,

Turning to swim on your back,
Each silent, thigh-shaking kick
Retilting the light,
Heaving the cool at your neck. (135)

It is mainly Marie that Heaney is adoring here, but there are flashes of otter: as if he is looking at Marie and thinking of an otter he had seen once swimming, kicking, surfacing. And at the end of the poem, while the poet has accomplished his apparent intention of celebrating the sensuous enjoyment of watching his wife, the otter is not completely absent. When the figure stops swimming,

suddenly you're out
Back again, intent as ever,
Heavy and frisky in your freshened pelt,
Printing the stones. (136)

Most often, when poets use an animal as a figurative vehicle, they squeeze out whatever metaphorical/symbolic resonance they can get from the animal and then, when the poetic conceit is completed, leave the animal figure empty and used up. But here, Heaney never abandons the otter: at the end of the poem, the effect of his luxuriant enjoyment of Marie has been also, in part, the enjoyment of the otter, or the otter of memory; and at the end of the poem, Marie is still a fusion of woman and otter, with her freshened pelt and her wet (foot/paw)prints on the stones.

Heaney has written numerous poems about Marie, proclaiming his profound and enduring love for her. Here, he taps into the shimmering enchantment he sees in animals to bestow some of it on his wife—or, more accurately, to share it with her so that both she and the otter coterminously share the spotlight of this poem. The person here really is, in part, the animal: the poem's perspective creates, in a sense, a co-essentiality between the two creatures. And Heaney's relationship with Marie, as described in many other poems, is one of intense symbiosis, interaction, correspondence. He characterizes their love as so vital that it is as if they are part of each other, forming a partnership of equal and shared souls. In depicting his wife as co-essential with an otter, Heaney also envisions himself by implication as part of that relationship. (An otter is not the only animal whose soul shares Marie: in "The Skunk," that animal, too, is an evocation/incarnation of the poet's wife.) Heaney's intense interactivity with Marie is here transposed, in part, onto/into the animal, and Heaney is thus describing, for himself, a manifestation of animal souls: part of his deepest soul is with the otter, in the otter.

Pattiann Rogers

For Pattiann Rogers, the perception of animals occasions unapologetically ecstatic celebration. "Rapture of the Deep: The Pattern of Poseidon's Love Song" is a love song to nature, populated with stunning incarnations of aquatic animals and patterned with the animals' movements, rhythms, and dynamics. Poetry, of course, is about pattern—poetry *is* pattern—and Rogers achieves a fundamental co-essence with animals by giving over the pattern of her poetry to the patterns of animals; she shares her own patterning authority with her poetic animals. "Rapture of the Deep," all in one endlessly impassioned breath, is mere observation of numerous animals, from bugs to sharks to plankton. In terms of narrative, the poem is about nothing: nothing except the rapture of nature, reverently observed and profusely conveyed. Rogers's love for animals resounds with an erotic, sensual pleasure that these animals inspire—though only an imaginative pleasure: the poet watches, but doesn't touch the animals. She doesn't need to be physically intimate with them to revel in the sensory and sensuous aura they generate.

> The blue ornata's spiderweb
> body sidles and pulses among the turning
> cilia wheels of the microscopic
> rotifera tilting over the feathery
> fans of the splendidum slowly extending
> and withdrawing
>   their fondling tongues
> inside the body of the summer solstice
> where the sun with its ragged
> radiances organizes transparent
> butterflies and paper kites of light
> into flocks of meadow-drifting
> throughout the green sea surrounding
> the design
>   of string worms palolo
> floating in the gripping and releasing
> event of their own tight coils
> toward a reef of chitons pulled
> from their rock bases by the violent
> bite and suck of a spinning
> squall
>   curling themselves then
> into their round coat-of-mail shells
> as if they were each one made
> by the sound of long O moaning
> inside a sailor's ancient prayer

to Mater Cara
                                    tumbled and tumbled
by the waves beneath which the frilled
shark a singular presence in a dimension
of lesser constellations suspended
mid-sea whips with a graceful pattern
of pitiful evil
                                    toward a nebula
of cephalopods undulating
below an arrangement of rain
shattering the evening suddenly
out of the linear into the million
falling moments. (*Bread* 74–5)

The animal patterns become the poetic patterns as the poetry (like the animals it describes) sidles and pulses, fondles, floats, tumbles, grips, and releases. The animals are the poem's aesthetics, its artistic effects. Their movements provide the poem's verbs, and their designs ("the feathery / fans of the splendidum"; "transparent / butterflies and paper kites of light"; "flocks of meadow-drifting / throughout the green sea") become its visually entrancing nouns.

The sea animals' motion and visual flair generate a kind of choreography. Rogers *uses* these animals to form her poem, but without *using* them up—without exploiting or manipulating them. The performers of this choreography are not the proverbial "dancing bears," but rather, butterflies, cephalopods *et al.*, that happen to be dancing, beautifully. Had we (who are not poets) looked at these animals ourselves, we might or might not have noticed the details and patterns of their extravagant dances, but Rogers focuses our gaze for us. Her words and images, the images of these animals sensitively transposed into poetry, emphasize for her readers the animals' dance, their color, their pattern—the elements of aesthetic form—but Rogers doesn't create or impose this form; she only points out to her readers what's already there. Her poems put us in an aesthetic frame of mind, as we watch, with her, uninvasively and naturally. We learn that animals can be aesthetically eloquent and rapturous just as they are: we need only let them do what they do. Throughout her oeuvre, Rogers seeks to foreground and celebrate the sublimities of animals.

Rogers's poetic animals often exhibit resonances of conventional Judeo-Christian depictions of God: she uses images of God to describe animals, I believe, to emphasize the consciously spiritual sense in which she is seeing animals. Two poems that exemplify this are "Mousefeet: From a Lecture on Muridae Cosmology" and "Fractal: Repetition of

Form over a Variety of Scales." "Muridae" is the family of the order rodentia that includes most common rats and mice, and the universe that Rogers's cosmology describes in this poem is one common to people and mice. She shows that the inscription of mice, the spirit of mice, the image and the prints of mice, are everywhere in our world—we share a world, and a cosmology; her implication, at the end of the poem, is that we may also share (as Mesoamericans do) a spirituality with the animals. The poem begins:

> Mousefeet are often as small, exact
> and precocious as eighth notes penned
> across a composer's score. Most are no
> larger than two quarter-inch W's printed
> side by side. All mouse toenails
> are just about the size of poppy seeds.
> Yet one encounters mousefeet
> everywhere.

Rogers starts off with analogy, the quintessential poetic device for asserting relationships of comparability and connection. The vehicles of the first analogies, music and writing, are human forms of cultural expression, which Rogers juxtaposes with the expressions of animals. Mousefeet indicate the records of mice' existence (i.e., their footprints, showing where they have been and how they live) as music and W's do for people. Feet transport mice, as symphonic scores and printed texts "transport" people. The comparability of these imprints are a poetic approximation of the connection asserted by animal souls. Rogers suggests that the detailed tracks of animals, which resemble our own mousefeet-sized markings, establish a common realm for people and animals. She goes on to describe, fancifully and figuratively, poetically, myriad incarnations of mousefeet in the world all around us:

> Raindrops hitting dusty cement
> sidewalks make trails of splayed mousefeet
> running in every direction. And there are pale,
> blue footprints of mice all over the moon.
> Just get a telescope and check
> for yourself some night. . . .
>
> Be careful where you tread.
> There are mousefeet, tiny folded fans
> of knuckles and pins, thousands of them, curled
> in the roll of the surf, inside the tight
> furl of marsh fog, planted deep in pea pods,
> and cockle rocks, in the earth in burrows
> below us as we speak. (71–2)

Mousefeet are a seemingly infinite trope. They appear as the leaves of wild radish ("simply green mousefeet / held bottomside up with thin toes spread / to the sun"), as "the flick of the rattlesnake's tail," as "dying dots of fire" in the skies above, and on and on. Mousefeet are everywhere—throughout people's world, throughout animals' world: which is to say that they are everywhere in a world *common* to people and animals, contradicting the predominant Western cultural sense of boundaries separating our worlds. In the last stanza, Rogers equates this universality with God's infinite presence:

> And be careful to listen
> to exactly what your prayers are meaning
> as you sing; for those mousefeet pervade
> and determine, ping and sloop, dicker
> and dodge through all invented cadences,
> imposing on every voice and ear the tittering
> character and mad, precise, alpha-and-omega
> pickering machinery heard so prominently
> every time in God's perfect reply. (73)

Our prayers are answered, Rogers asserts, and they are answered in mousefeet: that is, in the vocabulary of the little unnoticed animal elements that are everywhere in the world. God is in the (animal) details. The ubiquity of animals' presence, which people have mostly failed to perceive, equates with the ubiquity of the spiritual presence known as "God." To communicate with God, we need to go through animals—we need to appreciate mousefeet, as Rogers puts it in this poem, which means noticing and understanding animals, appreciating how their lives and their presence are the fundamental principles of animation in the world around us. God is nice, too, but the incarnation of God at the end of the poem is very much mediated by the mousefeet (which could just as easily, I think, be pigeonfeet or horsefeet—anyfeet, allfeet) signifying a presence by which we can appraise everything in the universe around us: so we have precisely, as the poem's title promises, a Muridae Cosmology.

In an essay entitled "Surprised by the Sacred," Rogers explains how she sees animals and nature as a pathway to the sacred and describes the importance of realizing the sanctity, and the marvel, of things (like mousefeet) that are already plentiful in the world all around us; we just need to attune ourselves to their holiness, in a spirit of pantheistic rapture. "I believe the world provides every physical image and sensation we will ever need in order to experience the sacred, to declare the holy, if we could only learn to recognize it, if we could only hone and refine our sense of the divine, just as we learn to see and distinguish with accuracy the ant on the trunk of the poplar, the Pole Star in Ursa Minor, rain coming toward us on the wind" (*Dream* 90).

In "Fractal: Repetition of Form over a Variety of Scales," again, we see God in the animal, God through the animal. "This moment is a single blue jay," the poem begins,

> a scramble of flint, sapphire iron,
> spiking blue among the empty brambles
> and vines wound like skeins back
> upon themselves through the dun forest
> of thistle spurs and thorns. (55)

This moment is also, as Rogers goes on to recount, the skeleton of the jay, and the "singular blue-black pod of jay heart / thiddering," and the jay's call, and the sun as it is caught in the jay's eye. Then the poem concludes:

> God is a process, a raveled nexus
> forever tangling into and around the changing
> form of his own moment—pulse and skein
> shifting mien, repeating cry
> of loss and delivery. (56)

God is a process, and a blue jay is also a process; while considering both of these processes, the poem dedicates considerably more attention to the bird's—its life force, its internal complexities, its interaction with the ecosphere outside—which comprises "this moment." In conventional Western religion, it is God who comprises "this moment" and every moment—the significance of God, the majesty of God, is inscribed in the ubiquitous immediacy, and the eternity, of this spirit. Just as in "Mousefeet," we see God through animals: tangled, changing form, borrowing the voice and the dynamics ("pulse and skein") of a living animal, a simple but sublime, moment-filling jay. It is like Blake's conceit in "Auguries of Innocence": we see the world in a grain of sand, and eternity in a wildflower—or here, a bird.[1] In "Fractal," it is the connection to the animal—the ability to revel in the moments of this animal—that leads to God. The subtitle, "Repetition of Form over a Variety of Scales," suggests that Rogers believes the divinity traditionally monopolized by a majestic God resides also (and is repeated in form) in a blue jay, and a mouse, and all the other creatures who share our world. This is Rogers's conception of animal souls.

Every critic should have the experience of discovering an artistic expression that voices, more concisely and immensely more effectively, what he or she has tried to say in academic prose. I am lucky to have come across Pattiann Rogers's insights after I had already completed the bulk of this book, because if I had read the following poem before I had tried to make my own statement, I might well have felt that it was superfluous to add anything more. So, having finished my own academic attempt at describing an ideal potential connection between people and animals as mediated by poetry, I would like to give the last word to Rogers's version of this and end my discussion of poetic animals with poetic animals.

I thank Rogers and Milkweed Editions for allowing me to reprint "Animals and People: 'The Human Heart in Conflict with Itself,' " which says it all better than I possibly could. It is a long poem, about all the ways people interact with animals: necessarily long, I think, simply because people do so many different things with animals, and to animals. The poem is, on the one hand, just an objectively descriptive account of all these interactions, but at the same time, it also embodies an intense moral undertone about our relations with each other. The effect, thus, is to make it seem—as it *should* seem, although as it rarely actually does—as if every human engagement with animals is inherently an ethical engagement, with ethical consequences. Our interactions with animals reflect our conscious choices about how to behave, and some choices are better than others. As I read this poem, I stop after each sentence, each point, and think of an example (mostly from my own life, my own immediate experience) of what Rogers is referring to; and I grapple with the ethics of each instance.

"Animals and People" describes ideal ways of conceiving animals and treating animals and also—often in jarring contrast with these ideals—conventional mainstream cultural realities. The poem is not, finally, less optimistic an iteration of animal souls than much of Rogers's other poetry. It is a somewhat cynical, or perhaps just accurate, account of how close we may come to finding our animal souls—and we *are* close, in many ways that Rogers recounts—and yet how far away we still remain. Full of paradoxes, the poem demonstrates how intimate people may be with animals, how dependent we are upon them, how aware we are of their power, and yet still, how unable to consecrate this awareness and to avoid the default conditions of exploitative oppression that define so many of our relationships with animals. Rogers illuminates the contradictions that color how we conceive and interact with animals. She demonstrates how complicated it is to sort all this out, as I have discovered myself during a decade of studying animals and their cultural representations: one insight leads to another, and perhaps a contradictory one; one resolution leads to a consequent quandary; a noble gesture begets a hypocrisy. There is no neat way to live with animals; there is no right way, no perfect way, in our imperfect world. But neither is there any way to repress the challenges animals present or to ignore them. They are out there, everywhere, and we are in here. We can't live with them, and we can't live without them. Rogers's poem captures all of this: where we are with respect to our consciousness of animals, and how far we still have to go.

Rogers's voice is not monolithic or absolutist, as her syntactical refrain (anaphora) proclaims that "some of us" do this, and, of course, others do something else... The poem's statements are not all-encompassing concerning any specific instance of people's relationship with animals, but overall, I think, the poem describes all of us and speaks for all of us. It represents the best example I have found of an ecocritical ethic in poetry that could lead our culture toward better relationships with animals if we grapple with it. Rogers finds, toward the end of the poem, our connection with animals despite ourselves—the affiliation that Mesoamericans realize to be necessary and inherent in our human (animal) existence. Their blood is our blood, and their fate is our fate, we discover. In our compulsions concerning animals, and in our ambivalent adoration of animals, Rogers finds our very life force, our connection to life, our inspiration to live.

Animals and People: "The Human Heart in Conflict with Itself"

Some of us like to photograph them. Some
of us like to paint pictures of them. Some of us
like to sculpt them and make statues and carvings
of them. Some of us like to compose music
about them and sing about them. And some of us
like to write about them.

Some of us like to go out
and catch them and kill them and eat them. Some
of us like to hunt them and shoot them and eat them.
Some of us like to raise them, care for them and eat
them. Some of us just like to eat them.

And some of us
name them and name their seasons and name their hours,
and some of us, in our curiosity, open them up
and study them with our tools and name their parts.

We capture them, mark them and release them,
and then we track them and spy on them and enter
their lives and affect their lives and abandon
their lives. We breed them and manipulate them
and alter them. Some of us experiment
upon them.

We put them on tethers and leashes,
in shackles and harnesses, in cages and boxes,
inside fences and walls. We put them in yokes
and muzzles. We want them to carry us and pull us
and haul for us.

And we want some of them
to be our companions, some of them to ride on our fingers
and some to ride sitting on our wrists or on our shoulders
and some to ride in our arms, ride clutching our necks.
We want them to walk at our heels.

We want them to trust
us and come to us, take our offerings, eat from our hands.
We want to participate in their beauty. We want to assume
their beauty and so possess them with our kindness and so
partake of their beauty in that way.

And we want them
to learn our language. We try to teach them our language.
We speak to them. We put *our* words in *their* mouths.
We want *them* to speak. We want to know what they see
when they look at us.

We use their heads and their bladders
for balls, their guts and their hides and their bones
to make music. We skin them and wear them for coats,
their scalps for hats. We rob them, their milk
and their honey, their feathers and their eggs.
We make money from them.

We construct icons of them.
We make images of them and put their images on our clothes
and on our necklaces and rings and on our walls
and in our religious places. We preserve their dead
bodies and parts of their dead bodies and display
them in our homes and buildings.

We name mountains
and rivers and cities and streets and organizations
and gangs and causes after them. We name years and time
and constellations of stars after them. We make mascots
of them, naming our athletic teams after them. Sometimes
we name ourselves after them.

We make toys of them
and rhymes of them for our children. We mold them
and shape them and distort them to fit our myths
and our stories and our dramas. We like to dress up
like them and masquerade as them. We like to imitate them
and try to move as they move and make the sounds they make,
hoping, by these means, to enter and become the black
mysteries of their being.

Sometimes we dress them
in our clothes and teach them tricks and laugh at them
and marvel at them. And we make parades of them
and festivals of them. We want them to entertain us
and amaze us and frighten us and reassure us
and calm us and rescue us from boredom.

We pit them
against one another and watch them fight one another,
and we gamble on them. We want to compete with them
ourselves, challenging them, testing our wits and talents
against their wits and talents, in forests and on plains,
in the ring. We want to be able to run like them and leap
like them and swim like them and fly like them and fight
like them and endure like them.

We want their total
absorption in the moment. We want their unwavering devotion
to life. We want their oblivion.

Some of us give thanks
and bless those we kill and eat, and ask for pardon,
and this is beautiful as long as they are the ones dying
and we are the ones eating.

And as long as we are not
seriously threatened, as long as we and our children
aren't hungry and aren't cold, we say, with a certain
degree of superiority, that we are no better
than any of them, that any of them deserve to live
just as much as we do.

And after we have proclaimed
this thought, and by doing so subtly pointed out
that we are allowing them to live, we direct them
and manage them and herd them and train them and follow
them and map them and collect them and make specimens
of them and butcher them and move them here and move
them there and we place them on lists and we take
them off of lists and we stare at them and stare
at them and stare at them.

We track them in our sleep.
They become the form of our sleep. We dream of them.
We seek them with accusation. We seek them
with supplication.

And in the ultimate imposition,
as Thoreau said, we make them bear the burden
of our thoughts. We make them carry the burden
of our metaphors and the burden of our desires and our guilt
and carry the equal burden of our curiosity and concern.
We make them bear our sins and our prayers and our hopes
into the desert, into the sky, into the stars.
We say we kill them for God.

We adore them and we curse
them. We caress them and we ravish them. We want them
to acknowledge us and be with us. We want them to disappear
and be autonomous. We abhor their viciousness and lack
of pity, as we abhor our own viciousness and lack of pity.
We love them and we reproach them, just as we love
and reproach ourselves.

We will never, we cannot,
leave them alone, even the tiniest one, ever, because we know
we are one with them. Their blood is our blood. Their breath
is our breath, their beginning our beginning, their fate
our fate.

Thus we deny them. Thus we yearn
for them. They are among us and within us and of us,
inextricably woven with the form and manner of our being,
with our understanding and our imaginations.
They are the grit and the salt and the lullaby
of our language.

We have a need to believe they are there,
and always will be, whether we witness them or not.
We need to know they are there, a vigorous life maintaining
itself without our presence, without our assistance,
without our attention. We need to know, we *must* know,
that we come from such stock so continuously and tenaciously
and religiously devoted to life.

We know we are one with them,
and we are frantic to understand how to actualize that union.
We attempt to actualize that union in our many stumbling,
ignorant and destructive ways, in our many confused
and noble and praiseworthy ways.

For how can we possess dignity
if we allow them no dignity? Who will recognize our beauty
if we do not revel in their beauty? How can we hope
to receive honor if we give no honor? How can we believe
in grace if we cannot bestow grace?

We want what we cannot
have. We want to give life at the same moment
we are taking it, nurture life at the same moment we light
the fire and raise the knife. We want to live, to provide,
and not be instruments of destruction, instruments
of death. We want to reconcile our "egoistic concerns"
with our "universal compassion." We want the lion
and the lamb to be one, the lion and the lamb
within finally to dwell together, to lie down together
in peace and praise at last. (31–6)

Notes

Chapter 2

1. Regarding the versification of this narrative, Gossen explains: "The verse format... follows the stylistic conventions of Tzotzil formal style, the foundation of which... consists of dyadic structure of ideas, sound, and syntax... the dyadic structures (and multiples thereof) that characterize Tzotzil narrative style are marked linguistically; therefore, my decisions regarding how to render the verse structure of narrative texts in translation are for the most part suggested by the original Tzotzil" (*Telling* 59–60).
2. My references to Menchú's writing deal with the cultural milieu in which she was raised; even critics of her disputed historiography concede that *I, Rigoberta Menchú* remains a valid account of Quiché social beliefs and practices.

Chapter 3

1. MGM's "product placement" is subtler in the original Spanish, though Pacheco still intends the same reference to the film company's famous opening credits: "el estruendo / que en pantallas crecientes / les dio el cine" (74).

Chapter 4

1. Since the poem is actually a metaphorical tribute to George Bernard Shaw, it is all the more appropriately anthropomorphic.
2. Linda Leavell, however, proposes that Moore does in fact have preferences: "Her favorite animals tend to be the burrowers, the nest and shell builders, and the armor bearers" (83). Leavell cites the archetypal imagery described by philosopher Gaston Bachelard in *The Poetics of Space*: "According to Bachelard, a shell is one of several 'primal images' of refuge, along with houses [and] nests... such images, he claims, are primal and universal because 'whenever life seeks to shelter, protect, cover or hide itself, the imagination sympathizes with the being that inhabits the protected space.' He quotes the painter Vlaminck: 'The well-being I feel, seated in front of my fire, while bad weather rages out-of-doors, is entirely animal. A rat in its hole, a rabbit in its burrow, cows in the stable, must all feel the same contentment that I feel.'" Moore's poems about these burrowers, nesters, and armored animals "overflow with images of animal well-being," Leavell writes (83).

3. Even as perspicacious an admirer as T. S. Eliot, no stranger to convoluted and opaque poetry, wrote in his introduction to Moore's *Selected Poems* of 1935 that it "would be difficult to say what is the 'subject-matter' of *The Jerboa*" (in Molesworth 268).
4. See my discussion of Moore and Dürer in *Reading Zoos*, pp. 324–41.
5. These poems, in the order of their appearance in *The Complete Poems*, are: "The Jerboa"; "No Swan So Fine"; "The Plumet Basilisk"; "The Frigate Pelican"; "The Buffalo"; "To a Prize Bird"; "The Fish"; "Critics and Connoisseurs"; "The Monkeys"; "Peter"; "Snakes, Mongooses, Snake Charmers, and the Like"; "An Octopus"; "Sea Unicorns and Land Unicorns"; "The Monkey Puzzle"; "An Egyptian Pulled Glass Bottle in the Shape of a Fish"; "To a Snail"; "Nothing Will Cure the Sick Lion but to Eat an Ape"; "To the Peacock of France" (all the previous poems originally published in *Selected Poems*, 1935); "Rigorists"; He 'Digesteth Harde Yron' "; "Bird-Witted"; "The Pangolin"; "The Paper Nautilus" (these previous five from *What Are Years*, 1941); "The Wood-Weasel"; "Elephants" (these two from *Nevertheless*, 1944); "His Shield" (from *Collected Poems*, 1951); "Apparition of Splendor"; "Tom Fool at Jamaica"; "The Sycamore" (from *Like a Bulwark*, 1956); "To a Chameleon"; "A Jellyfish"; "The Arctic Ox (or Goat)" (from *O to Be a Dragon*, 1959); "To a Giraffe"; "Blue Bug"; "To Victor Hugo of My Crow Pluto" (from *Tell Me, Tell Me*, 1966); and, from a section of "Hitherto Uncollected" poems, "Tippoo's Tiger." Other significant animal poems that are not collected in *The Complete Poems* include "Black Earth" (*Egoist* IV, April 1918: 55–6); "Old Tiger," "Dock Rats" (*Observations*, New York: Dial P, 1924: 53–4), and "Pigeons" (*Poetry* 47.2, November 1935: 61–5).

Chapter 5

1. And note also in Blake's poem the prevalence of animal images and analogies (often, representing the mistreatment of animals) as a device to suggest the need for people to establish a more perfect spiritual connection with God. I quote a few lines at random: "He who shall hurt the little Wren / Shall never be belovd by Men. / He who the Ox to wrath has movd / Shall never be by Woman lovd. / The wanton Boy that kills the Fly / Shall feel the Spider's enmity. . . . The Caterpillar on the Leaf / Repeats to thee thy Mother's grief. / Kill not the Moth nor Butterfly, / For the Last Judgment draweth nigh." Blake's perspective is not identical to Rogers's, as his animals are largely used to prove an anthropocentric point, but like her, he notices the richness and ubiquity of nonhuman life, and uses this as a platform for describing the ideal of a rich and ubiquitous spiritual consciousness.

Works Cited

Adams, Richard N. and Arthur J. Rubel. "Sickness and Social Relations." In *Handbook of Middle American Indians* vol. 6. Ed. Manning Nash. Austin: University of Texas Press, 1967, 333–56.

Ardolino, Frank. "Raging Bulls, Tigers 'Burning Bright,' and Other Animals in Boxing Literature and Films." *Aethlon: The Journal of Sports Literature* 6.2 (Spring 1989): 47–77.

Asian Elephant Art & Conservation Project. <www.elephantart.com>

Baker, Steve. *Picturing the Beast: Animals, Identity and Representation.* Manchester: Manchester University Press, 1993.

——. *The Postmodern Animal.* London: Reaktion, 2000.

Bate, Jonathan. *The Song of the Earth.* Cambridge: Harvard University Press, 2000.

Baudrillard, Jean. *Simulacra and Simulation.* Ann Arbor: University of Michigan Press, 1994.

Berger, John. "Why Look at Animals?" In *About Looking.* New York: Pantheon, 1980.

Beston, Henry. *The Outermost House: A Year of Life on the Great Beach of Cape Cod.* New York: Doubleday, 1928.

Birke, Lynda and Luciana Parisi. "Animals, Becoming." In *Animal Others: On Ethics, Ontology, and Animal Life.* Ed. H. Peter Steeves. Albany: State University of New York Press, 1999.

Bleakley, Alan. *The Animalizing Imagination: Totemism, Textuality and Ecocriticism.* London: Macmillan, 2000.

Branch, Michael P., Rochelle Johnson, Daniel Patterson, and Scott Slovic. *Reading the Earth: New Directions in the Study of Literature and the Environment.* Moscow: University of Idaho Press, 1988.

Carolan, Trevor. "The Wild Mind of Gary Snyder." *Shambhala Sun Online,* 1996. <www.shambhalasun.com/Archives/Features/1996/May '96/Snyder.htm>

Colby, Benjamin N. "Psychological Orientations." In *Handbook of Middle American Indians* vol. 6. Ed. Manning Nash. Austin: University of Texas Press, 1967, 416–31.

Conniff, Richard. *Every Creeping Thing: True Tales of Faintly Repulsive Wildlife.* New York: Henry Holt, 1998.

Costello, Bonnie. *Marianne Moore: Imaginary Possessions.* Cambridge: Harvard University Press, 1981.

Croke, Vicki. *The Modern Ark: The Story of Zoos, Past, Present and Future*. New York: Scribner, 1997.

Davis, Charles B. *The Animal Motif in Bamana Art*. New Orleans: The Davis Gallery, 1981.

Deleuze, Gilles, and Félix Guattari. *Kafka: Toward a Minor Literature*. Trans. Dana Polan. Minneapolis: University of Minnesota Press, 1986.

——. *A Thousand Plateaus*. Trans. Brian Massumi. Minneapolis: University of Minnesota Press, 1987.

Doudoroff, Michael J. "José Emilio Pacheco: An Overview of the Poetry, 1963–86." *Hispania* 72.2 (May 1989): 264–76.

Elder, John. *Imagining the Earth: Poetry and the Vision of Nature*. Second ed. Athens: University of Georgia Press, 1996.

Fish, Stanley E. *Self-Consuming Artifacts: The Experience of Seventeenth-Century Literature*. Berkeley: University of California Press, 1972.

Fowles, John. "Seeing Nature Whole." *Harper's Magazine* (November 1979): 49–68.

Fudge, Erica. *Perceiving Animals: Humans and Beasts in Early Modern English Culture*. London: Macmillan, 2000.

Franklin, Adrian. *Animals and Modern Cultures: A Sociology of Human–Animal Relationships in Modernity*. London: Sage, 1999.

Frost, Laurie Adams. "Pets and Lovers: The Human-Companion Animal Bond in Contemporary Literary Prose." *Journal of Popular Culture* 25.1 (Summer 1991): 39–53.

Gossen, Gary H. "Animal Souls, Co-essences, and Human Destiny in Mesoamerica." In *Monsters, Tricksters, and Sacred Cows: Animal Tales and American Identities*. Ed. A. James Arnold. Charlottesville: University Press of Virginia, 1996.

——. "Animal Souls and Human Destiny in Chamula." *Man* 10.3 (1975): 448–61.

——. "From Olmecs to Zapatistas: A Once and Future History of Souls." *American Anthropologist* 96.3 (1994): 553–70.

——. *Telling Maya Tales: Tzotzil Identities in Modern Mexico*. New York: Routledge, 1999.

Hancocks, David. *A Different Nature: The Paradoxical World of Zoos and Their Uncertain Future*. Berkeley: University of California Press, 2001.

Harrison, Jane. *Themis: A Study of the Social Origins of Greek Religion*. 1911. London: Merlin Press, 1963.

Harrod, Howard. *The Animals Came Dancing: The Native American Sacred Ecology and Animal Kinship*. Tuscon: University of Arizona Press, 2000.

Heaney, Seamus. *Selected Poems 1966–1987*. New York: Farrar, Straus, and Giroux, 1990.

——. *Squarings*. In *Seeing Things*. New York: Farrar, Straus, and Giroux, 1991.

Hollander, John, ed. *Animal Poems*. New York: Knopf, 1994.

Holley, Margaret. *The Poetry of Marianne Moore: A Study in Voice and Value.* Cambridge: Cambridge University Press, 1987.

Komar, Vitaly and Alexander Melamid. *When Elephants Paint: The Quest of Two Modern Artists to Save the Elephants of Thailand.* New York: HarperCollins, 2000.

Kowalski, Gary. *The Souls of Animals.* Walpole, NH: Stillpoint, 1991.

Lawrence, Elizabeth Atwood. "Seeing in Nature What Is Ours: Poetry and the Human–Animal Bond." *Journal of American Culture* 17.4 (Winter 1994): 47–53.

Leavell, Linda. *Marianne Moore and the Visual Arts: Prismatic Color.* Baton Rouge: Louisiana State University Press, 1995

Lévi-Strauss, Claude. Totemism. Trans. Rodney Needham. Boston: Beacon, 1963.

Lippit, Akira Mizuta. *Electric Animal: Toward a Rhetoric of Wildlife.* Minneapolis: University of Minnesota Press, 2000.

Lutwack, Leonard. *Birds in Literature.* Gainesville: University Press of Florida, 1994.

Malamud, Randy. *Reading Zoos: Representations of Animals and Captivity.* New York: New York University Press, 1998.

Menchú, Rigoberta. *I, Rigoberta Menchú: An Indian Woman in Guatemala.* Trans. Ann Wright. London: Verso, 1984.

Mendelson, E. Michael. "Ritual and Mythology." In *Handbook of Middle American Indians* vol. 6. Ed. Manning Nash. Austin: University of Texas Press, 1967, 392–415.

Mitman, Gregg. *Reel Nature: America's Romance with Wildlife on Film.* Cambridge: Harvard University Press, 1999.

Molesworth, Charles. *Marianne Moore: A Literary Life.* New York: Atheneum, 1990.

Montagne, Renee. "Elephant Music." Morning Edition, National Public Radio, 12 February 2001. <http://search.npr.org/cf/cmn/cmnpd01fm.cfm?PrgDate = 2%2F12%2F2001&PrgID = 3>

Moore, Marianne. *The Complete Poems of Marianne Moore.* New York: Penguin, 1967.

——. *The Complete Prose of Marianne Moore.* Ed. Patricia C. Willis. New York: Viking, 1986.

——. "Pigeons." *Poetry* 47.2 (November 1935): 61–5.

——. *The Selected Letters of Marianne Moore.* Ed. Bonnie Costello *et al.* New York: Knopf, 1997.

Morphy, Howard. "Introduction." *Animals Into Art.* Ed. Howard Morphy. London: Unwin Hyman, 1989, 1–17.

Muldoon, Paul, ed. *The Faber Book of Beasts.* London: Faber, 1997.

Nagel, Thomas. "What is it Like to Be a Bat?" *Philosophical Review* 83.4 (October 1974): 435–50.

Nash, Ogden. *I Wouldn't Have Missed It.* Boston: Little, Brown, 1975.

Noske, Barbara. *Beyond Boundaries: Humans and Animals*. Montreal: Black Rose Books, 1997.

Oliver, Mary. *American Primitive*. Boston: Back Bay Books, 1978.

Pacheco, José Emilio. *An Ark for the Next Millennium*. Trans. Margaret Sayers Peden. Austin: University of Texas Press, 1993.

Palmatier, Robert. *Speaking of Animals: A Dictionary of Animal Metaphors*. Westport, CT: Greenwood Press, 1995.

Pitt-Kethley, Fiona. *Sky Ray Lolly*. London: Sphere, 1990.

Pollan, Michael. *Second Nature: A Gardener's Education*. New York: Dell, 2000.

Preece, Rod. *Animals and Nature: Cultural Myths, Cultural Realities*. Vancouver: University of British Columbia Press, 1999.

Quinn, Bernetta. "The Artist as Armored Animal: Marianne Moore, Randall Jarrell." In *Marianne Moore: Woman and Poet*. Ed. Patricia C. Willis. Orono, ME: National Poetry Foundation, 1990, 287–96.

Rich, Louis. "Dragons of Legend Come to Bronx Zoo." New York *Times*, 19 September 1926: X, 5, 11.

Ritvo, Harriet. *The Animal Estate: The English and Other Creatures in the Victorian Age*. Cambridge: Harvard University Press, 1987.

Rogers, Pattiann. *The Dream of the Marsh Wren*. Minneapolis: Milkweed, 1999.

——. *Eating Bread and Honey*. Minneapolis: Milkweed, 1997.

Ross, Bruce. "Fables of the Golden Age: The Poetry of Marianne Moore." *Twentieth Century Literature* 30.2–3 (Summer-Fall 1984): 327–50.

Rotella, Guy. *Reading and Writing Nature: The Poetry of Robert Frost, Wallace Stevens, Marianne Moore, and Elizabeth Bishop*. Boston: Northeastern University Press, 1991.

Scigaj, Leonard M. *Sustainable Poetry: Four American Ecopoets*. Lexington: University Press of Kentucky, 1999.

Seelye, John. "Cats, Coons, Crocketts, and Other Furry Critters: Or, why Davy Wears an Animal for a Hat." In *Crockett at Two Hundred: New Perspectives on the Man and the Myth*. Ed. Michael A. Lofaro and Joe Cummings. Knoxville: University of Tennessee Press, 1989, 153–78.

Shepard, Paul. *The Others: How Animals Made Us Human*. Washington: Island Press, 1996.

——. *Thinking Animals: Animals and the Development of Human Intelligence*. New York: Viking, 1978.

Smith, Stevie. *New Selected Poems of Stevie Smith*. New York: New Directions, 1988.

Smith, Zadie. *White Teeth*. New York: Random House, 2000.

Snyder, Gary. *Turtle Island*. New York: New Directions, 1974.

Soper, Kate. *What is Nature? Culture, Politics and the Non-Human*. Oxford: Blackwell, 1995.

Steele, Cynthia. "An Ark for the Next Millennium" (review). *Review—Latin American Literature and Arts* 51 (Fall 1995): 90–2.

Stevens Wallace. *The Palm at the End of the Mind.* New York: Vintage, 1972.

Strickland, Sarah. "Variations on a Tune by Tadpole the Elephant." *Independent* 8 November 2000. <www.independent.co.uk/news/World/Asia_China/2000-11/tadpole081100.shtml>

Sugatananda, Anagarika P. "The Place of Animals in Buddhism." <www.web.ukonline.co.uk/buddhism/fstory4.htm>

Tallmadge, John. "Beyond the Excursion": Initiatory Themes in Annie Dillard and Terry Tempest Williams." In Branch *et al.*, 197–207.

Twain, Mark. *Mark Twain's Best: Eight Short Stories by America's Master Humorist.* New York: Scholastic, 1962.

Weiss, David. "Refusing to Name the Animals." *Gettysburg Review* 3.1 (Winter 1990): 233–41.

Willis, Patricia C. " 'Rigorists.' " *Marianne Moore Newsletter* 5.2 (Fall 1981): 14.

Wolch, Jennifer and Jody Emel, eds. *Animal Geographies: Place, Politics, and Identity in the Nature-Culture Borderlands.* London: Verso, 1998.

Index

7 - Nagel - role of imagination
33 - brevity of poetic experience → sustained imaginative engagem
43 - how do representations impact?
45 - proclaim animals' moral innocence